...erybody loves
the Last Kids on Earth series!

"TERRIFYINGLY FUN! Max Brallier's *The Last Kids on Earth* delivers big thrills and even bigger laughs." —JEFF KINNEY, author of the #1 *New York Times* bestseller *Diary of a Wimpy Kid*

★ "A GROSS-OUT GOOD TIME with surprisingly nuanced character development."
—*School Library Journal*, starred review

★ "Classic ACTION-PACKED, monster-fighting fun." —*Kirkus Reviews*, starred review

★ "SNARKY END-OF-THE-WORLD FUN."
—*Publishers Weekly*, starred review

"The likable cast, lots of adventure, and GOOEY, OOZY MONSTER SLIME GALORE keep the pages turning." —*Booklist*

"HILARIOUS and FULL OF HEART." —*Boys' Life*

"This clever mix of black-and-white drawings and vivid prose brings NEW LIFE TO THE LIVING DEAD." —Common Sense Media

Winner of the Texas Bluebonnet Award

THE MONSTER-BATTLING FUN DOESN'T STOP HERE!

TheLastKidsOnEarth.com

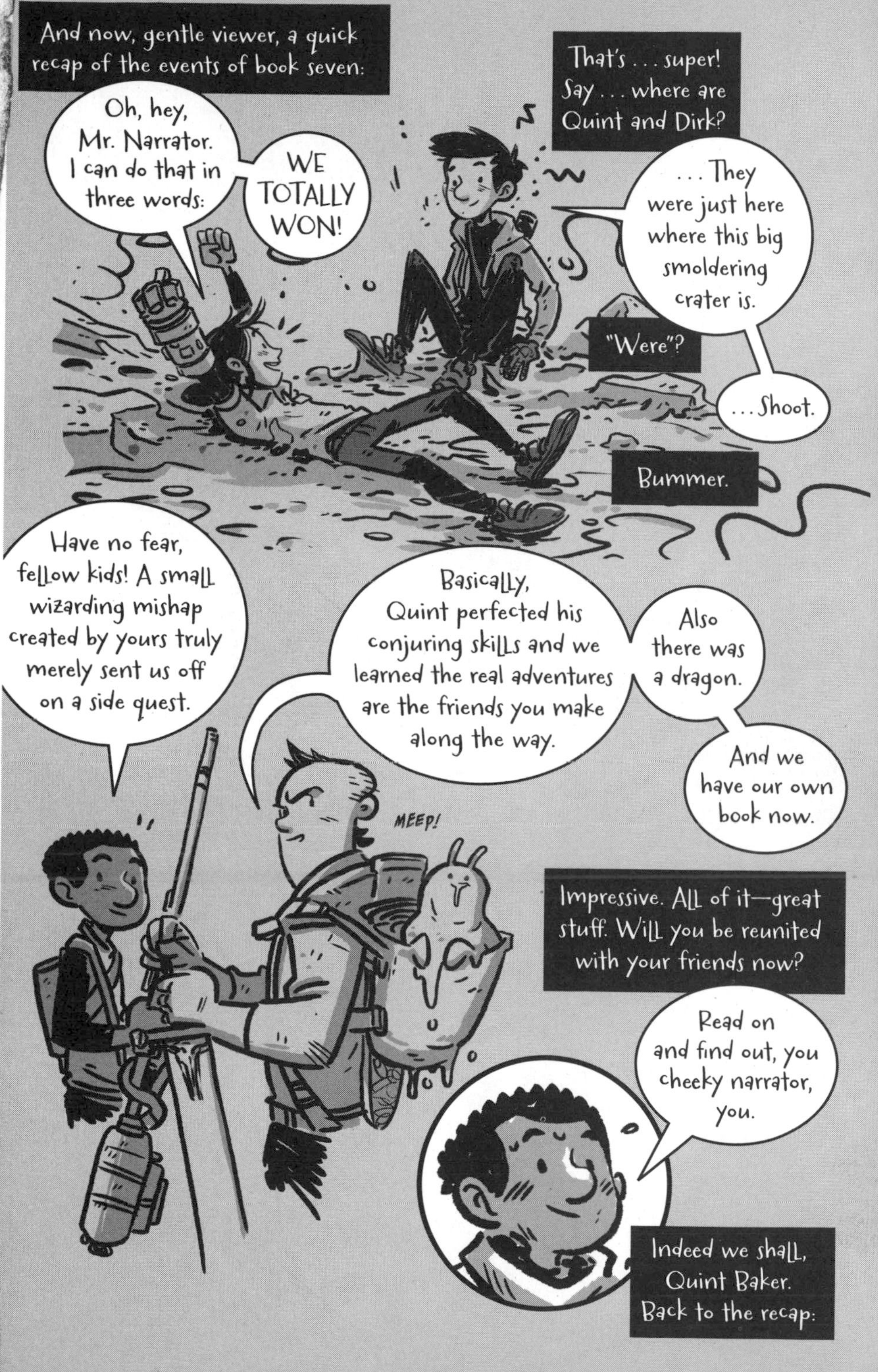
And now, gentle viewer, a quick recap of the events of book seven:
Oh, hey, Mr. Narrator. I can do that in three words:
WE TOTALLY WON!
That's . . . super! Say . . . where are Quint and Dirk?
. . . They were just here where this big smoldering crater is.
"Were"?
. . . Shoot.
Bummer.
Have no fear, fellow kids! A small wizarding mishap created by yours truly merely sent us off on a side quest.
Basically, Quint perfected his conjuring skills and we learned the real adventures are the friends you make along the way.
Also there was a dragon.
And we have our own book now.
MEEP!
Impressive. All of it—great stuff. Will you be reunited with your friends now?
Read on and find out, you cheeky narrator, you.
Indeed we shall, Quint Baker. Back to the recap:

...Traveling on a giant caterpillar with a mall on its back is not as straight-forward as it sounds.

Our heroes run into old foes:

Apocalypse PARTY!

Well, you can just imagine how well that goes.

A special election is held—a referendum on the Mallusk Mall's current administration. An owl wins. And inevitably...

A battle pits Thrull against Ghazt, and the outcome does not bode well for the world's most beloved Cosmic Terror that's been reanimated into the body of an action-figure rat.

YOU KNOW, I KEEP GETTING BLAMED FOR GHAZT'S AILING STATE. IT WAS THE DEL TORO GIRL WHO DID THIS, NOT I.

...Are you hauling his half-lifeless carcass away to do nice things to him?

...No.

Pardon? Didn't hear—

NO!

OW.

I rest my case. And now...on to BOOK EIGHT:

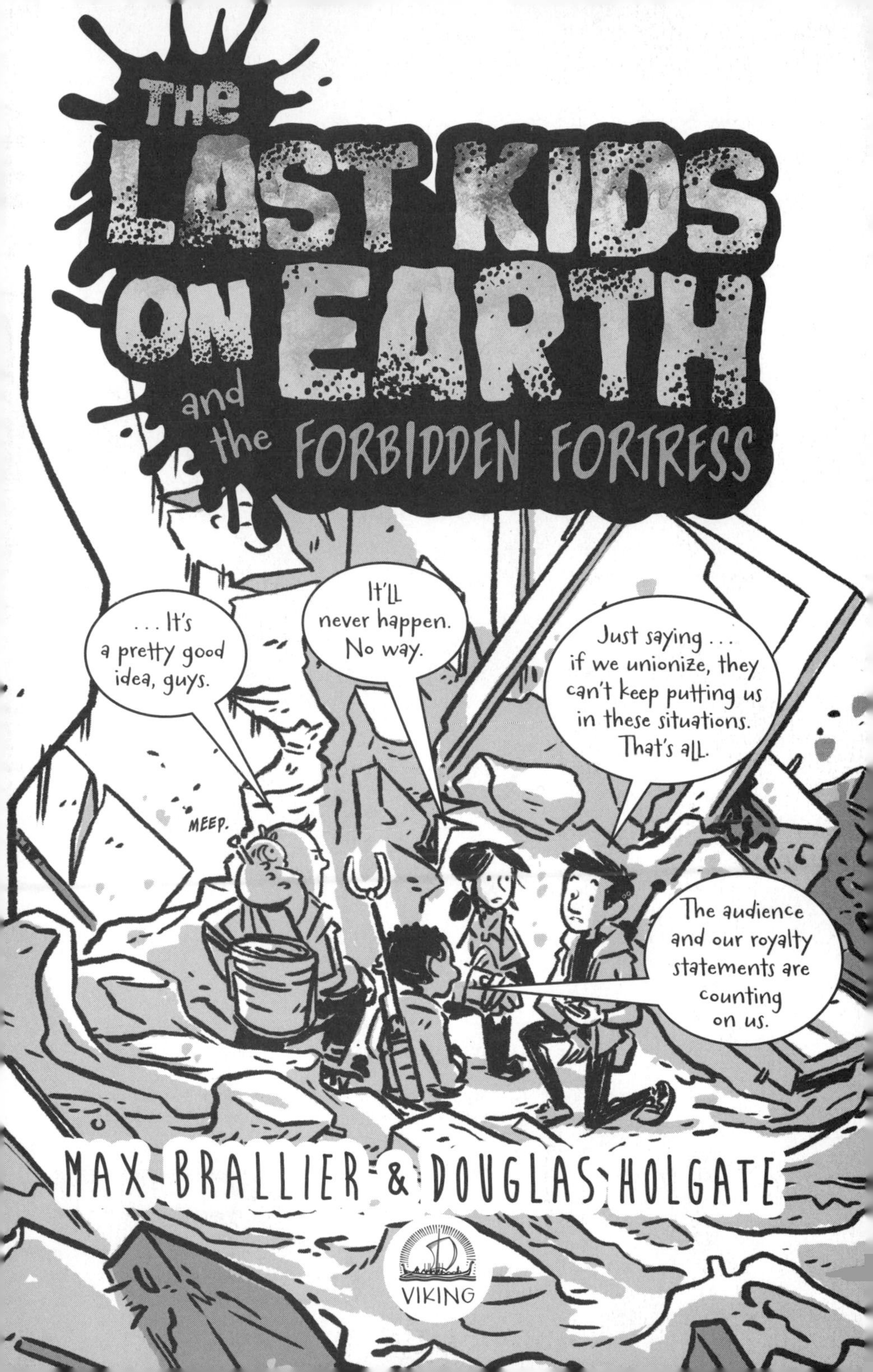
The LAST KIDS ON EARTH
and the FORBIDDEN FORTRESS
. . . It's a pretty good idea, guys.
MEEP.
It'LL never happen. No way.
Just saying . . . if we unionize, they can't keep putting us in these situations. That's aLL.
The audience and our royalty statements are counting on us.
MAX BRALLIER & DOUGLAS HOLGATE
VIKING

VIKING
An imprint of Penguin Random House LLC, New York

First published in the United States of America by Viking,
an imprint of Penguin Random House LLC, 2022

Visit us online at penguinrandomhouse.com.

Library of Congress Cataloging-in-Publication Data is available.

Printed in the United States of America

ISBN 9780593405239 (Hardcover)

1st Printing

ISBN 9780593528938 (International Edition)

1st Printing

LSCH

Book design by Jim Hoover
Set in Cosmiqua Com and Carrotflower

For Lila.

—M. B.

For Illy
(the golden bear)
and Frankie
(the chaos agent).
The best good girls.

—D. H.

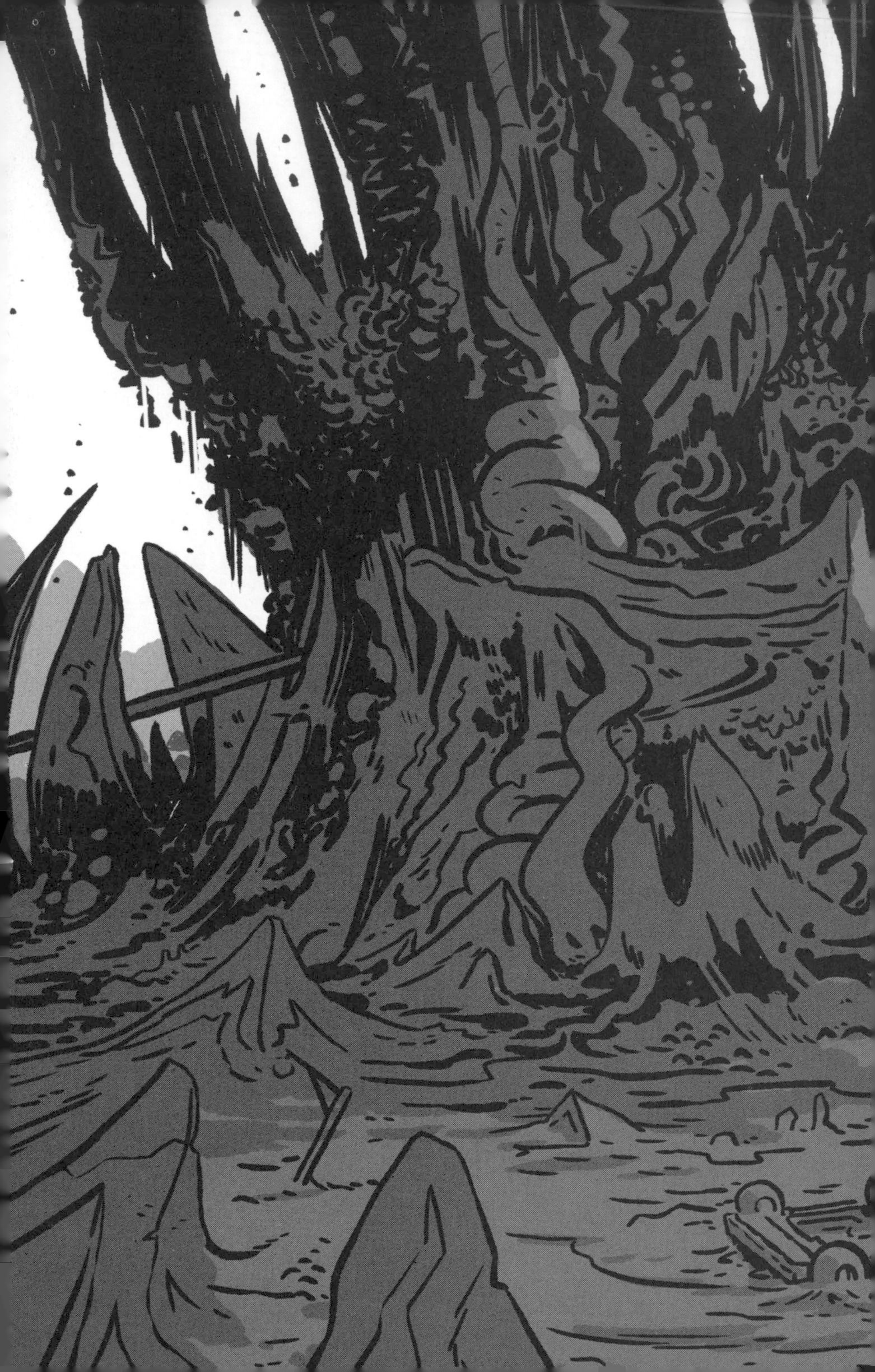

chapter one

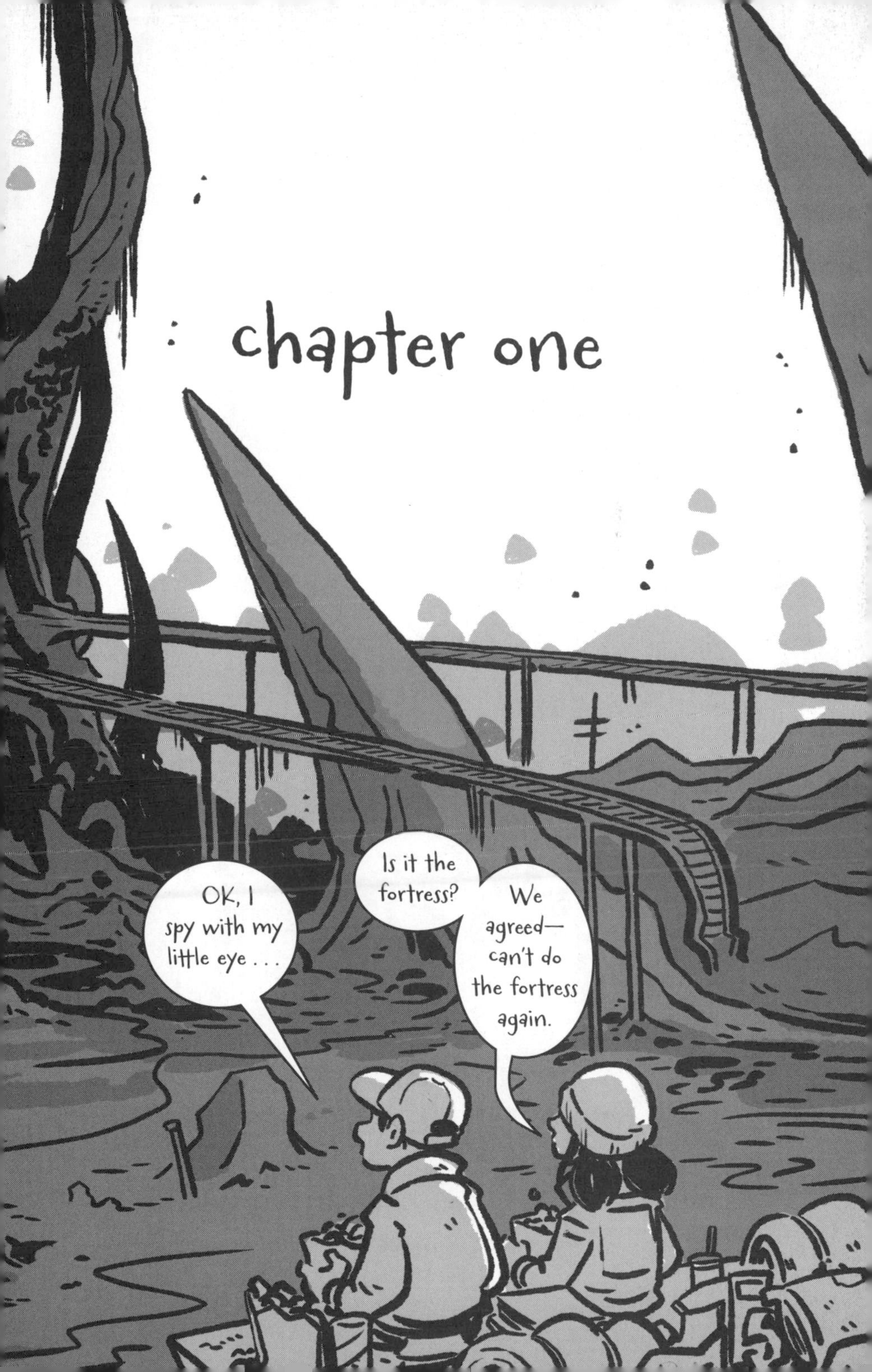
OK, I spy with my little eye . . .
Is it the fortress?
We agreed— can't do the fortress again.

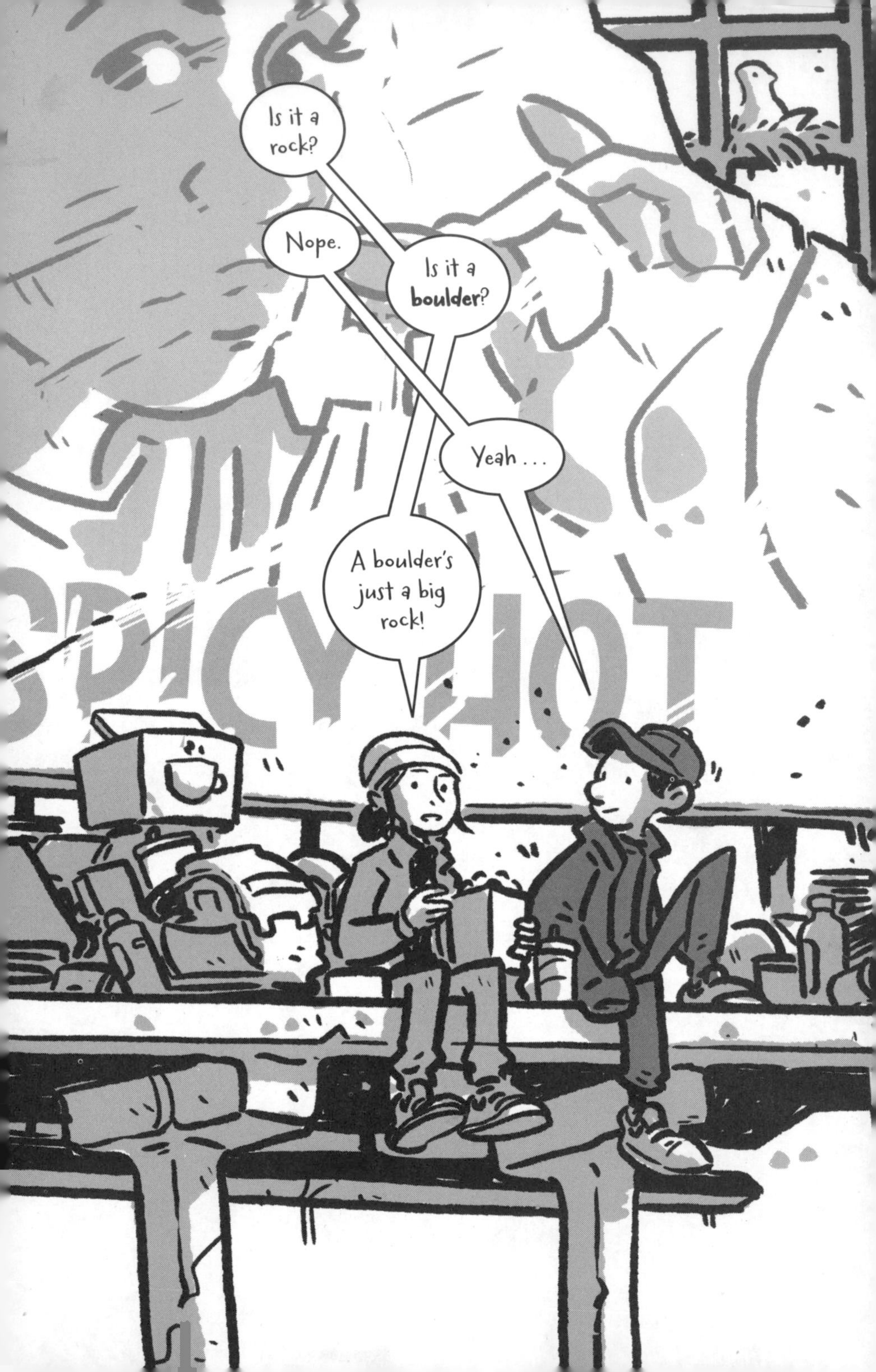

Is it a rock?
Nope.
Is it a **boulder**?
Yeah . . .
A boulder's just a big rock!
SPICY HOT

I shrug. I can't help the scenery. I can't help that our games of I Spy are getting repetitive. We've been sitting in the same spot, looking at the same thing, for a long time.

And not a long time like hours. Nope. June and I have been perched on this billboard—staring out at that fortress—for *weeks*.

We're doing a surveillance stakeout thing. We're basically spies. Spies who do their spying from *really far away*.

And spying from far away is good, because the whole vibe of the fortress messes with my head. Like staring at an optical illusion that you can't quite figure out.

We've been at it so long that we've pretty much turned this billboard into our home away from home (away from home). It's darn near cozy now. We've got ball-game butt pillows, a solar-powered hot cocoa machine, and enough reading material to last us until the *next* end of the world.

On the plus side—it's given June and me some quality one-on-one time. We've got about two hundred inside jokes, and we're pretty much super chums who never, ever argue . . .

It's been a very long and very weird few weeks. How weird? Oh, let me count the ways . . . and the locations.

Right here: June and me, perched on the billboard's walkway. June's hunkered down in a knit cap and an army jacket—it's a cool look, and I'm bummed she thought of it first. All I've got is a plain baseball cap and my camera.

And *down below*: an elevated train track.

That track leads to the thing *in the distance*: the fortress that looks like the sorta joint Skeletor would rent out for a Sweet 16 bash.

It's spooky strange. Has it been built here? Constructed by some mad monster architect? We don't know. We just know it's *not normal*.

Also not normal: the Cosmic Hand. The sucker-covered other-dimensional monster-tentacle glove that is forever wrapped around my wrist and fingers. The Cosmic Hand used to do one thing and one thing only: allow me to wield the Louisville Slicer and use the Slicer's other-dimensional energy to control zombies.

But then I did something *huge*. I controlled a zombie without the Slicer—with *only* the Cosmic Hand.

Since then, the Cosmic Hand has been, like . . . *evolving*.

Um, that's not good.

And in the past few weeks, it's changed *a ton*.

Which is scary. Scary enough that I've kept it secret.

I feel like that character in every vampire movie who gets bit but doesn't want anyone to know, so they have to go around hiding the bite marks, and it keeps making them more and more paranoid and nutso-feeling.

For real, I even got this extra-baggy, super-long-sleeved jacket to keep the growing, changing part of the Cosmic Hand hidden. But if you look beneath it, you'll see—

BIGGER! SCALIER!
MORE UP-MY ARM-IER!
ALSO REALLY, ITCHY!

The Cosmic Hand is starting to feel like . . . *part* of me.

Or worse—like I'm part of *it*. And there's nothing I can do about it. I mean, if my monster buddy Skaelka were here, I'm sure she'd have some suggestions for how to get rid of it—but I don't much like imagining them . . .

But Skaelka's not here. Neither is Rover. And—worst of all—neither are Quint and Dirk and Drooler. They're missing.

I'm worried about them.

And I'm worried I'm starting to become an actual *MONSTER*.

All of this worrying is too much to keep bottled up inside. Something's gotta give.

I know what I need to do. I need to tell June about the Cosmic Hand—how it's been physically *changing*, like, a *lot*. 'Cause maybe that'll help free up some space in my conscience.

I've been trying to work up the courage to tell her for the past few weeks, but haven't been able to get the words out of my throat. Every time I start, I lose my nerve, and it's like . . .

But today's the day.

I'm gonna tell her. Spit it out. No excuses. I'm just gonna say it. Out loud. With my mouth.

Right . . . NOW.

"June, listen," I start, working up my loopy guts to make the confession. "I gotta tell you . . . a thing. And it's a thing that could be really, really—"

Just then, my teeth start clanging together. The billboard rattles. We hear the spine-scraping sound of rusty metal grinding against even rustier metal.

The train is coming.

"Put a pin in that thought, duder. Train's almost here," June says. "It's time." She's trying to sound calm even though what we're about to do is nothing anyone could *ever* be calm about.

Suddenly, the train appears—racing beneath us, wheels screeching and shrieking.

June stands. "There he is." She points. "Tiny Splotcher."

Tiny Splotcher is the single monster sentry perched atop the train. We call these sentries Splotchers 'cause of the splotchy ooze-stains they leave behind them when they walk. And we call this one Tiny Splotcher 'cause, well, he's tinier than the others.

June hoists herself over the billboard's ledge. I gulp, following, as June shouts, "JUMP!"

And we do . . .

See, I was campaigning for mayor of Mallusk City, the community of (mostly) friendly monsters who live inside the Millennium Super Mall—which is fused atop a massive centipede monster we call the Mallusk.

Then a few things happened real fast.

First, we learned that the Mallusk was traveling straight toward our archenemy, Thrull, after being secretly hijacked by one of his evil servants. And . . . it was kinda my fault. I had pledged to protect the monsters aboard the Mallusk, but the whole time, I was—unwittingly—delivering them to their doom, to become Thrull's eternal servants. And it was all due to my careless, ill-thought, impulsive decision to use the Cosmic Hand.

So I abandoned my campaign for mayor—and decided to stop being polite and start getting *real*. To tell THE TRUTH.

That fight I told you about? It's here now, sooner than it needed to be—and that's because of me.

I used this power that I don't understand, and it revealed our location to Thrull's forces.

That's why the Howlers attacked before, and that's why Thrull himself is coming now.

But that's when Thrull showed up with an army. He was seconds from destroying all of us when Ghazt entered the fight, tackling Thrull. YAY!

But then Thrull stabbed Ghazt with a bone spike. SORTA YAY, SORTA NOT!

As Thrull clutched the wounded Ghazt—he said something. Something that changes *a lot* for us:

"I have big plans, Ghazt. To complete them, I need what is in your head. And I will get it. I know a creature who will pry the information from your brain."

And whatever Thrull needs from Ghazt's brain is something we want, too. It doesn't even matter what the info is because the first rule of defeating an evil warlord: *never* let that evil warlord get what it wants.

Thrull vamoosed with Ghazt—off to deliver him to this mysterious creature who, apparently, specializes in prying information from brains? Weird job. How does one even get into that? Is it like an apprenticeship deal?

It was far from anything like victory. The Mallusk was hurt, bad.

But it could have been a whole lot worse.

Wait, nope, it *was* a whole lot worse.

Because after Thrull escaped, we discovered that Quint, Dirk, and Drooler were gone. Just totally and completely disappeared!

The only reason I'm not paralyzed by sadness and fear right now is because Yursl—the mall's resident conjurer and Quint's sorta-teacher—swears that Quint and Dirk are alive, somewhere. She says they were only teleported. And I have to believe her because we're talking about my best friend here. And my . . . Dirk. Plus Drooler, who's adorable, essential, and perpetually gooey.

Johnny Steve, the true mayor of Mallusk City, helped us gather search parties. Monster volunteers raced off, riding Carapace creatures, in search of our buddies.

We should be going with them.

I know. I want to . . . more than anything. But we **have** to find Thrull—and Ghazt.

There's a lot to do and no time to waste.

Because Thrull is building the Tower. And when it's finished and activated, Ṛeżżőcħ the Ancient, Destructor of Worlds, will come into *our* world and do the thing he does so well it's actually *part of his name*: DESTRUCT THE WORLD!

So June and I left the Mallusk to heal and the Carapace search party to find our friends, and went chasing after Ghazt and Thrull ourselves.

Thrull actually wasn't too hard to track. We just followed the wake of destruction and excess foliage. And it led us here.

To the fortress.

That's where Thrull's trail stopped. Which means that's where he took Ghazt.

The Mallusk eventually caught up to us and parked itself under a nearby underpass. Now June and I use it as a base of operations, returning each night to see if the Carapace search party has any Quint-and-Dirk updates.

And every morning, we return to the billboard for more fortress-watching, trying to come up with a plan to stop this creature-buddy of Thrull's from getting the info out of Ghazt's brain.

Except our plans always begin and end with "get inside the fortress and find out what's going on."

Getting inside the fortress will *not* be easy. We thought about hopping onto the train tracks and slipping through one of the fortress's muscly crevice-doors. But then we saw a wayward bird attempt it, and that put our idea to bed real fast . . .

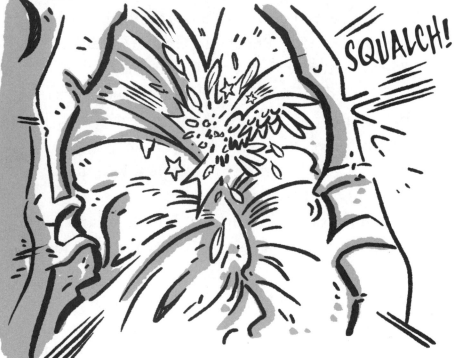

So we came up with a new plan: leap on top of the train, abduct Tiny Splotcher, and pump him for information!

And that new plan got underway, moments

earlier, when we did that big ridiculous jump and—

OK, you're caught up—back to the present moment, resuming the real-deal action!

"AAAAAAAGH!"

Somebody yells that. Might be June. Might be me. Might be both of us, because . . .

Our plan is off to a lousy start. We *totally* mistimed our jump, and now we're plummeting, *not* on a trajectory to grab and nab Tiny Splotcher.

chapter two

Yep, we completely *miss* Tiny Splotcher and instead just crash through the train's roof panel like a pair of fleshy missiles.

Ever fallen through the roof of a train, then capped it off with a face-plant into a monster? I don't recommend it.

"We would've been better off going with the exploding-bird plan," I groan, sitting up.

We just landed in a tin can packed with monstery badness, a train hurtling toward a door that will explode us on contact. Also, I think I rolled my ankle, so yeah, *nothing is going well right now.*

"Just mortifying," I continue. "Sorry to intrude. We'll get outta your hair," I add in my most nonchalant voice, as I attempt to casually grab the train's EMERGENCY EXIT lever.

One Splotcher barks something to the others, which, if I had to guess from their reaction, roughly translates to, "GET 'EM!"

"From now on," June says as she leaps to her feet. "Leave the big action plans to me, 'K, Jack?"

"This WAS your plan!"

"No, no. I don't think that's true."

"It was totally your plan!" I say.

And then I don't say anything else for a bit because it's battling time.

It's almost too chaotic to describe. A prize fight in a bread box. Monstrous claws lash out, talons slice and cut through the air—it's a whirlwind tornado of action.

I hear a muffled boom, and two Splotchers shoot upward into the ceiling. "And stay off!" June says, dusting off her Blasty arm.

The Slicer feels at home in my hand—but it's not totally at home in this train car. I try to unleash some home-run-derby, crush-the-cover-off-the-baseball-level destruction, but when I swing—

THUNK!

The blade jams into the wall—and stays there.

"Argh! Stupid Slicer, stupid wall . . ." I mutter as I try to rip it out. A Splotcher cocks back its arm—which is not *really* an arm, but more of a jagged, meat-and-bone sword appendage.

"OK, it is simply too *tight in here to fight*!" I say. "I mean—can we at least agree on that?"

Suddenly, my head whips back. Another Splotcher has grabbed a handful of my jacket and is ripping me off my feet. Guess he doesn't agree.

"Hey, hey, hold on a sec, would ya!" I stammer. "Wanna talk this out? We just need to put our heads together!"

And with that—

OK, I need a heavy swig of Tylenol. Extra strength. Also, my "put our heads together" line didn't sound as cool as I thought it was going to.

But it worked. The Splotcher drops me—probably surprised by the pure stupidity of the head-butt maneuver.

I finally manage to rip the Slicer out of the

wall, then I dive between the monster's legs,
sliding toward the emergency lever.

I reach for it, just . . . a few . . . more inches.
But then—

"ACK! Get . . . OFF!"

It's June—her angry cry fills the car, followed
by a—*THWOCK!*

June cries out in pain. Through the melee, I
see her.

Seeing my friend in peril gets my Cosmic Hand pulsing and starts my heart crashing around in my chest. I gotta help her! I—

WHAMM!

A Splotcher belts me. I hit the floor, hard. Something heavy—I'm guessing the creature's ooze-soaked foot—steps onto my back, pushing down.

Hard.

Harder.

Mashing me into the floor like I'm a juicy, Jack-shaped cockroach.

Something inside me pops. Possibly a kidney. I hope it's a kidney—at least I have two of those.

There's only one thought in my mind: help June.

The Cosmic Hand starts *thud, thudding*— practically *gnawing* at the arm flesh beneath it as I reach out for her. Spots fill my vision— not sure if that's because the Cosmic Hand's doing strange stuff or if it's the Splotcher's foot pushing the last bit of air out of my lungs.

I reach and reach, straining my outstretched arm, wishing it were about five times longer.

But I'm so far away.

And more monsters are upon June. Their hulking frames crowd closer around her, until she's completely out of view.

But still, I keep reaching. The otherworldly, unknowable weirdness of the Cosmic Hand digs deep into my arm, like jagged fingernails, clamping down, trying to draw blood until suddenly—

Well, I don't know what happens, exactly.

The Cosmic Hand *erupts*, tearing open my sleeve, becoming a swirling black-and-purple tendril, lashing up, knocking the Splotcher off my back, then going stiff as it thrusts outward, and—

WHA-KKKSSSSSHHHH!

Before I can say, "What the huh?"—it's over.

As quickly as the Cosmic Hand changed—it returns back to its original form. The fleshy spear is yanked back into my hand. Blood pounds in my ears, but over the throbbing, I hear . . .

June. Screaming.

Blinking away the black dots that cloud my vision, I see the Splotcher nearest June spinning wildly, grunting, grabbing his shoulder in pain. He staggers into the far wall, and I see—

June.

Her scream was a *good* scream.

She's safe now.

I saved her.

No, not quite.

The Cosmic Hand saved her.

But . . .

A thin smear of blood streaks her cheek. A few strands of just-sliced hair drift onto her shoulder.

The Cosmic Hand. It cut her face.

It *hurt* her.

I stare at the monstrous thing on my arm, horrified. *What did you DO?!*

June snaps her arm upward, bringing her
elbow into the gut of the Splotcher behind her.

Ooze spills. The Splotcher wails.

Darting ahead, June barks, "GET THAT DOOR
OPEN, JACK!"

It takes me a second to move.

June is going full rock 'em, sock 'em on the
monsters—but all I see is the blood on her face. *I*
did that. The Cosmic Hand did that. Because for

an instant, it turned into a fleshy, Cosmic *Spear*.
It's not supposed to do that. It's not supposed to
do anything, especially not without my *express
permission*. If it *is*, that means—

KLUNK!

Suddenly, Tiny Splotcher—the one we were
supposed to capture in a quick grab-and-go—
tumbles through the roof.

June's eyes flash—and she raises Blasty. Her
arm-weapon jumps, and there's a *twang*! A lasso-
line flies out, tangling Tiny Splotcher tight.

"Jack, c'mon!" she shouts.

"Huh?" I ask, my head still half-lost in
thought, pondering the Cosmic Hand—and what
it just did.

"The door!" June cries again. "What are you
waiting for, Christmas?"

"Right!" I say, finally snapping out of it. I
scramble to my feet, grab the lever, throw all my
weight into it, and—

KA-CHUNK!

The door slides open. Wind whips into the car.

"Time to get out of here!" June shouts. "And
we're leaving with a souvenir!"

June slams into me, dragging Tiny Splotcher

behind her. All three of us topple across the floor, then—

Out of the car.

I'd love to turn around, take a moment to tip my cap to the other snarling monster guards, but—alas—my cool undercover-agent hat was whipped off by the wind during our jump.

We hit the ground like a bouncy ball flying out of a fifty-cent machine—and instantly Blasty's lasso-line ensnares all three of us as we tumble down a steep, hilly street in one cartoonish, entangled avalanche of bouncing bodies . . .

chapter three

When we finally stop tumbling and tilt-a-flipping, we're sprawled out on concrete. My eyes keep spinning for a long time—and when they finally *stop* and focus, I see hair. June's hair, in my face. It tickles.

"When's the last time you washed your hair?" I ask her. "You might wanna do it soon 'cause it kinda stinks like maple syrup."

June groans. "That's not my hair, dumb dumb. Look around."

Sitting up, I see that we've landed in the parking lot of a roadside breakfast joint: Suzie Stacks Pancake Barn. Flies buzz around in lazy patterns. They're loud.

But not as loud as the sound of bones snapping and cracking.

It's Tiny Splotcher—he's rising. Joints and limbs pop at impossible, unnatural angles, allowing him to free himself from the lasso-line.

But June and I—and our darn non-snappable-and-re-snappable appendages—are still stuck fast.

The monster's glowing, oozing claw-appendage flashes open, revealing a terrifying array of needle-spikes.

"Whoa, whoa, whoa—WAIT!" June says, holding up a hand. "Could you, maybe, go easy on us? Because, uh . . ."

"Because, well . . ." I start, before June jumps back in.

"Because my friend here is *super* scared right now. *Huge* needle-phobe."

"What the—HEY!" I shout. "Am not; *you're* the one—"

"See," June says, smiling at the Splotcher while nodding her head my way. "A little defensive, too. He hates needles. At the doctor's, he closes his eyes—but he makes the nurse tell him when the shot is coming because he also hates *not knowing*."

"We never went to the doctor together!" I exclaim.

What's going on here? Has the monster apocalypse finally gotten to her? And, yeah, I hate shots. Everyone hates shots. If I ever met someone who *liked* shots, I'd step away slowly, 'cause—

"At the school nurse's one time, he just flat-out fainted," June says. "Not a criticism, just saying."

Tiny Splotcher snaps one last limb, and a

dangling arm fixes back into place. His shoulder makes a sound like two canned hams hurled against a brick wall. Leaning forward, he hisses, "I have had many shots. Many injections. But unlike this cowardly young human, I welcome them!"

"Oh, had a lot of shots, eh?" June says. "From the school nurse?"

Tiny Splotcher makes a wet, hacking sound. "From Wracksaw! Bear witness: we are now in the shadow of his fortress—where me and my fellow monsters have been made great. *Been given purpose!*"

And that's when I get it. June doesn't have to say it—I know what she's doing. It's almost like—proof that she and I have a special connection, maybe? I'd like to think so.

"Ahh, Wracksaw," I say, jumping in. Seems like maybe that's the creature Thrull was taking Ghazt to, but I have to know for sure. "Weird name for a school nurse—"

"He is no school nurssssse! He is a brilliant mind!"

"Ooh, that's actually perfect! 'Cause one of your buddies gave me this little cut here," June says, turning her injured cheek toward

Tiny Splotcher. "Maybe Wracksaw could stitch me up?"

My throat tightens at that. So does the Cosmic Hand. Because that cut was made by me. Not a Splotcher.

"He would do more than stitch. He has not yet had a human body to *experiment on*. But . . . NO! I will not deliver you to him. He is too busy with Ghazt."

"Oh, you know Ghazt?" June asks. "*We* know Ghazt!"

"You do not *know* Ghazt," the guard says, hissing. "You only *knew* Ghazt." Tiny Splotcher's narrow, insect-like face rearranges into something like a knowing grin. "Was he a companion of yours?"

Not sure how to answer that one.

Truly.

What do you call a Cosmic General you've been fighting for what feels like *forever*? An interdimensional rat monster whose powers were stolen by Thrull—and then stolen again, *from* Thrull, *by me*, when the Scrapken tentacle on my hand sucked away Ghazt's powers, turning the Scrapken tentacle into the Cosmic Hand?

"We were more like . . . colleagues?" I say finally. "We actually ran for the same office. It was a hard-fought campaign, but I suppose there's a begrudging mutual respect after something like that—"

"Then I will take great joy in your sadness," Tiny Splotcher says, his horrible mouth twisting into an arrogant smile, "when I tell you that . . ."

GHAZT IS DEAD.

WHAT??

Dead?! Wait . . . No. That's not . . . *Dead?*

In case my brain-thoughts didn't make it clear enough, I shout, "Dead?! Wait . . . No. That's not . . . *Dead?!?*"

I mean, Ghazt wasn't in great shape when Thrull carried him off . . . but dead? Could he really be gone? For good?

June catches my eye. I suspect she's thinking what I *should* be thinking: What about the info inside Ghazt's brain? That's what matters. If he's dead, does that mean Thrull's already gotten what he was after?

"Wow," June says. "That's . . . just a real shock. For both of us. Is there going to be, like, a funeral? I'd love to look upon his beautiful . . ." June pauses, like she's swallowing down puke, before finishing with "rat face one last time."

Tiny Splotcher cackles. "There will not be much left of him for funeraling once Wracksaw has finished the knowledge-extraction."

"Hold up!" June says. "That can't happen yet!"

Tiny Splotcher looks at June questioningly. "And why is that?"

"We are his, uh—"

"Emergency contacts!" I say.

June sighs. "Yes. What Jack said, I guess. We were Ghazt the Cosmic General's *emergency contacts*."

"And you can't start a knowledge-extraction without informing the emergency contacts! Assuming knowledge-extraction is what we think it is . . ." I say, not finishing the sentence and hoping that Tiny Splotcher will help me out.

"Knowledge-extraction," Tiny Splotcher says, "is drilling into Ghazt's dead *brain* to find and remove the Tower Schematics."

That piece of news hits me like a bomb drop. While we've been sitting around, watching the fortress, this Wracksaw dude has been inside trying to scrape blueprints out of Ghazt's noggin.

But *why*? The Tower is *already* being built. I saw it when I grabbed Blargus with the Cosmic Hand, psychically linking me to Thrull for a brief, horrifying moment. And it looked like Thrull was making fine progress . . .

"Oh right, the schematics for Thrull," June says. "Ghazt told us all about that. 'Cause we were friendly, like I said. Thrull must be happy."

"Thrull is not *happy*!" Tiny Splotcher roars. "All work on the Tower has stalled. Now thousands of skeleton soldiers and monsters— just sitting around, playing knuckle bites! Nothing to do. Thrull will not be happy until the knowledge-extraction is complete and the schematics are in his possession."

I breathe a sigh of relief so big it probably looks like a Monday-afternoon yawn. The knowledge-extraction isn't finished yet, and neither is the Tower. There's still time!

So, uh, just out of curiosity . . . is Ghazt's dead body in there with **just** monsters? I'd like to think of him surrounded by his friends.

HA! HAPPY TO TELL YOU NEWS THAT WILL NOT MAKE YOU HAPPY. NO FRIENDS. NO MORE PRISONERS. JUST WRACKSAW, GUARDS, AND GHAZT'S DEAD BODY NOW.

Tiny Splotcher smiles. "Wracksaw cannot be distracted now. That is why I will finish you here . . ."

With that, Tiny Splotcher raises his claw-arm high. Needles flash in the afternoon sunlight.

"Well, this has been informative and fun," June says, clicking her tongue. Then she turns to look at me. "Now?"

"Now what?" I ask.

"Really, duder?" she asks, reaching to tap a button on Blasty. "Now, like, as in—"

Click!

"NOW!"

June taps the button on Blasty—and in a flash, the lasso-line releases.

"Wait, you could have freed us the whole time?!" I exclaim, scrambling to my feet faster than Tiny Splotcher can react.

"Yeah, Jack, try to keep up!"

I reach for my Slicer, when—

STOMP!

Tiny Splotcher's rough foot clomps down on it.

His monstrous body *changes*. Muscles tear, bones split and reaffix as he grows larger, rising, making clear that Tiny Splotcher was probably *not* a great name for this guy . . .

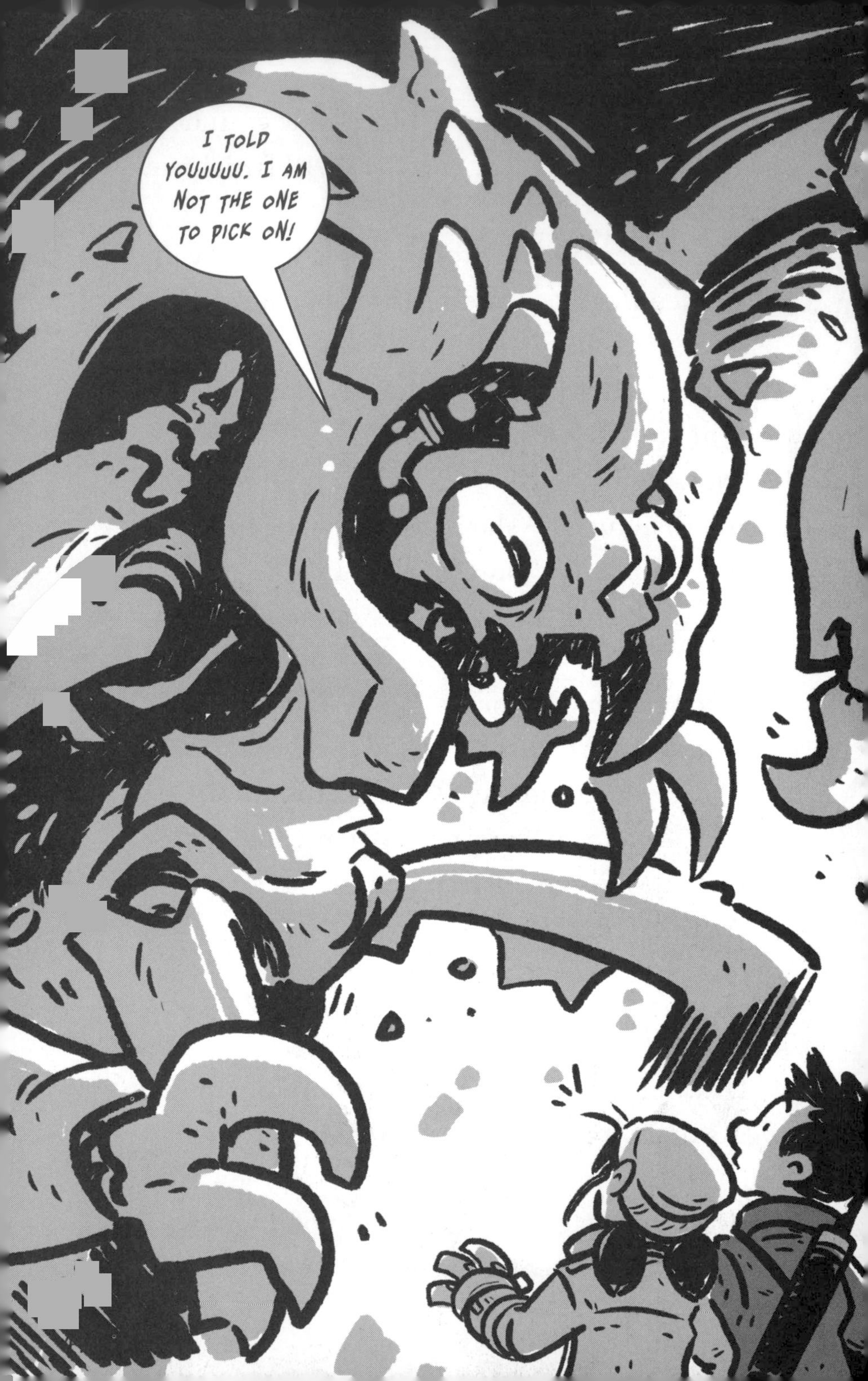
I TOLD YOUUUUU. I AM NOT THE ONE TO PICK ON!

chapter four

June and I take three nervous steps back.

Not-So-Tiny Splotcher approaches. Then, suddenly, a voice—booming from the trees—

"I COME BACK TO YOU NOW AT THE TURN OF THE TIDE."

Huh? I glance around, looking for the source of the voice, but finding nothing. Then—

Tiny Splotcher is gone! Obliterated! Little scraps of paper flutter onto the parking lot, floating down like feathers on the wind. Each piece of paper has a small image of a Splotcher on it, like baseball cards.

"Uh . . ." I say, looking suspiciously at my Cosmic Hand.

June lifts Blasty and shakes her head. "Wasn't me."

Noise above us. June and I both jerk our heads up to see . . .

He's been dying to say that "turn of the tide" thing.

"QUINT! DIRK!" I exclaim. "You're alive!"

"Sure are. And we saved your butts," Dirk says, grinning. And seeing that grin just about makes my heart explode with happiness.

Drooler slides from the hilt of Dirk's sword and hits the ground with a happy wheeze. *Whoa.* Drooler's not totally a squashy little baby anymore.

"Quint did the saving," a voice growls—and again, I'm hit by a wave of shock and surprise. It's Skaelka, coming up behind them, riding a Carapace. She's in full armor—*Quint-built armor*, I realize—and bearing a giant ax.

"Skaelka, too!" June shouts. "Hey, girl!"

In a flash, we're all racing toward each other. "We're all alive and back together!" I cry.

Quint, is that a proton pack??

Conjurer's cannon! I've almost got conjuring under control now!

Almost?

It's a long story. Read the book.

MEEP!

"But how are you . . . like . . . *here*?" I'm still so stunned that I can barely put my thoughts into a coherent question. "Yursl promised you'd survive the teleporting—but oh man, we were so scared, you have no idea, I can't even . . . We sent out about a zillion monsters looking for you!"

"We know," Quint says. "We ran into Smud and Johnny Steve; they told us where to find you."

I wish I had a minute alone with Quint. I want to hear everything, about where he's been, what they did, who they—

Wait.

Skaelka's back, too.

Which means—Rover should be here. I glance around, scanning the surrounding cars and stores—expecting him to leap out, doing a big puppy-dog surprise thing. But as I catch Skaelka's eye, my stomach goes sickly hollow and my body twitches, just slightly.

"Skaelka . . ." I start. "Where's Rover?"

Skaelka takes a step forward, then kneels in front of me. "I swore an oath to you, Jack. And I regret that I could not keep it."

Dread—shaky-leg, mind-racing dread—floods through me. "What do you mean you—but . . . ? Is Rover . . . ?"

"He's OK, bud," Dirk says, jumping in. "He's alive. Just . . . not here. Out there."

Skaelka bows her head—then explains . . . "Enemies caught Rover and me unaware. They swept down from the sky. Skaelka leapt into battle and—as I vowed—I kept Rover alive. They turned their fury on Skaelka. And as they carried me away, the last thing I saw was Rover, unharmed, but alone . . ."

I try to swallow, but my mouth is desert dry. Alone! Rover's out there—all by himself? Who's going to give him scritches? Who's going to tell him he's the best boy?

"He's a monster. He can handle himself,"
June says, trying to reassure me.

"Maybe! But he's not supposed to *have* to!"
I say, trying not to shout and mostly failing.
"We're supposed to be together! We're supposed
to all be . . ."

I trail off, suddenly feeling very tired. I shut
my eyes, and all I see is Rover out there, on
his own in the wilds, hunted by Thrull's awful
soldiers. I never should have let him go with
Skaelka.

I failed him.

Skaelka looks up at me. "Jack, I swear to
you—I will right my wrong. I will—"

"It's fine, Skaelka," I say, cutting her off.
That's a big fat lie, it's *not* fine, but whatever.
"I'm the one who let him go. I'm the one who
failed him."

And that part isn't a lie.

"Now, please stand up, Skaelka. You're
making me super uncomfortable."

I feel everybody staring at me.

I know they want me to act like everything's
OK. But it's not. Although, right now, it sorta
has to be . . .

I turn to Dirk and Quint. "I wanted to go out and look for you guys more than I've ever wanted anything. But I couldn't. And now . . . it's the same thing again. I can't go looking for Rover. Because . . . Thrull. Ghazt. That fortress. But as soon as we're done with all this . . ."

"We're gonna find him," Dirk swears. "That's a promise. Like you promised me we'd get Drooler back."

I nod and quickly turn away—my eyes are watering, and I don't want my friends seeing that. There's too much going on. "OK," I say softly.

Quint suddenly gasps. He's looking up at the fortress. From the parking lot, it looms high, like a mountain. "What did you find here?"

"Not only what did we find—what did we *learn*," June says.

June's words help recharge me. They're a reminder that big, world-hanging-in-the-balance things are happening. And we have stuff to do. Soon.

"It's something BIG," I say, forcing a bit of optimism into my voice. Gonna need to fake it till I make it right now.

"Ghazt is . . ." June starts. "Wait for it. Wait for it."

"Wait for it one more time," I add, grinning. "Ghazt is . . ."

"Dead," Dirk says. "We know. We heard that part."

"Oh." June and I frown. We were both pretty amped to deliver that monumental news ourselves.

We quickly fill our friends in on the parts they *didn't* hear: Wracksaw, the knowledge-extraction, and the Tower Schematics thing being sucked out of Ghazt's noggin.

"Wait . . ." Quint says as we finish. I see a smile growing on his face. "Did you two pull a . . . REVERSE INTERROGATION?!"

June grins. "Sure did. Black Widow–style. And it worked like a charm."

"Then why were you two about to eat it when we got here?" Dirk asks.

"That was *after* the reverse interrogation," I say.

I notice Skaelka has stepped a few feet away— her eyes fixed on the fortress in the distance.

With a low hum, she says, "The fortress fell through from my dimension."

Um . . . what? I didn't know that could happen. I wonder what else can fall through . . .

All of a sudden, Dirk and Quint share a glance—they know something we don't.

"We've seen that thing before," Quint says. "In Skaelka's memories."

"That fortress," Dirk says, his eyes narrowing. "It's where the Drakkor was messed with."

I'm about to ask what a Drakkor is and how exactly Quint and Dirk *saw* Skaelka's memories, when Skaelka speaks up—and her words completely derail my train of thought, because they are chilling to the bone.

"It's also where I was held prisoner," Skaelka intones. "Where I was tortured by Wracksaw. He is . . . cruel. Worse than you can imagine."

"Wait, what?" June asks. "Prisoner?"

"And you were . . . *tortured*?" I ask, horrified.

Dirk fills in the rest. "They messed with Skaelka's brain—stirred her memories all up like alphabet soup. It's . . ." He trails off with a shudder. Drooler offers a comforting *meep*.

"Hold up," I say. "This all happened *there*? The same place we've been staking out? Where this Wracksaw creature is trying to remove the Tower Schematics from Ghazt's brain??"

You know how you drop quarters into a vending machine, and right before you get your Snickers, there's that satisfying *ka-CHING* when the money falls into place? That's the sound I imagine all our brains making.

"The Tower Schematics . . ." Quint repeats. "Are still in Ghazt's brain."

And then I imagine the sound again: another *ka-CHING* as June says, "That means, if we can get the schematics *first* . . . and destroy them . . ."

TR!PLE KA-CHING!

We can WIN!

Without the schematics, Thrull can't finish the Tower!

THIS IS TRUE. AND WITHOUT THE TOWER, REŻŻÓCH WILL NEVER BE ABLE TO GAIN ENTRY TO THIS DIMENSION.

We can END this! Like . . . ONCE AND FOR ALL!

chapter five

I feel all tingly. Like eating Tropical Skittles while chugging Dr Pepper. A gush of happiness that's so sweet and so refreshing.

June eagerly taps Blasty. "So that's it, right? We just *blow up* the fortress? One big blasteroni with cheese—and then we're done-zo?!"

"A little aggressive," Dirk says. "But I like it."

"The fortress can only be destroyed from within," Skaelka explains.

Quint nods, rubbing his chin. "OK, so, Jack, June—how do we get inside?"

June looks at me. I look at her. Our faces tell the same story.

Dirk sighs. "You forgot to ask that monster how to get inside, didn't you . . ."

"But I had that question right here!" I exclaim. "On my list. Look!"

Questions to ask Splotcher
during interrogation.

• Where's Ghazt?
• What does Thrull want from his brain?
• Who else is in the fortress?
• How do we get inside?

Bonus questions if we have the time.
• What's the longest you've ever let your
toenail get before you clipped it?
• Do monsters like bowling?
• You ever try origami, or is that strictly
a good guy/neutral fellow thing?

"Y'know what," I say, balling up the paper. "June was supposed to ask that one."

June scowls, all fake-offended. "No, I wasn't! If I was, I would have asked."

"If *I* was," I say. "*I* would have asked."

"It matters not," Skaelka says, silencing us. Her words are quiet but heavy as she stares into the distance. "As I gaze upon that ghastly place, my memories return to me one by one. And I now know how to gain entry. I know, because . . ."

I shudder, knowing Skaelka is staring out at the same place she was tortured. From our vantage point, the cliff is visible—and it's no bunny slope.

"It is known as the Cliff of Infinite Fatalities. Two hundred talons tall. Nearly impossible to climb," Skaelka says. "Winds crash like the Pitiless Plains. Razorkaw birds wet their beaks with the blood of any who attempt the climb. They will peck and pluck your eyeballs."

I clear my throat. "But it *is* possible."

The sun is behind us, but Skaelka still squints as she eyes the fortress, like it pains her to look but she knows she has to. It's like watching a scary movie, hands over your eyes, but peeking through your fingers because you still *gotta* see what happens.

"Even if we did manage entry," Skaelka says, "we would need to reach the heart of the fortress. From there, it would take an untold amount of explosive energy to destroy it. There is—"

"Fusion!" Quint guesses, then excitedly guesses again, "FISSION!"

"No," Skaelka says. She turns to us, her face grim. "There is *nothing* from this dimension that powerful."

chapter six

We all deflate.

Nothing?

I look at Quint—expecting him to light up with a solution. But even *he* isn't capable of cobbling together a makeshift monster-fortress-destroying bomb. It's not like we can just scavenge a bunch of plutonium from an abandoned Home Depot. Not where we are anyway. Nevada, maybe . . .

We stand there, contemplating solutions to this conundrum, when June says—

"We'll figure it out! We always do!"

And she's right. When have we ever let a little thing like lack of fusion stop us? It's just a bump in the road, a snag in the plan, a—

"Blowing up a monster fortress sounds impossible," Dirk says. "But doing the impossible is sorta our area of expertise now."

And with that, we begin the trek back to the Mallusk . . .

Soon, the fortress is well behind us—but the Mallusk is still about a mile ahead. The sun's starting to go down. A lot of purply reds and reddy purples and stuff.

I catch June looking at it with a secretive smile.

I give her a nudge. "What are you grinning about?"

"We're still gonna have to fight Thrull," Dirk points out. "Even if he fails to bring Ṛeżżŏċħ here, he's still got a giant skeleton army."

And that's true. But what's one more massive fight against an other-dimensional terror? We've thwarted him before. We took down Blarg. And the King Wretch. There's been SO much thwarting!

"The world will be far from perfect," Quint points out. "We can't unzombify the zombies."

"Or get back the ones eaten by the Tree of Entry," I add. "Or devoured by Dozers or any of the other monsters."

"It's not a magic fix, but it's *something*," June says. It doesn't matter what we throw at her, she won't let it rain on her parade. "But if—no, WHEN—we do, it will be *some* sort of real world again! We'll figure out where our parents are— and we'll get them back. Heck, we'll get other *people* back."

"Not sure I consider that a plus," Dirk mumbles.

We're all smiling when we crest a ridge and finally reach our new home base: the still-healing Mallusk, sheltered beneath a half-crumbled highway overpass, munching on a landfill. Stretching out in front of her is our makeshift camp.

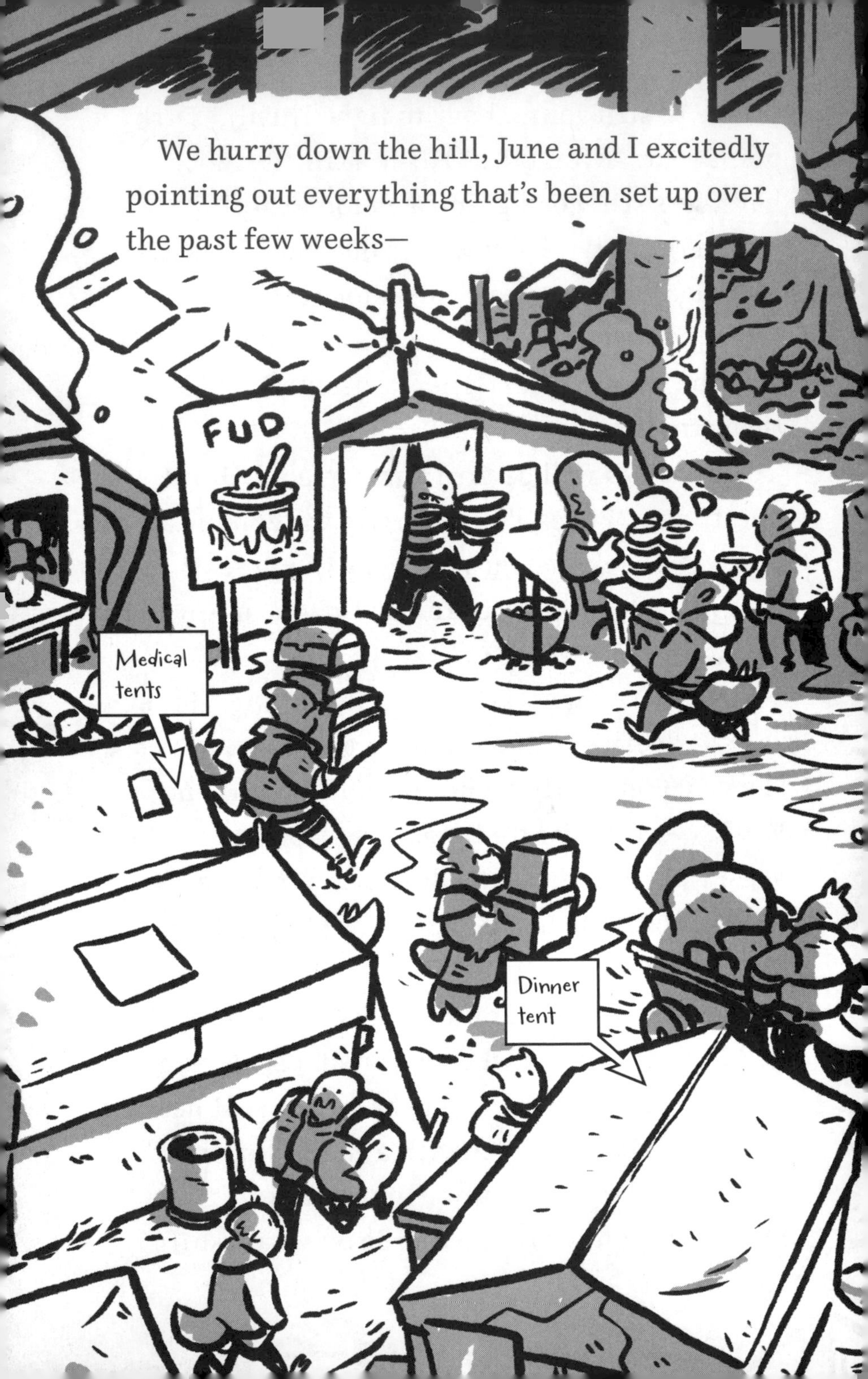
We hurry down the hill, June and I excitedly pointing out everything that's been set up over the past few weeks—
FUD
Medical tents
Dinner tent

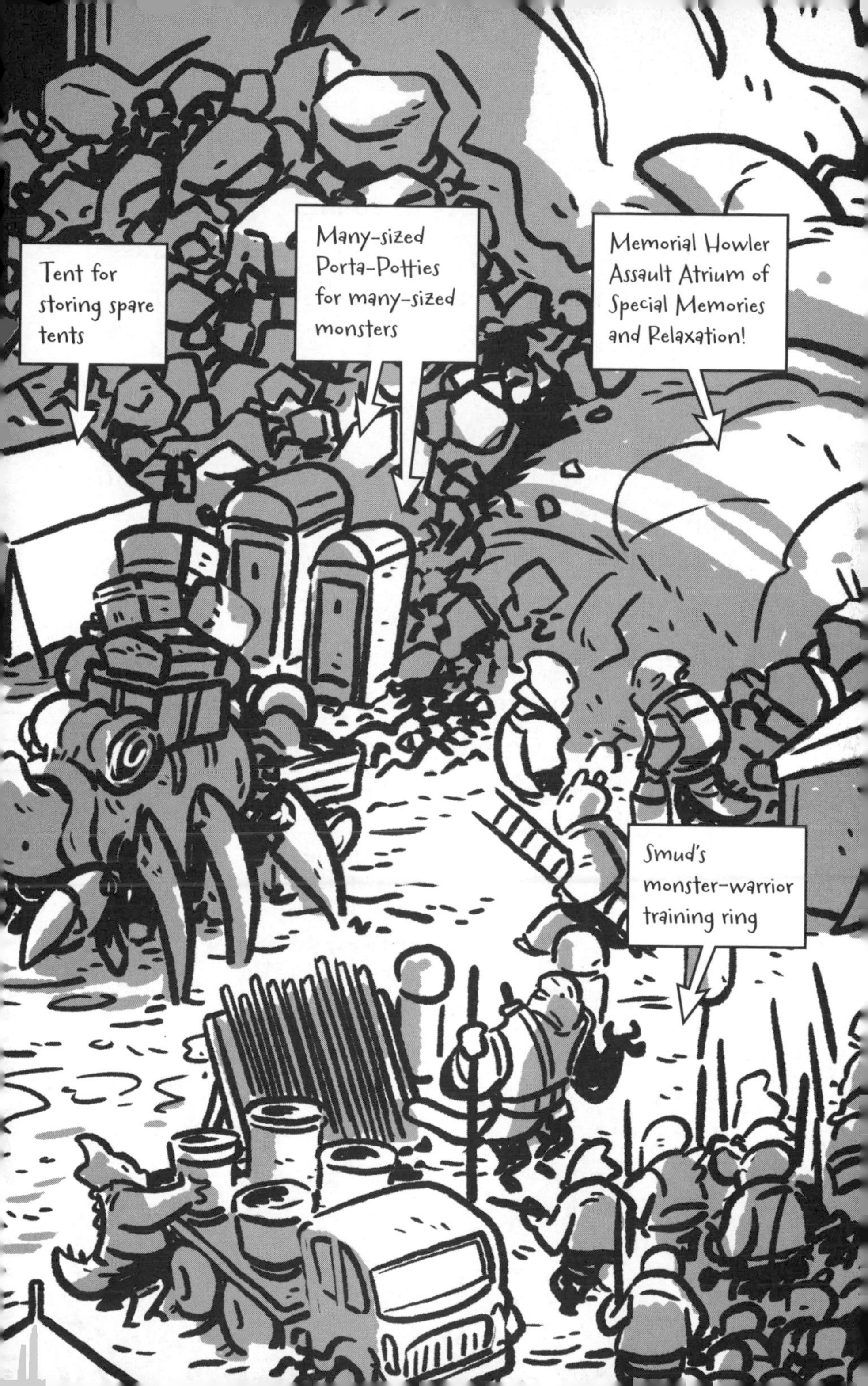
Tent for storing spare tents
Many-sized Porta-Potties for many-sized monsters
Memorial Howler Assault Atrium of Special Memories and Relaxation!
Smud's monster-warrior training ring

Dirk spots Smud. The goofy brute—formerly Ghazt's henchmonster—is busy training the citizens of Mallusk City in combat, getting them ready for the fight to come when we reach the Tower. "Hard to get used to bad guy monsters turned good-ish guy monsters," Dirk says.

I nod—it's true. But it happens a lot during the monster-zombie apocalypse, and it's confusing. Especially because, in the beginning, the *opposite* happened. Thrull, the WORST villain of them all, pretended to be our friend. Then he betrayed us. And killed my friend Bardle . . .

"QUINT!" a friendly voice exclaims. I turn to see Quint reuniting with our favorite conjurer, Yursl. I hurry to join the conversation. Gotta keep up with all the goings-on. They're discussing that Drakkor thing again.

YOU DID WHAT NOW?!

An **intentional** teleportation. I sent the Drakkor to the Neat-O Buzz factory, far enough to keep it away, but strategically located to keep it **there**.

Makes sense, good choice, exactly what I would've done.

Yursl eyes me questioningly, but I just keep on nodding like I know all about the Drakkor. But so far, I only know enough to know that I feel like I missed out on something epic.

Yursl's face scrunches up—can't tell if she's happy, infuriated, or possibly just experiencing mild indigestion. Finally, her face settles on something like . . . *grandmotherly pride*.

"I gave you the conjuring guidebook because it was essential that you learned conjuring on your own," Yursl says. "And it seems you have, toots!"

"Indeed!" Quint says, lifting his cannon, showing it off. "I've got a mean Kinetic Volley now."

I agree. "And he can turn Splotchers into trading cards!"

Quint elbows me sharply. "Ixnay on the ardscay."

Yursl frowns. "I can't think of a conjuration that should cause—"

"No, no, that was just a, uh . . . Jack's blood sugar level was low, and he was seeing stuff—" Quint says quickly, trying to shuffle us away.

I hear Yursl murmur, "What an odd pair," as we hurry off.

Back at Hey, Sport—our former campaign headquarters and general living, sleeping, and hanging-out spot—we have big plans for a movie marathon.

My Zombie Squad greets us with trays of popcorn and candy. A single box of Raisinets—Dirk's favorite—is set off to the side so it won't contaminate the other candy with its lousiness.

But as soon as we spot our makeshift beds, the plan changes.

My friends and I collapse. Tired bodies, for sure, but also just overwhelmed and beat from the day's torrent of reunions, new information, and newfound hope.

In seconds, I'm sprawled out on my trampoline bed. When my eyes flutter closed, I see Rover. All two tons of him, furry and happy to see me, like nobody else has ever been happy to see me.

Rover and I used to gallop through Wakefield like He-Man and Battle Cat—but did you ever see He-Man play fetch with his trusty steed? I think not. Rover and I used to have the best games of fetch, even if he did eat the Frisbee half the time . . .

Gulp!

Rover, fetch!

I'm gonna find you, Rover, I think. *And we're gonna play the most **epic** game of fetch ever.*

It's a nice drifting-off-to-sleep image.

Unfortunately, it's not my last drifting-off-to-sleep image. As I slip into that half-asleep, half-waking state, I see one last thing.

It's the Cosmic Hand. Turning me into something I don't want to be . . .

NOOOooOOO!!

chapter seven

I figured a day of leaping onto speeding trains
and evil monster interrogations would earn me
a little extra snooze time, but Drooler disagrees.

My eyes flutter open and I see Drooler,
perched on my chest, chirping, *"MEEP! MEEP!
MEEP!"*

Dirk stands over us, grinning. "You ready for
a dudes-on-a-mission type mission, Jack? 'Cause
we're doing a dudes-on-a-mission type mission!
Quint and June and Skaelka have already been
planning for *hours*."

"What day is it?" I yawn.

"The day after yesterday. That's how days
work."

I grumble.

"Y'know," Dirk says, "when Quint and I were
out on our just-the-two-of-us hero quest, we
didn't have any trouble wakin' up when a big
fight was awaitin'."

"FINE, FINE, I'M UP!" I start—but it's a moment too late. Dirk has decided he will get me up. *All the way up.*

Dirk and I follow a breadcrumb trail of Lego bricks through the mall—a green- and orange- and yellow-brick road to our friends. I've been living in this mall for more than a month now, and I have the layout memorized like a Mario Kart track—with all the shortcuts.

Two turns, just past the giant Howler gash in the wall, we reach our destination: the Hobby Horse.

When I see Quint, I wake up, fully. Because my friend is *back*.

The past few weeks—not knowing where he and Dirk were or if they were OK—have been the longest weeks of my life. To think that my *stupid* Cosmic Hand could've led to my friends maybe being *dead*? To swallow my pride and admit to the mall citizens that I had messed up—that I was *not* a leader? It was a lot to handle for one kid.

And it only got worse after I saw that smoldering hole in the ground—where Quint and Dirk had vanished.

After that, I felt even less capable of leading. And still do. How can I lead if so many of the choices I've made have been the *wrong* choices? If it weren't for my careless use of the Cosmic Hand, Thrull wouldn't have Ghazt—Thrull wouldn't be one step away from bringing Ŗeżżőcħ here.

"Where we at?" Dirk says. He enters the Hobby Horse, glaring at the goofy mascot at the door like he's daring it to start something.

Quint eagerly dives in. "We combined what little Skaelka remembers of the fortress, along with—"

"All the rad recon Jack and I did, plus his photos," June says, jumping in. "To create—"

"Drumroll, please!" Quint says.

"How about a cinnamon roll, *then* a drum-roll?" I ask. "Any food around here? Morning meetings require pastries or something, don't you think—"

"THE FORTRESS!" they say together, as they step aside, revealing—

"OK, this is better than pastries," I say, circling the model. I whistle under my breath. It's too bad there aren't awards for Best Toy Replica of a Monster Torture Fortress, because this would definitely take the prize.

"We will each have a specific role to fill," Quint announces.

"I can guide us through once we're in," Skaelka says with certainty. "My memories of the fortress are still hazy—but they *will* return once I see it again in the flesh."

"One big problem remains, though," Quint says. Using a bubble wand, he points to the model's small-scale representation of the cliff. "Like Skaelka said, getting inside is nearly impossible."

June asks, "How'd you get down, then?"

"I jumped," Skaelka replies. "Only Quint's armor—and the ooze-swamp surrounding the base—saved me. But for you to attempt it, with your brittle human bones . . . would be ugly, wet, leaky death."

"We're hoping to avoid death—ugly, wet, leaky, or otherwise," Quint says.

With that, June, Dirk, and Quint begin hurling out ideas for how to get up that giant cliff and into the fortress . . .

"Mega-Catapults!" Quint says.

"Giant birds!" Dirk suggests.

"Giant birds launched from Mega-Catapults!" June says.

Now, usually, tossing around ideas—especially super lousy ones—is my jam.

But not right now.

I barely hear my friends. They're just background noise as my eyes focus on the model, practically zooming in on the cliff face.

And then I feel it.

The Cosmic Hand. It's pulsing. Tightening and throbbing. It feels like a standoff. Me. The model. The hand.

It's not until I taste blood that I realize I'm gnawing on the inside of my cheek.

"Jack?"

"Huh?" I say, snapping out of it.

Quint says, "I asked you what you think, Jack. You've been quiet."

"What's up?" June asks. She smiles. "Usually, tossing around ideas—especially super-lousy ones—is your jam."

"Uh, one sec," I say, my insides wobbly. I'm suddenly desperate for fresh air.

My eyes dart around the Hobby Horse. I spot an impulse-buy, sure-to-cause-a-tantrum Dum-Dums display on the counter. I reach for it, knocking over the box as I grab one, fingernail stabbing at the wrapper as I quick-walk through the store, through the exploded far wall, and outside, out of sight.

Before I have a full-blown panic attack, I jam the lollipop into my mouth.

I'm scared.

So scared I can taste the fear.

Wait, nope—that's just my cheek blood mixing with blue raspberry. It's the limited-edition flavor no one ever asked for.

The cool air settles my stomach and slows my brain's spiraling.

The Cosmic Hand tightens, squeezing and squashing the bare flesh underneath. My arm feels like a washcloth being wrung out.

I watch the otherworldly suction cups that cover the hand slowly flicker open and closed.

The suction cups make the hand perfect for gripping things: the Louisville Slicer, the last piece of pizza, the keystone nacho that holds the nacho pile together . . . and also . . .

Cliffsides, probably.

Even supposedly unclimbable, death-trap cliffsides.

It feels like the Cosmic Hand is telling me what to do. I mean, not literally *telling* me. The hand doesn't *talk*. And if it ever does start talking, well, that's when I'll know I've truly gone stone-cold crazy.

But the hand *does* have a habit of thumping and throbbing just before a hand-related idea pops into my noggin.

And right now, that hand-related idea is: climb the cliff. Because the clock is ticking, and I don't see any two-hundred-talon-tall ladders lying around.

Except so far, using the Cosmic Hand to do anything *but* wield the Louisville Slicer has led to near disaster. It's like . . .

And when I reached out to help June, it did something *monstrous*. *Unforgivable*.

It *hurt* my friend.

I'm no leader. I don't want to be. But I know that I may need to be. And being a leader doesn't mean having all the answers. It means doing the thing that's scary when you DON'T have all the answers.

At least, that's what Rogue said in Ultimate X-Men one time . . .

There's no time. This Wracksaw guy didn't have the schematics *yesterday*, but he might have them tomorrow. Evil's like summer vacation, always moving faster than you want it to.

Any moment, the knowledge-extraction will take place. Wracksaw will turn the Tower Schematics over to Thrull. And then . . . game over. Otherworldly EVIL AND DESTRUCTIVE GOD comes here and destroys *everything*.

So I take a final chomp out of the lollipop, flick it into the Mallusk's landfill food pile, and step back inside.

chapter eight

Everybody explodes in exclamations.

Dirk starts to fight me on it. June shouts something about how it's madness. Skaelka begins talking about eye-pecking birds again.

But I just shake my head until my pals' shoulders slump with grim understanding.

I'm the one who *can* do this, so I'm the one who *must* do this. My nerves twang like a banjo, but my hand hums in satisfaction.

June catches my eye. I nod. And she reluctantly nods back.

"I suppose," Quint begins, sounding unsure, "that I could rig something for you to carry up. Once you reach the entrance, you can lower it down for the rest of us."

Everyone else is quiet—and I realize they're gonna stay that way until I make clear that I *really am* OK with this. Even if I'm not.

"Your proposed title for this Mission Operation is a tad lengthy," Quint says. "But OK! So . . . like I said, we'll each have a role to fill. Jack will get us inside . . ."

Dirk perks up. "Ooh! I'm gonna be the Muscle! All silent and sneaky when needed—and then, also, super 'BOOM, FIST TO YOUR FACE, BAD GUY!' Hmm . . . I'm gonna need some special extra-quiet shoes for this . . ."

"Boom? Did someone say boom?" June asks. "'Cause I call dibs on making stuff go boom. I might not know anything about conjuring or interdimensional cosmic blow-ups—but you know what I *do* know about?" She slaps her Blasty hand onto the table. "BLASTING! And I'm *pumped* to blast that evil place to bits, because that means I'm one step closer to reuniting with my family!"

"This is a delightful new side of you, June," I say with a teasing grin.

She points her regular, normal, not-Blasty hand at me and grins back. "BOOM."

Skaelka cocks her head. "How you four are not yet dead, I do not know," she says, before announcing, "I will be your guide on this perilous journey, navigating you to the heart of that foul fortress."

Quint says, "And now that we know how we're getting in, here's how it's all going to go down . . ."

"THE PLAN"

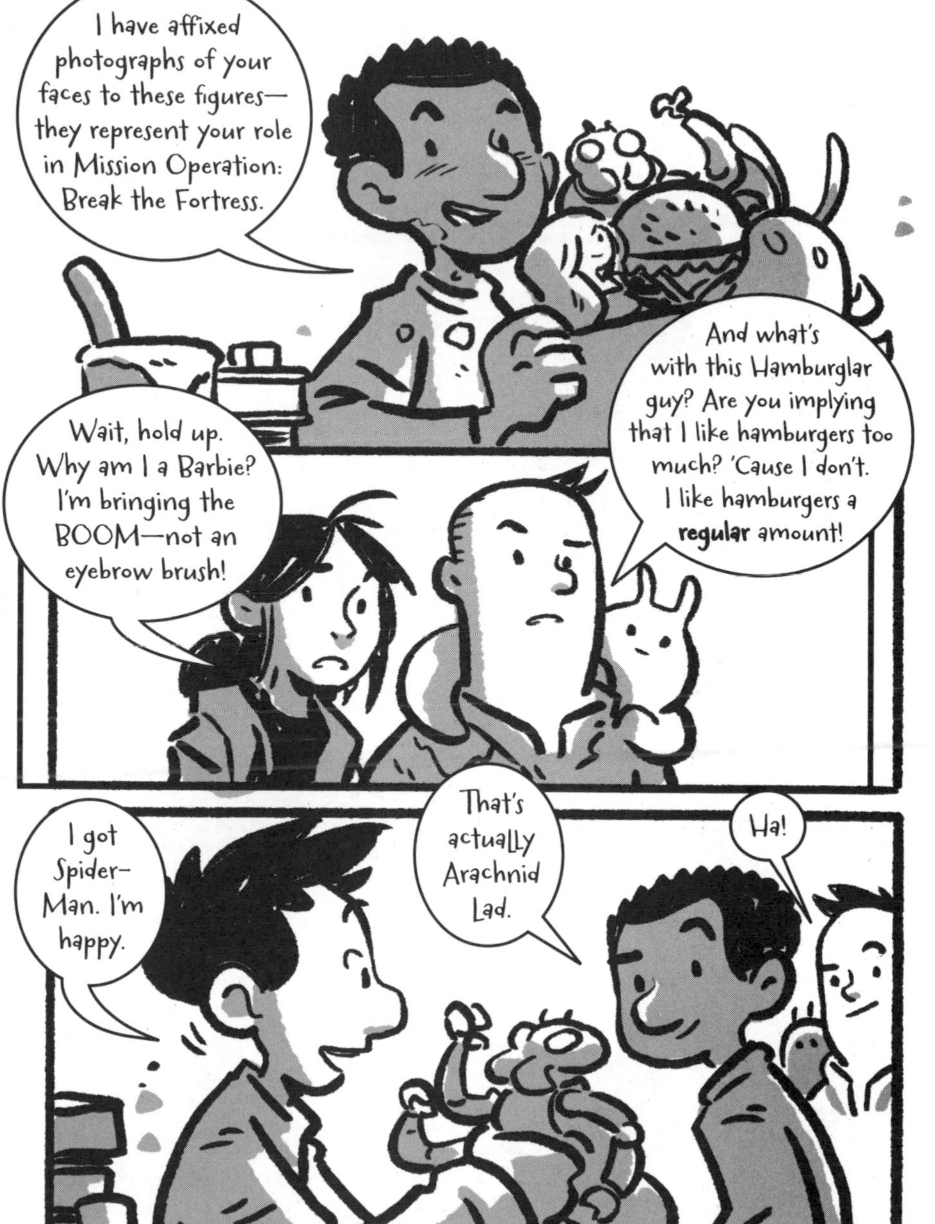
I have affixed photographs of your faces to these figures—they represent your role in Mission Operation: Break the Fortress.
Wait, hold up. Why am I a Barbie? I'm bringing the BOOM—not an eyebrow brush!
And what's with this Hamburglar guy? Are you implying that I like hamburgers too much? 'Cause I don't. I like hamburgers a **regular** amount!
I got Spider-Man. I'm happy.
That's actually Arachnid Lad.
Ha!

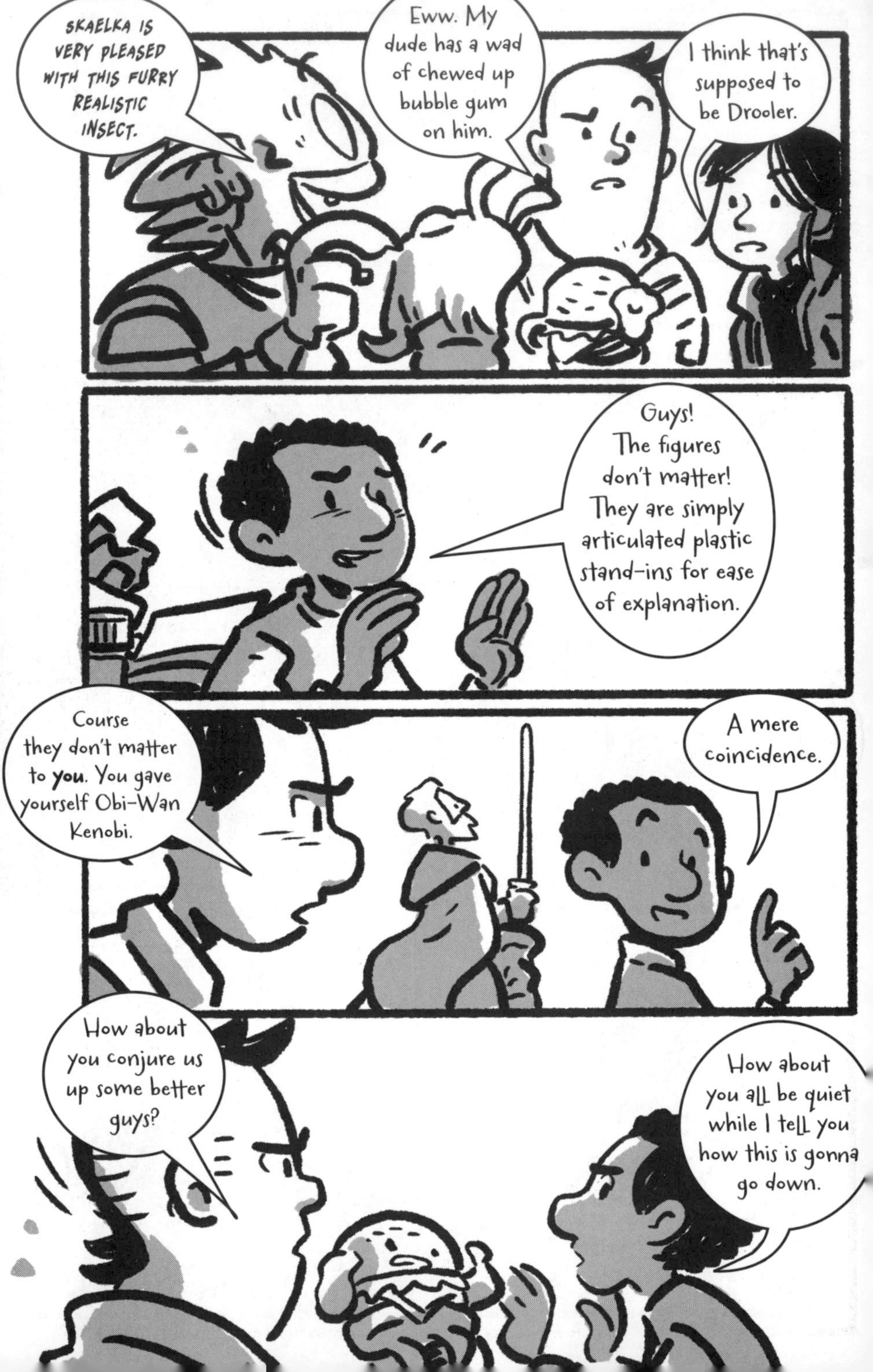
SKAELKA IS VERY PLEASED WITH THIS FURRY REALISTIC INSECT.
Eww. My dude has a wad of chewed up bubble gum on him.
I think that's supposed to be Drooler.
Guys! The figures don't matter! They are simply articulated plastic stand-ins for ease of explanation.
Course they don't matter to **you**. You gave yourself Obi-Wan Kenobi.
A mere coincidence.
How about you conjure us up some better guys?
How about you all be quiet while I tell you how this is gonna go down.

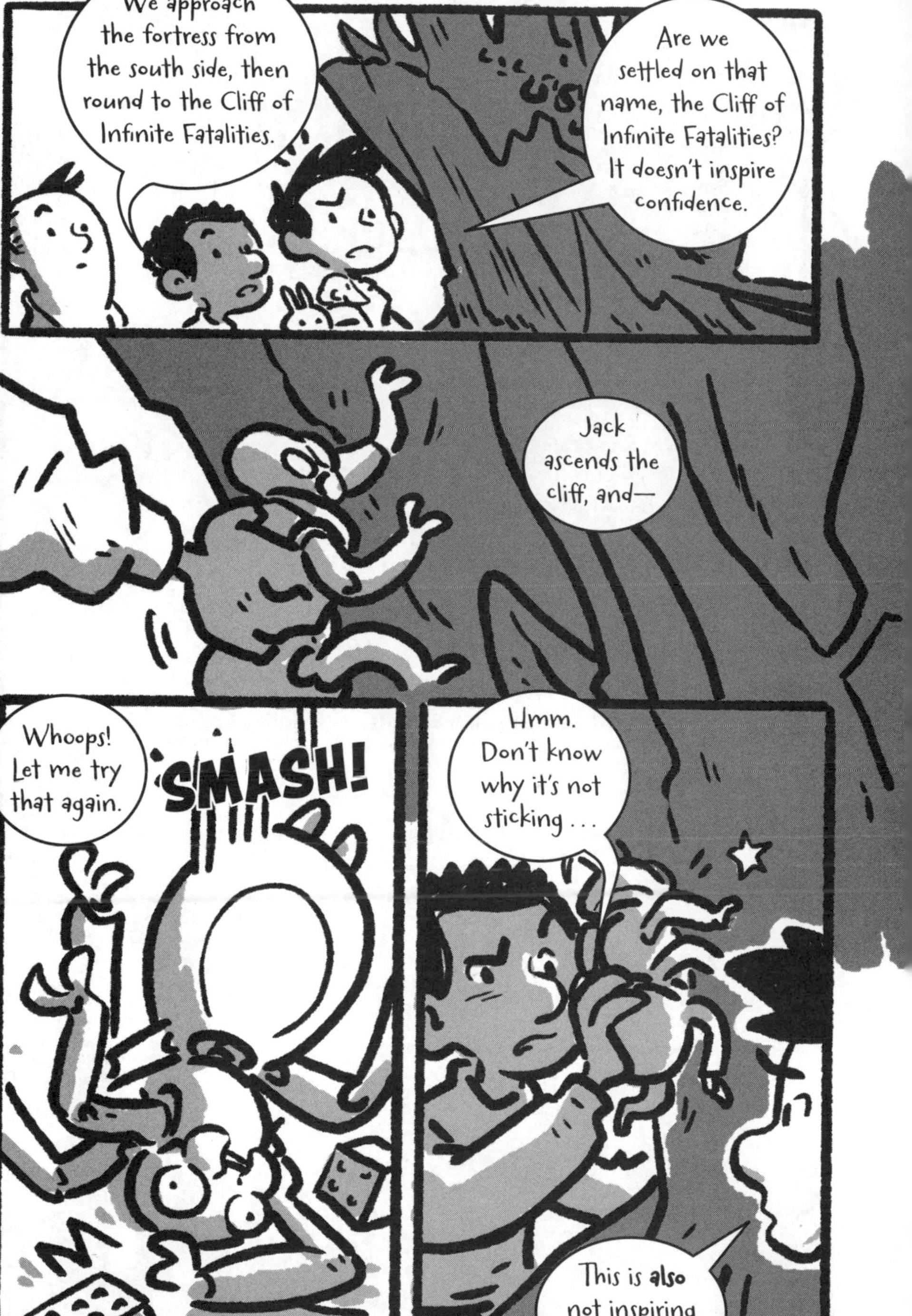
We approach the fortress from the south side, then round to the Cliff of Infinite Fatalities.
Are we settled on that name, the Cliff of Infinite Fatalities? It doesn't inspire confidence.
Jack ascends the cliff, and—
Whoops! Let me try that again.
SMASH!
Hmm. Don't know why it's not sticking . . .
This is **also** not inspiring confidence . . .

Whatever! We get it! If I have to keep watching little Jack smash against Lego rocks, I'm never gonna do this. Let's just skip ahead to me getting up—with my head still attached.

Fine. With Jack successfully up the cliff, he will lower a lift device that I will construct. I'm thinking a human hamster ball, but I still need to noodle.

Wait, human hamster ball?

Please roll with it.

HA, good one!

And then we enter.

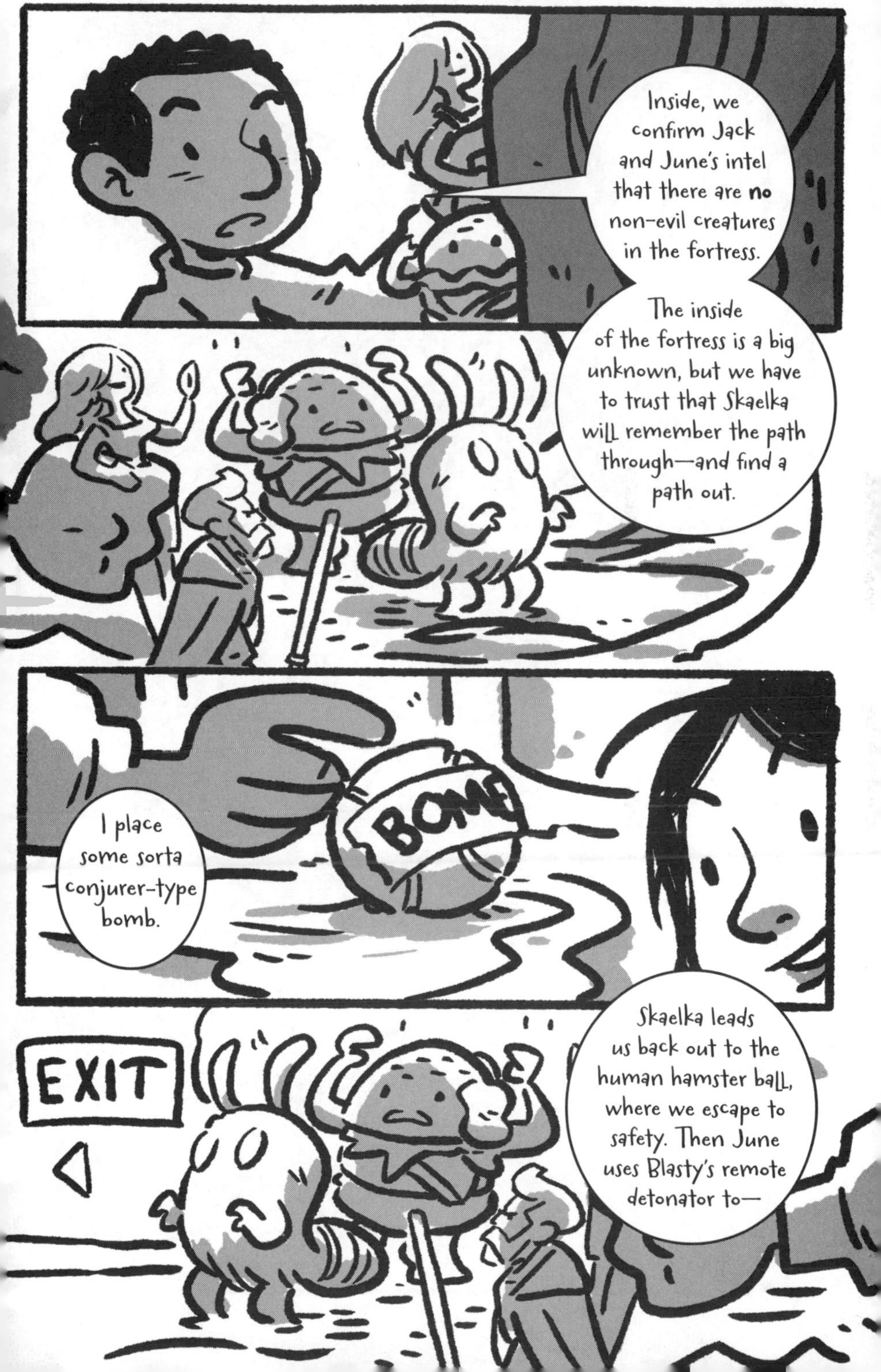
Inside, we confirm Jack and June's intel that there are **no** non-evil creatures in the fortress.
The inside of the fortress is a big unknown, but we have to trust that Skaelka will remember the path through—and find a path out.
BOMB
I place some sorta conjurer-type bomb.
EXIT
Skaelka leads us back out to the human hamster ball, where we escape to safety. Then June uses Blasty's remote detonator to—

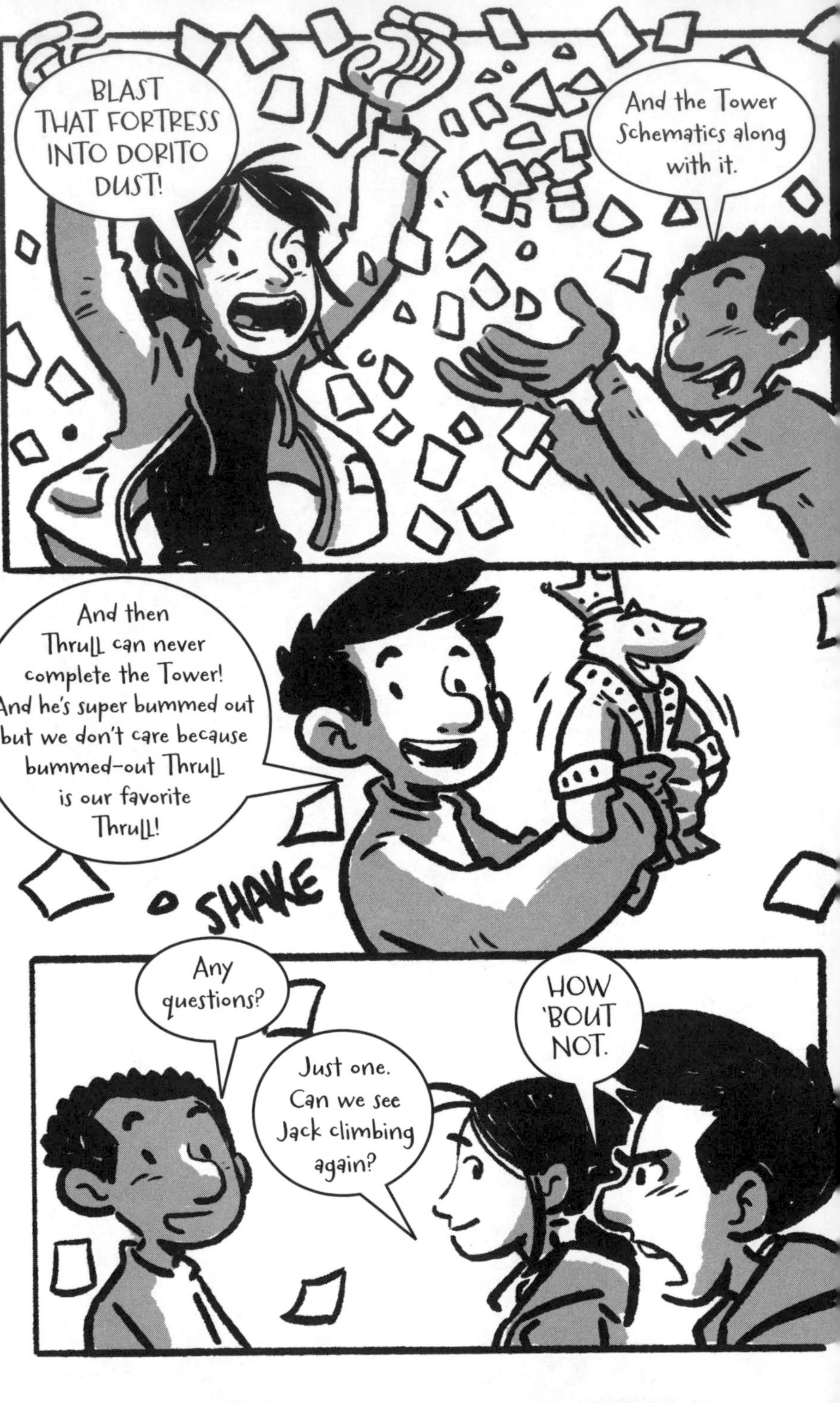
BLAST THAT FORTRESS INTO DORITO DUST!
And the Tower Schematics along with it.
And then Thrull can never complete the Tower! And he's super bummed out but we don't care because bummed-out Thrull is our favorite Thrull!
SHAKE
Any questions?
Just one. Can we see Jack climbing again?
HOW 'BOUT NOT.

"And that, my friends, is the plan," Quint says, snapping his bubble wand away and clicking his heels together with military precision. "Though it is still missing one key ingredient."

"Mayonnaise?" I ask. "Don't be mayonnaise—I hate mayonnaise."

"He means the thing that will actually *destroy* the joint," June says. "The uh . . . hmm . . . Fortress Breaker! And I've got an idea for how to go about getting one!"

With that, June darts out of the store, setting off a chain reaction of hasty departures.

Skaelka leaves to spar with Smud's warriors-in-training, convinced that combat will get her blood pumping and her memories returning. Quint rushes to begin work on his "human hamster ball." Drooler scampers off, too, mimicking everyone else's hurried exits—and Dirk follows.

"You might wanna get one of those toddler leashes for him!" I call after Dirk.

"NEVER!" Dirk cries as he speeds after the little slimeball.

And then it's just me. Staring at the model of the fortress. And that cliff.

And then at my hand.

I sigh.

If I'm gonna climb the Cliff of Infinite Fatalities, I should probably—well—learn how to climb . . .

chapter nine

So, here's my problem—

There's no real way to *practice* climbing a monstrous cliffside—especially when the only thing you've ever climbed before was the fifth-grade jungle gym. And double-especially when the only thing you know about the cliff you've gotta climb is that it's supposedly unclimbable.

But I gotta do *something*. Everybody else is busy preparing for the big Mission Operation: Break the Fortress. Though most of Dirk's time is spent chasing after Drooler . . .

So I head off in search of a cliff to test out.
A small one. Like, y'know, a starter cliff.

But it ends up not being a cliff at all.

I'm halfway up the side when the cliff *stands* and I realize it's actually a *giant rock monster*.

So I'm left stuck, dangling from this boulder beast, while it goes on a freaking leisurely five-hour afternoon hike . . .

The monster walks about three more miles before I'm finally able to slide off.

I'm headed back into camp, exhausted, when—

"HEADS UP!" June calls, speeding past me.

"Geez, June, where's the fire?" I call.

"It's about to start," she shouts, turning as she runs to flash me a mischievous smile. I realize she's carrying a cardboard box and wearing huge science-class safety goggles. "I'm beginning Fortress Breaker tests if you wanna watch!"

Um, yeah, duh.

"So, what exactly are you testing?" I shout, chasing after her.

"Conjurer thingamabobs! Each one chock-full of other-dimensional destructive energy!" she calls. Then, by way of explanation, she says, "I paid a little visit to our local conjurer . . ."

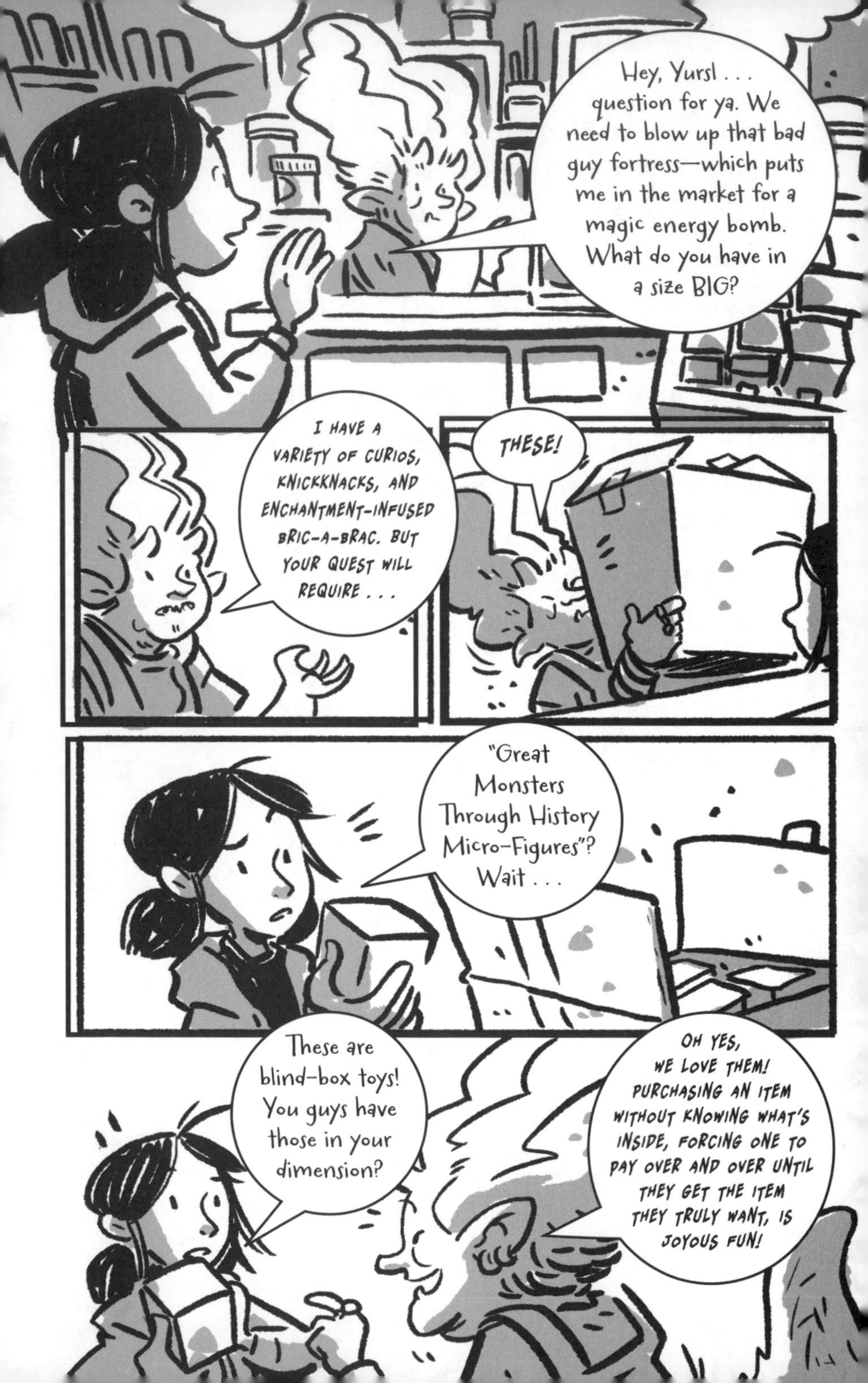
Hey, Yursl . . . question for ya. We need to blow up that bad guy fortress—which puts me in the market for a magic energy bomb. What do you have in a size BIG?
I HAVE A VARIETY OF CURIOS, KNICKKNACKS, AND ENCHANTMENT-INFUSED BRIC-A-BRAC. BUT YOUR QUEST WILL REQUIRE . . .
THESE!
"Great Monsters Through History Micro-Figures"? Wait . . .
These are blind-box toys! You guys have those in your dimension?
OH YES, WE LOVE THEM! PURCHASING AN ITEM WITHOUT KNOWING WHAT'S INSIDE, FORCING ONE TO PAY OVER AND OVER UNTIL THEY GET THE ITEM THEY TRULY WANT, IS JOYOUS FUN!

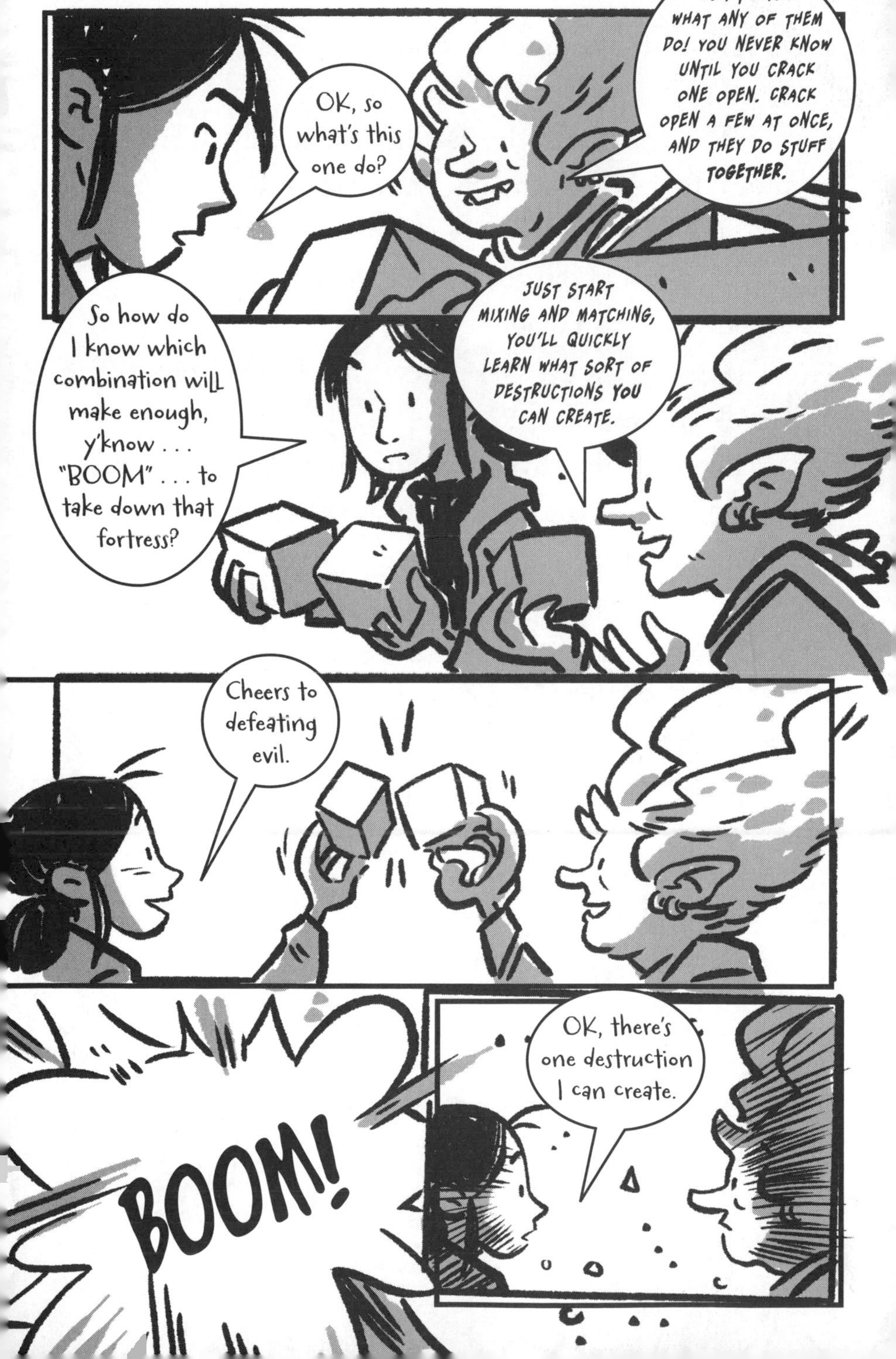
OK, so what's this one do?
DON'T KNOW WHAT ANY OF THEM DO! YOU NEVER KNOW UNTIL YOU CRACK ONE OPEN. CRACK OPEN A FEW AT ONCE, AND THEY DO STUFF TOGETHER.
So how do I know which combination will make enough, y'know . . . "BOOM" . . . to take down that fortress?
JUST START MIXING AND MATCHING, YOU'LL QUICKLY LEARN WHAT SORT OF DESTRUCTIONS YOU CAN CREATE.
Cheers to defeating evil.
BOOM!
OK, there's one destruction I can create.

That's all too much for me to process, so I just say, "This sounds incredibly unsafe."

We race around the Mallusk. Up ahead, two football field lengths past the camp, I see—

"THE BLASTING ZONE!" June announces proudly. I'm about to commend her on the elaborate setup when—

"Hold up," I say. "What's with all the ancient Greek statue things?"

"Needed something to actually *blast*," she says. "Ended up going a little nuts at the fancy lawn ornament store . . ."

I nod, thinking that *kinda* makes sense, when—

"HEY!" I exclaim. "My face! That one's got MY FACE!" Then, half-horrified, half-honored, I realize they've ALL got my face.

"June," I say. "These statues are . . ."

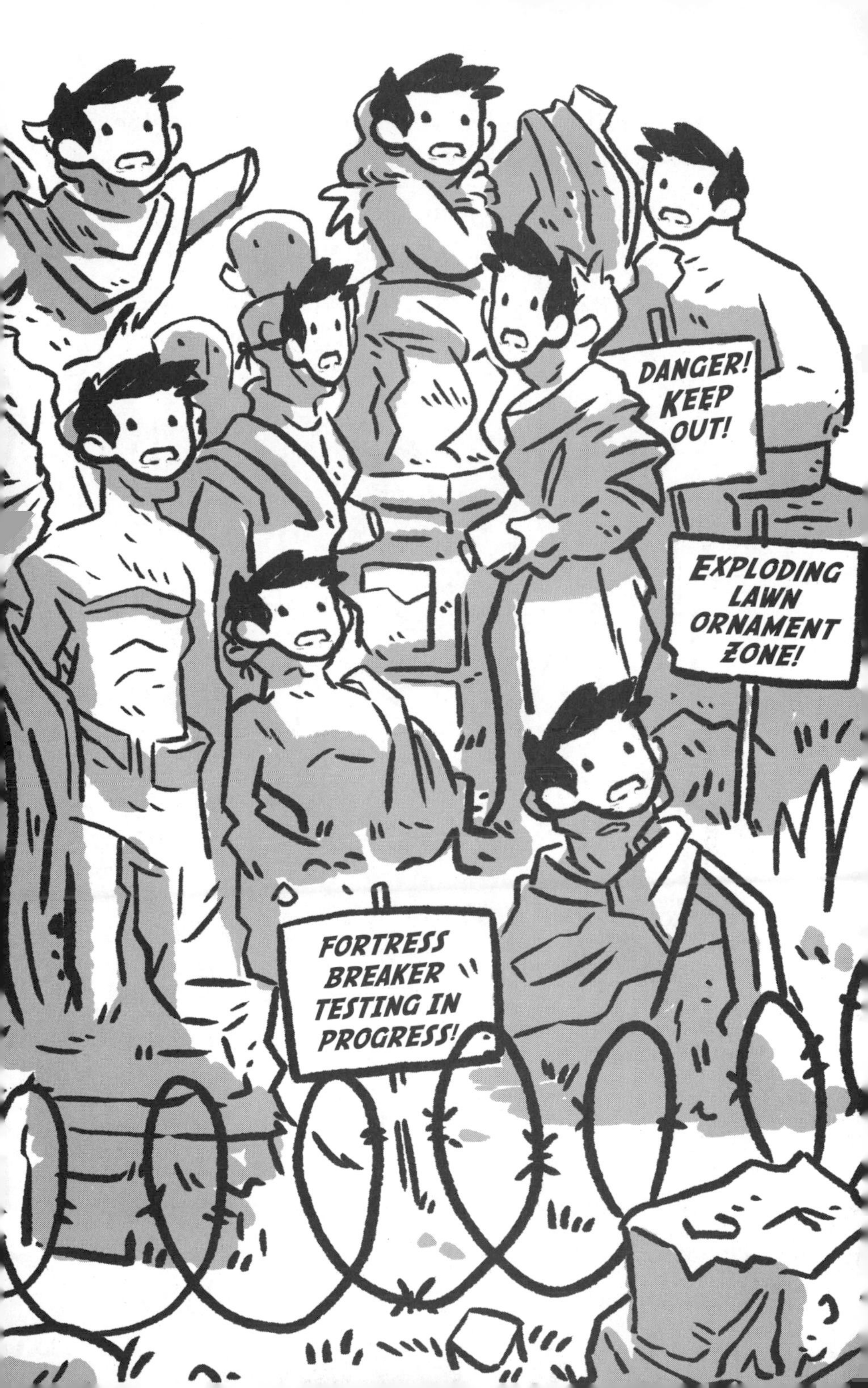
DANGER! KEEP OUT!
EXPLODING LAWN ORNAMENT ZONE!
FORTRESS BREAKER TESTING IN PROGRESS!

"You really doubled down on Quint's printing-out-faces thing, huh?" I ask.

"Revenge for your June Bait," she says, grinning.

"I guess I did kinda start it," I admit, thinking back to a *really bad zombie-catching plan* we had long ago . . .

June Bait!

June tears open the first tiny blind-box carton, revealing a lumpy blob-monster figure made from something like other-dimensional plastic.

"Zorgal the Mildly Repugnant," I read.

June pulls out a fistful of wireless transmitters, pulled from walkie-talkies. She sticks one to Zorgal and slides the other one into Blasty. She dashes into the blasting zone, drops Zorgal next to a statue, then darts back. She's practically giddy as she hops over a rusted refrigerator and ducks down beside me.

June tosses me a pair of safety goggles. Then, in a very official-sounding voice, she announces, "Blast test number one—Zorgal the Mildly Repugnant—will now commence."

I throw on my goggles and June nudges my shoulder.

"Hope you're prepared for an earth-shattering kaboom, Jack." She reaches down, flicks a switch on Blasty, and—

There's a little *PWEEF* sound, Zorgal's left arm falls off, then he topples face-first into the dirt.

"Good thing I was prepared," I say.

June rolls her eyes. "Still helpful! Now we know that Zorgal does a pweefy thing," June says, undeterred. "Let's see what happens when I start combining these bad boys."

She unboxes three more figures: a neon skull, a metallic spine covered in teeth, and something that looks like a melting labradoodle.

Moments later, she commences blast test number two. It's way more successful—and way louder. We might need to get our hearing checked soon . . .

The next three days are a whirlwind of preparation: June playing mix-and-match blind-box blow-up, Skaelka dueling with Smud's monsters, and Quint assembling his lift-device.

And me? Well, I spend about nineteen hours playing an old Spider-Man arcade game. 'Cause like I said, there's no real way to prepare to *climb a giant wall brimming with unknowable terror*.

The whole scary plan fills me with fear. But maybe . . .

Hmm. Maybe I can prepare for *that part*? Prepare for *the scary*?

Back in middle school, Dirk was the scariest kid around—so I seek him out. I figure I'll find him doing judo moves or something, preparing to be the Muscle. But . . . nope. He's plopped in a recliner, running a needle and thread through a stuffed possum while watching ninja movies.

Before I can even ask, he says, "Don't question my process."

I shrug. Fair enough.

"So, uh, look . . ." I start. "I need to face some fear. *Any major fear*. Like, overcome it."

Dirk stops sewing and looks up. "So, what scares you the most?"

Turning into a monster, I think, but I definitely *do not* say that.

"Well, I have this recurring dream where my teeth fall out. Also, beating a mega boss in a video game and forgetting to save—that's a big one. Finding Rover but he doesn't recognize me. Not finding Rover. Finding Rover but he has a human head. Great white sharks, hammerhead sharks, that toothless goalie on the San Jose Sharks—I guess all sharks, really. Hummingbirds really freak me out, too—they're *so tiny* but their wings move *so fast*. Oh, back in school, when we had to read out loud in front of the class. Also . . ."

"Bingo," Dirk says.

And soon . . .

Jack Sullivan—why don't you pick up where we left off.

Oh crud. Um, where were we?

MR. SAVAGE! JACK WASN'T PAYING ATTENTION!

CHAPTER TWELVE, JACK!

FLIK

So . . . that was a bust.

And time is running out. Quint has finished building his "human hamster ball," and June swears she's close to perfecting the Fortress Breaker. Which means it's just about time for Mission Operation: Break the Fortress to get underway, and I'm still—

"Jack! I have something for you to climb," Johnny Steve says, waddling over. He's grinning like he was reading my mind. "And if you can climb *this thing*, you can climb anything."

It turns out that *this thing* is a massive tower of monsters—the world's gnarliest cheerleader pyramid.

Suddenly, an earsplitting whistle cuts through the air. Johnny Steve claps his hands together and yells, "Let's go, Jack! Ascend!"

And I do . . .

And I'm actually . . . succeeding?

I step on a lot of monster heads, and my fingers poke around in a lot of monster mouths— which is so gross that it prevents me from even thinking about the many ways this could go bad. And before I know it . . .

I reach the top! I'm throwing my arms up, mid-Rocky-pose, when something like a sonic boom of mystical energy crashes through camp—

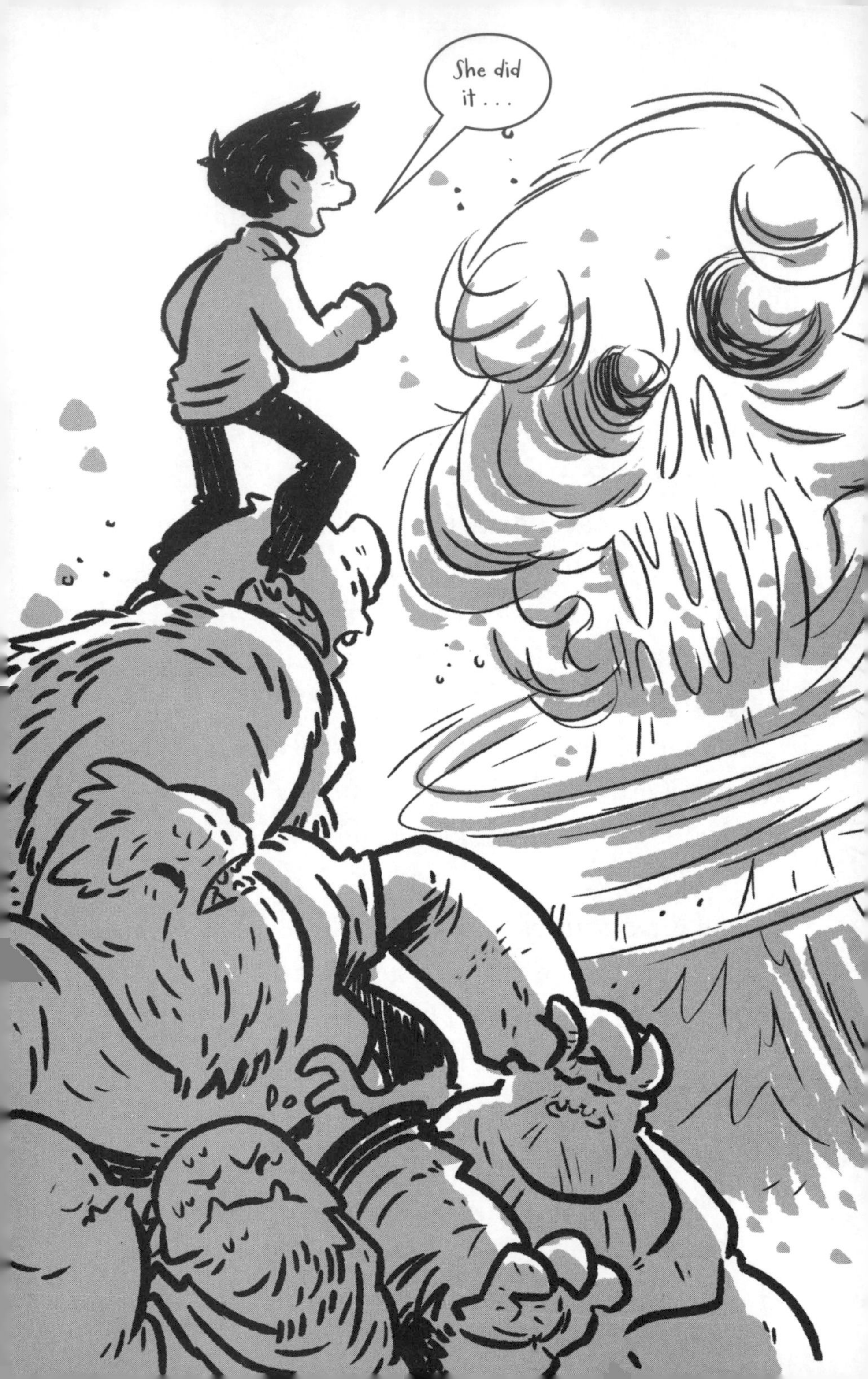
She did it . . .

A moment later, I spot June in the way-off distance, dashing back toward camp. Hands cupped around her mouth, she cries out, "THE FORTRESS BREAKER IS READY!"

That means . . . gulp . . . It's just about time to do this *for real*.

That night, we feast. Gotta fill our bellies—no idea what the food situation will be inside the fortress, but I highly doubt there's gonna be, like, an other-dimensional Dairy Queen or something.

Quint sits, clipboard in hand, checking things off, confirming we're fully prepared.

"Check, check, check, check, and check," Quint announces. But he doesn't sound fully satisfied. He pops a tater tot into his mouth and says nervously, "I just hope Skaelka will be able to lead us through the fortress."

"Smud's little monster battalion is definitely helping her get her groove back," Dirk says, nodding. "Look at her swinging that Nerf ax . . ."

"Sparring has allowed me to recall many of my favorite attacks," Skaelka says as she hops off the mound of groaning monsters and strides toward us.

"On that note . . ." Quint says. "Once we're inside the fortress . . . are you certain you'll recall how to reach the location where we'll need to place the Fortress Breaker?"

Skaelka looks nervous—but she nods. "Skaelka will remember," she says. "As well as Skaelka remembered the path out of that vile corn labyrinth."

What?? I think, sighing. *I missed out on a corn labyrinth, too?*

Pressing her hands together formally, Skaelka says, "I will lead you directly to the *heart* of that fortress—so that you can destroy it."

Just then, we hear the crashing roar of a charging Carapace—one of the search parties, speeding back to camp. Atop the Carapace are three monsters: members of the mall's resident rock band, the Brutal Gaspers.

"BIG NEWS!" the guitarist, Cliq, shouts. "No sign of Quint, Dirk, and Skaelka. But still . . . BIG NEWS!"

"Uh, we're right here," Dirk says, waving. "Got back a few days ago."

"But what's the big news??" June asks.

A cloud of dust puffs up as the rock band skids to a stop in front of us.

My friends and I exchange a heavy glance.
June says, "Sounds like something big is about to
go down."

Skaelka nods. "I suspect Wracksaw is close to
retrieving the Tower Schematics."

Grim, Dirk says, "There's only one way to find
out."

My hand throbs as I grip the Slicer and stand.

"Buddies," I say, "we leave at first light . . ."

chapter ten

Moonbeams shine through the windows of Hey, Sport—it's not even dawn, but we're all geared up, about ready to go. I wave the Louisville Slicer and gather my Zombie Squad.

"Alfred, Lefty, Glurm—you gotta sit this one out," I say as they shamble across the store. "This Wracksaw guy is bad news for monsters . . . and probably for zombies, too."

They groan softly in reply—almost sounding disappointed. But I don't care. All I care is that they're safe.

Soon, we're marching through the mall, booming monster snores coming from stores and kiosks—and I've never been more jealous of someone else's sleep time.

My heart is doing yoga, and my stomach is working on macramé. I'm tense, tied up in knots, and nervous . . . *very* nervous.

But at the very least—we *look* like some buddies who are ready to do a Mission Operation thing. And that fills me with hope.

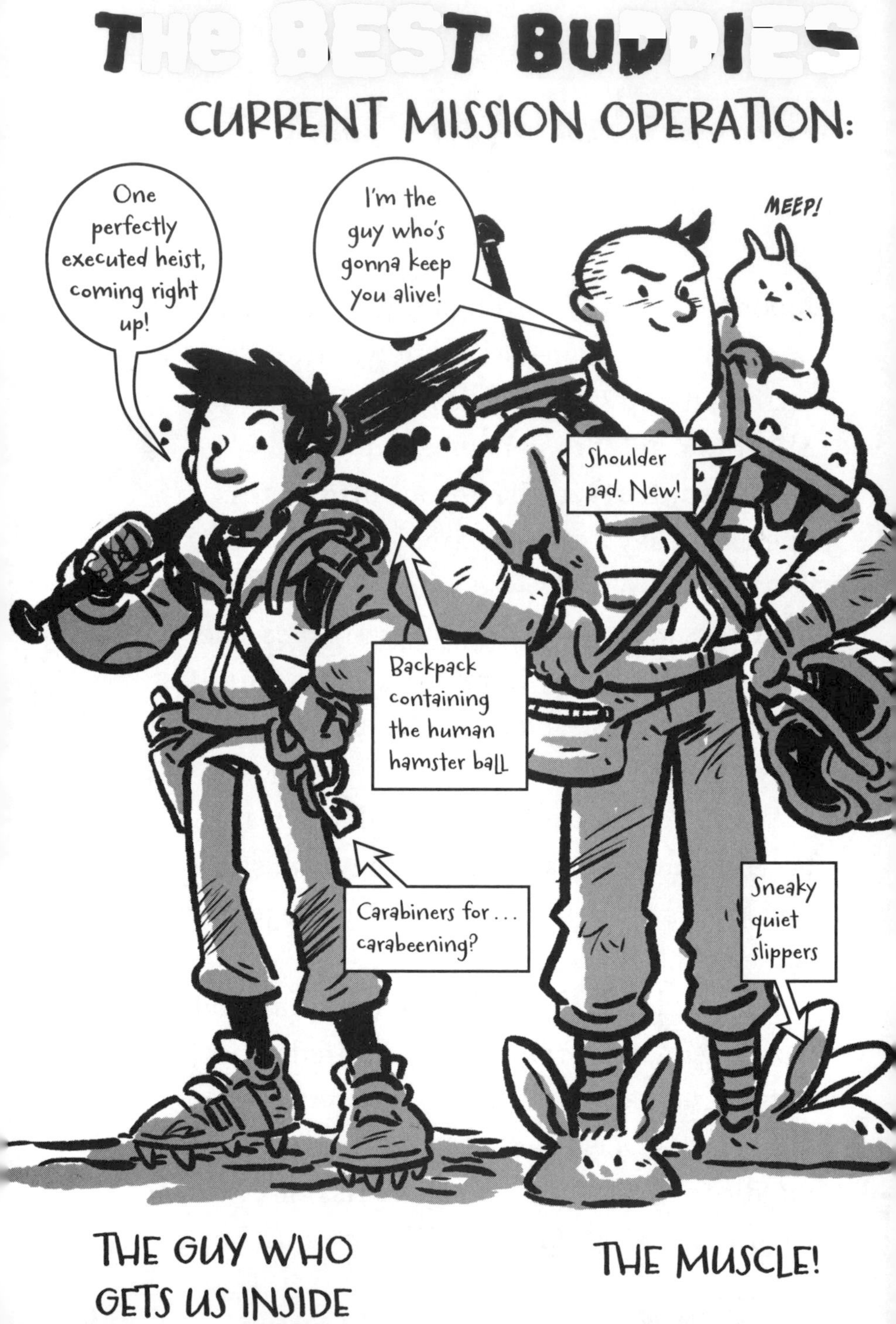
THE BEST BUDDIES
CURRENT MISSION OPERATION:
One perfectly executed heist, coming right up!
I'm the guy who's gonna keep you alive!
MEEP!
Shoulder pad. New!
Backpack containing the human hamster ball
Carabiners for . . . carabeening?
Sneaky quiet slippers
THE GUY WHO GETS US INSIDE
THE MUSCLE!

MISSION FORCE!

BREAK THE FORTRESS

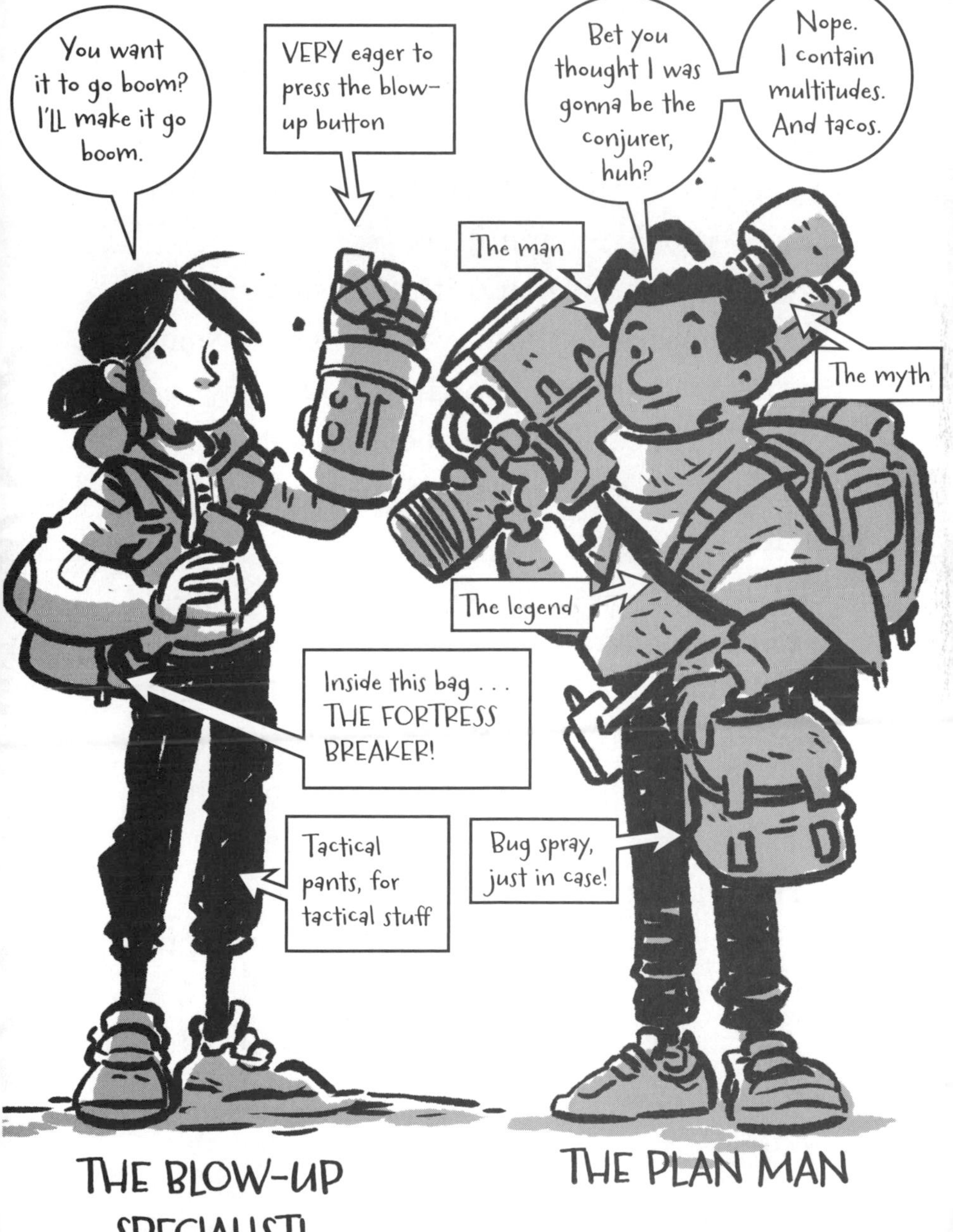

You want it to go boom? I'LL make it go boom.
VERY eager to press the blow-up button
Bet you thought I was gonna be the conjurer, huh?
Nope. I contain multitudes. And tacos.
The man
The myth
The legend
Inside this bag . . . THE FORTRESS BREAKER!
Tactical pants, for tactical stuff
Bug spray, just in case!
THE BLOW-UP SPECIALIST!
THE PLAN MAN

Streaks of morning light slice through the sky as we step out into camp. A cold wind blows, and I zip up my jacket. The sleeve is tight around my changing arm, keeping it hidden.

A voice calls, "Jack Sullivan! My fourth-favorite human!"

It's Johnny Steve, flanked by Yursl and Smud. I grin. A goodbye committee.

"Lift me up so I can initiate a good-riddance-high-five parade!" Johnny Steve says to Smud.

"Think you mean 'good luck'," June says.

But Smud's still half asleep, so instead it's Yursl who scoops up Johnny Steve, setting him on her shoulders.

It feels like the end of a Little League game, when both teams line up so everybody can slap hands. I guess it's supposed to teach kids about good sportsmanship—but in reality, it's just a chance for the winning team to gloat and the losing team to grumble. And I was always terrible at Little League, so when the game ended, all I really cared about was getting to the promised pizza party.

But there's no pizza party waiting for us where we're going now . . .

As we march across camp, June says, "That was a nice surprise."

"Let us hope it is the last surprise today," Skaelka says, hefting her ax over her shoulder. "Nice . . . or otherwise."

It's nearly midday when we pass beneath our billboard lookout post, and what lies ahead of us sends a shiver down my spine. The fortress has *changed* . . .

The fortress tilts at an impossible angle, like it *should* fall over at any moment—but won't.

"We're really going to win," June whispers. I glance over—and her cheeks flush.

"Whoops," she says. "I didn't, uh . . . I didn't mean to say that out loud."

But just then, the sun seems to catch the whole world just perfect. And we look . . . *right*. We don't look like kids just barely hanging on, trying to survive. We look like we're supposed to be right here, right now.

We're not on our back feet for once. No, this time, we're fighting back.

I smile at June. "You can say it out loud. And you can say it again, too, 'cause you're right. We *are* gonna win."

"Hey, chatterboxes, let's keep it movin'!" Dirk calls, huffing ahead of us. Drooler waves to us over Dirk's shoulder. "Double time!"

"You heard the Muscle. Time squared," Quint says as we march ahead.

A spooky, otherworldly swamp surrounds the base of the fortress, teeming with oozing fungus and debris. At the water's edge, an oily bubble grows—then pops as we pass.

"We circle around the corrosive swamp. Beyond it lies a path to the solid soil beneath the cliff," Skaelka announces, carefully treading forward.

"Yeah," I start. "We'll *definitely* wanna avoid the corrosive—"

I shut up.

Out of the corner of my eye, something moves.

A patch of glowing algae on the swamp's surface is suddenly sucked under. And then—

SPLLLAAAASH!

"Fightin' poses, gang!" Dirk barks. "I'm takin' lead!"

Spiderlike legs that previously belonged to another monster

Guard dog leash?

-THE ARACHNACANID-

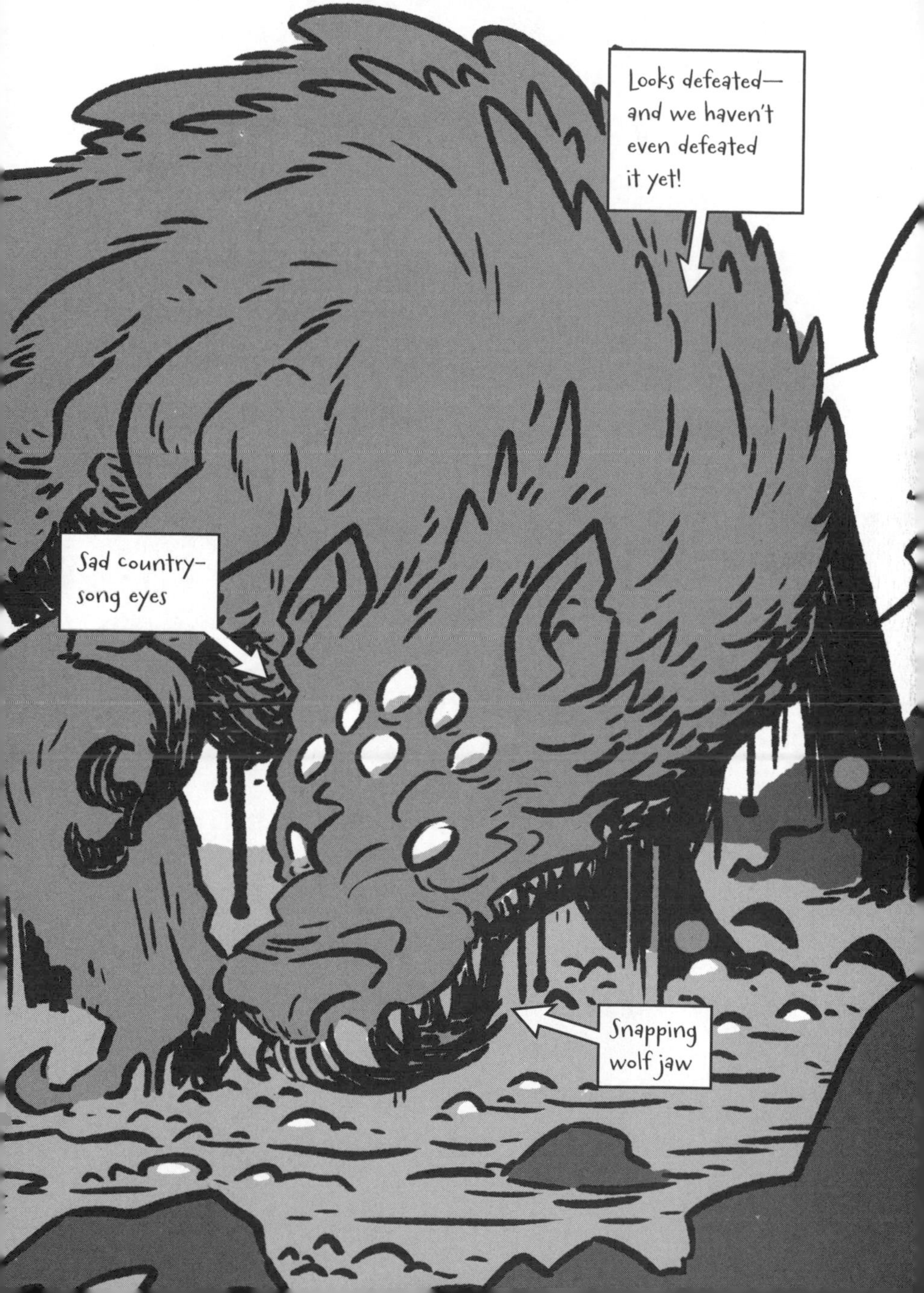
Looks defeated—and we haven't even defeated it yet!
Sad country-song eyes
Snapping wolf jaw

The fight ends before it begins—something I wish happened more often.

"Wracksaw did this," Skaelka says. "Wracksaw turned him into . . . this unnatural beast."

With her hands out, like she's trying to calm an angry dog, Skaelka wades out into the swamp.

The Arachnacanid stops yanking against its chain. Each breath is a low groan.

"It doesn't look like a threat now," I say. "It just looks like it's in pain."

"Like the Drakkor," Dirk says.

"I was about to say the same thing, friend," Quint replies.

I shoot them both a "we get it, you went on a cool adventure and became bosom buddies with something called a Drakkor, don't know what that is, but I'm guessing it's probably like a sentient beachball and I'm 92 percent sure that guess is correct" look.

Water splashes as the Arachnacanid settles into the swamp. Its mouth slowly opens . . .

"L'œ Ŵōŏ§ţʃ Ħðeśţ."

"Whoa," I whisper. "It can talk."

"The language is not entirely familiar to me," Skaelka says. "But Skaelka will do her best to translate."

The Arachnacanid's head sinks into the watery ooze for a moment—then jerks up again. Its words come in long, slow gasps. "Ħðeśfť . . ."

"It tells Skaelka it was the final innocent

creature in the fortress. Wracksaw experi-mented on it," Skaelka says, turning from the Arachnacanid to us. "Wracksaw chained the monster here to guard the cliff-entrance during the pivotal moment of knowledge-extraction . . ."

"I mean this in the least-jerky way possible," I say, inching forward. "But it doesn't appear to be the most effective guard."

"It does not attack because . . . it recognizes me," Skaelka says. "It saw Skaelka inside the fortress. It knows Wracksaw has hurt Skaelka, too."

I'm suddenly struck by a realization. A weakness—a blind spot—in Wracksaw, in Thrull, and maybe even in Ṛeżżŏcħ. Evil understands nothing *but* evil. Wracksaw must not have counted on one of his experiments sympathizing with a fellow survivor because Wracksaw probably doesn't even know the meaning of the word. Real, true evil—it can't contemplate the idea of "good."

"Đæß Çðêl Ďděĝ."

Skaelka takes a deep, shuddering breath. I've never seen her like this before. "Our friend tells me only evil remains inside the fortress."

June's face lights up—if there's only evil

inside, that means there's no roadblocks to her big Fortress Breaker moment.

She starts to punch the air, but Dirk catches her fist. "Read the room, dude."

"Right. Sorry."

The Arachnacanid surges up again. "IJŝşšt."

Skaelka looks like her ax suddenly weighs two tons. It almost seems like . . . the Arachnacanid asked for something . . .

"I am bound to oblige. My ax is sharp, and I will be swift," Skaelka says matter-of-factly. Then, softly, she adds, "The creature will be dead soon regardless. Wracksaw's foul experimentation has seen to that."

I look away as Skaelka lifts the ax high.

There's no sound for a long moment. Then the air whistles as she brings the blade crashing down.

CLANG!

The metallic sound spins me around. I exhale, relieved, when I see that Skaelka has only sliced through the chain. The Arachnacanid slips beneath the surface. Free of this place.

Skaelka wades back to the water's edge, then sits down, hard. Barnacles glow around her. Her eyes shut, and she rests her arms on the hilt of her ax.

"I . . . I could not do what it asked," Skaelka says. Her voice is shaky as she lifts her head and looks at us. "Nor can I enter the fortress again. I am too afraid of encountering Wracksaw. I . . . I cannot."

June inhales sharply.

"But . . . sure you can," she starts, but Dirk grabs her hand and pulls her into a huddle.

"Quint and I spent a *lot* of time with Skaelka," Dirk whispers. "Inside her head, too. If she says she can't, she can't. We gotta respect that."

Dirk's right. I know that. June does, too. But—this is bad. We were counting on Skaelka to get us through the fortress.

The ground rumbles beneath us, and we all look up. A geyser of something like steam erupts from the peak of the fortress. As it dissipates in the cold wind, we hear a sudden—

KRAK!

Skaelka has slammed her ax into the ground, using it to stand.

"That exhalation of air," she says, nodding toward the plume. "It causes a memory to return . . . Inside the fortress is a Directarium—it will show you the location of the heart."

"And that's where we place the Fortress Breaker," June says, her spirits lifting.

"The Directarium is similar to your Maparatus; they are living maps, connected," Skealka says. "The Maparatus can lead you to the Directarium. Find the Directarium, steal its data, and then you will find the heart."

"We will do as you say," Quint says, lifting his cannon and tapping the Maparatus.

"The Plan Man," Dirk says. "Coming through in a pinch."

With that, we head for the cliff side of the fortress. Skaelka remains behind—a bit broken, a lot sad.

"Be safe . . ." she says softly.

chapter twelve

Well . . . you're doing it, Jack. You're really doing it.

Yep. I'm climbing the cliff.

No amount of Spider-Man movie-watching and Spider-Man video-gaming could have prepared me for this.

The cliff is everything Skaelka promised: gross, scary, and BIG. Two hundred feet, er—talons, looks like a lot when you're staring up at it—but, trust me, it *feels* like even more when you're *clinging to the side of it*.

When I pictured the climb, I figured my friends and I would say a bunch of emotional stuff first, before I started. But that didn't happen. I think we all knew it wouldn't help.

Instead, Dirk was just like—

And with that, I was off.

My backpack—with Quint's human hamster ball packed inside—digs hard into my shoulders.

My body is all pain.

The good thing about the pain, though, is that it distracts from everything else. My mind is blank, unthinking, as I climb: hand over hand, foot finding foothold.

I don't stop until I'm nearly a quarter of the way up. And I only stop because my arms have turned to rubber. I find a small recess, just large enough to fit my butt and one leg. I wait for the blood to return to my limbs and the air to my lungs.

I'm just inching out of the nook, reaching for a handhold, when—

A crashing gust of wind suddenly pounds the cliffside, swinging me away from the wall like a screen door crashing open, turning me nearly horizontal.

Seconds before I'm hurled into oblivion—

SCHLURP!

The Cosmic Hand finds a protruding rock and clamps down, hard as a vise.

When the wind finally lets up, I crash back into the cliff face, dangling like the most perilously placed ornament on the Christmas tree.

The Cosmic Hand squeezed harder than hard—harder than I ever could—during the blast.

I don't love the way the Cosmic Hand is, like, starting to *know* things. But I won't argue now. Not the time to complain when it just saved me from a death drop.

The higher I climb, the stranger the cliff becomes. The more . . . unearthly. Goop bubbles out of cracks and crevices. The jagged stone glistens like it's made of gelatin.

I'll say it again: no amount of Spider-Man movie-watching and Spider-Man video-gaming could have prepared me for this. Though Quint might disagree. Back in the day, before the monster apocalypse, we spent *a lot* of time talking about the logistics of Spider-Man's abilities . . .

FOCUS, JACK! I scream at my own brain. *Stop thinking about Quint! Stop thinking about the time **before** you had the Cosmic Hand! There's no point, and it won't help any—*

But . . .

But what about June? On the train?

*I wanted to help her, but I couldn't—so the Cosmic Hand did it for me. And the Cosmic Hand **cut** her. It was just a scratch, sure. But what about next time?*

My mind is suddenly racing, out of control. Is what I'm doing right now making a next time *inevitable*?

What if it's like upgrading a weapon or a power in a video game—and the more you use it, the more powerful it gets, the more it changes? Am I going to become some creature my friends have to *vanquish*? Am I really gonna fully turn into a—

"AUGH!"

My brain goes quiet again. I focus on the pain and on finding the next handhold.

The sun has passed behind the fortress and the air has turned frigid when I finally allow myself to check how far I've gone—and, hardly believing it, I realize I'm nearing the top.

I can see the rocky overhang that leads to the tunnel. Just a few dozen feet to go.

I'm just starting to think I'm actually going to make it when—

The fortress shifts. The cliffside trembles.

Something splats against my shoulder, then slithers down my arm. Something . . . *chunky*.

Another drop. Then a splash.

"No, no, no," I say, feeling my hand slip.

Get a grip, Jack! Literally. *GET A GRIP!*

I barely have time to find a handhold when a shiver runs through the cliffside. The wall quakes, sways, and—

FLOOSH!

A tidal wave of black oil-goop explodes from the mouth of the tunnel. The sudden waterfall seems to hang above me for a lifetime—almost frozen—as it arcs out and then rains down, a storm of foul liquid.

My fingers grip the rock so tight it's like I'm trying to squeeze juice out of it. The crag I'm clinging to begins to crack, and suddenly—

CAWWW!

A horrible, snapping *beak* explodes through the wall! One of the Razorkaws Skaelka warned me about. My handhold crumbles, and I can do nothing but . . .

GRAB!

CAWWW!

Trust me, I hate this way more than you do.

The Razorkaw squawks louder, struggling to retreat back into its hidey-hole crevice and avoid the coming vertical tsunami of mystery wetness.

Actually, nope, it's not mystery wetness.

It's blood. Monster blood.

It rains down. Along with coils of guts and other grisly debris: teeth and whiskers and jagged nails the size of surfboards. Something splashes into my ear, and—not to be an alarmist, but I'm probably gonna need a new ear.

My hand is slipping down the Razorkaw's wet neck when—

PAIN. I feel the same sharp pain in my arm that I felt just before the Cosmic Hand transformed into a Cosmic *Spear*.

Energy cracks through me, and the Cosmic Hand changes.

I want to look away . . . but I can't.

Shimmering purple tendrils are slithering up my arm, around my shoulder, then leaping out from behind my back, creating something like a protective bubble, shielding me from the downpour.

Crackling energy fills the space around me.

The Razorkaw's eyes lock on to mine.

And . . . it speaks.

The demon bird speaks the language of
Ŗeżżŏch. And I understand the words—though
I wish I didn't . . .

The words are too awful to hear. The
Razorkaw is too terrible to look at.

My eyes clamp shut.

I don't know how much time passes before the gruesome downpour finally stops—but when it does, the Cosmic Hand has returned to normal. I feel foggy, half-conscious.

The Razorkaw squawks again—this time just a snarling, mean bird sound.

I need to get off this cliff. *Stat.*

My sneakers squeal against the slick stone, and I scramble up, focused on nothing but reaching the top.

A final gust of wind surges past—

It lifts me, sending me tumbling through the air, swinging upside down, then right side up, until I see the overhang. I'm about to sail *past* the ledge when—

chapter thirteen

I manage to unpack Quint's human hamster ball, despite his obscenely long list of deployment instructions. When I finally reach the last step, I pull the tag, and— POOF!

I roll the ball toward the overhang, then step back as it topples over the side.

Soon, the pulley whines, the rope goes taut, and my friends are on the move.

My jacket is torn and shredded where the Cosmic Hand went all bubble protector. I retrieve a roll of duct tape from my backpack and loop it around my sleeve to keep the horror hidden.

I finish just as my friends reach the top, arriving in something like a see-through New Year's Eve ball. Dirk doesn't seem to have enjoyed the trip . . .

Quint secures the hamster ball to the landing, unzips the bubble, and my friends step out onto not-totally-solid ground.

"Nice climbing," June starts to say, before losing her balance, staggering toward the mouth of the tunnel.

And then—all together—we step inside.

"We have just entered our first other-dimensional fortress," Quint says, looking around in awe. Tubules of fluid rush behind the walls—and the tunnel radiates a ghostly, icy blue. "The construction is *fascinating.*"

Sure, I think. *Fascinating if you're into architecture that feels like it might close in and squash you at any moment.*

Quint flips open the Maparatus. The screen glows a startling white. "I should be able to locate the Directarium once we're out of this tunnel and into the fortress proper."

"Then," Dirk says, "let's enter the fortress proper."

I'm about to ask if "entering the fortress *proper*" means we're supposed to walk like fancy butlers or something, but I decide this isn't really the moment.

Almost like we've infiltrated other-dimensional fortresses before, we fall into place. Dirk, in his role as the Muscle, takes the lead. The ceiling is thick with glistening lengths of something like rope. It pulses like a python swallowing hamsters . . .

"Anyone else feel like they're being watched?" June asks nervously.

I know what June means. It's like walking through some haunted house, when you know there's *something* awful waiting around each corner but you don't know *what*. So you're stuck forever bracing yourself for some big scary SURPRISE.

But no matter how horrifying the haunted house is, you can usually get through it by doing one of two things: shutting your eyes the instant anything pops out, or telling yourself "None of this is real," over and over.

The problem here, though, is if I shut my eyes I'm liable to stumble over the uneven ground and bust a kneecap. And no amount of convincing can get me to believe this isn't all *very real*.

"Watch your feet," Dirk says, turning a corner. He holds Drooler out at arm's length, his Ultra-Slime-soaked body glowing like a lantern.

"This place is lovely," I say, stepping over a puckery hole in the floor that's vomiting up a puddle of . . . well, let's just call it a puddle and leave it at that.

"SCREECH!"

The fist-sized daddy-longlegs-tick monster crackles, sounding like a broken speaker as it scuttles into the distance.

We're nearly to the end of the tunnel when Dirk suddenly holds up a hand. "You guys hear that?"

A surge of wind erupts behind us, funneling cold air through the tunnel. I hear a noise at our backs—like something softly swirling over the puddles.

Then a loud *whoosh*, like breathing.

Something flashes in the darkness, and we all jump to the side, terrified, then realize—

"Oh, no. That was the—"

"The hamster ball!" I cry as it tumbles past us. "It's free!"

The human hamster ball catches air, soaring through the tunnel.

"BY GOD I HATE THAT HAMSTER BALL, BUT IT'S OUR WAY OUT!" Dirk cries, charging ahead.

I speed past Dirk, knocking him aside. Drooler's Ultra-Slime splashes my face.

"Almost got it!" I cry, just a few short steps behind the ball as it bursts through the mouth of the tunnel.

I reach out to grab it, but Dirk snatches me by the scruff of my jacket just as—

It's gone.

Carried over the edge, down into the chasm.

And as we get our first look at the fortress, *proper*, we realize—we were not prepared.

chapter fourteen

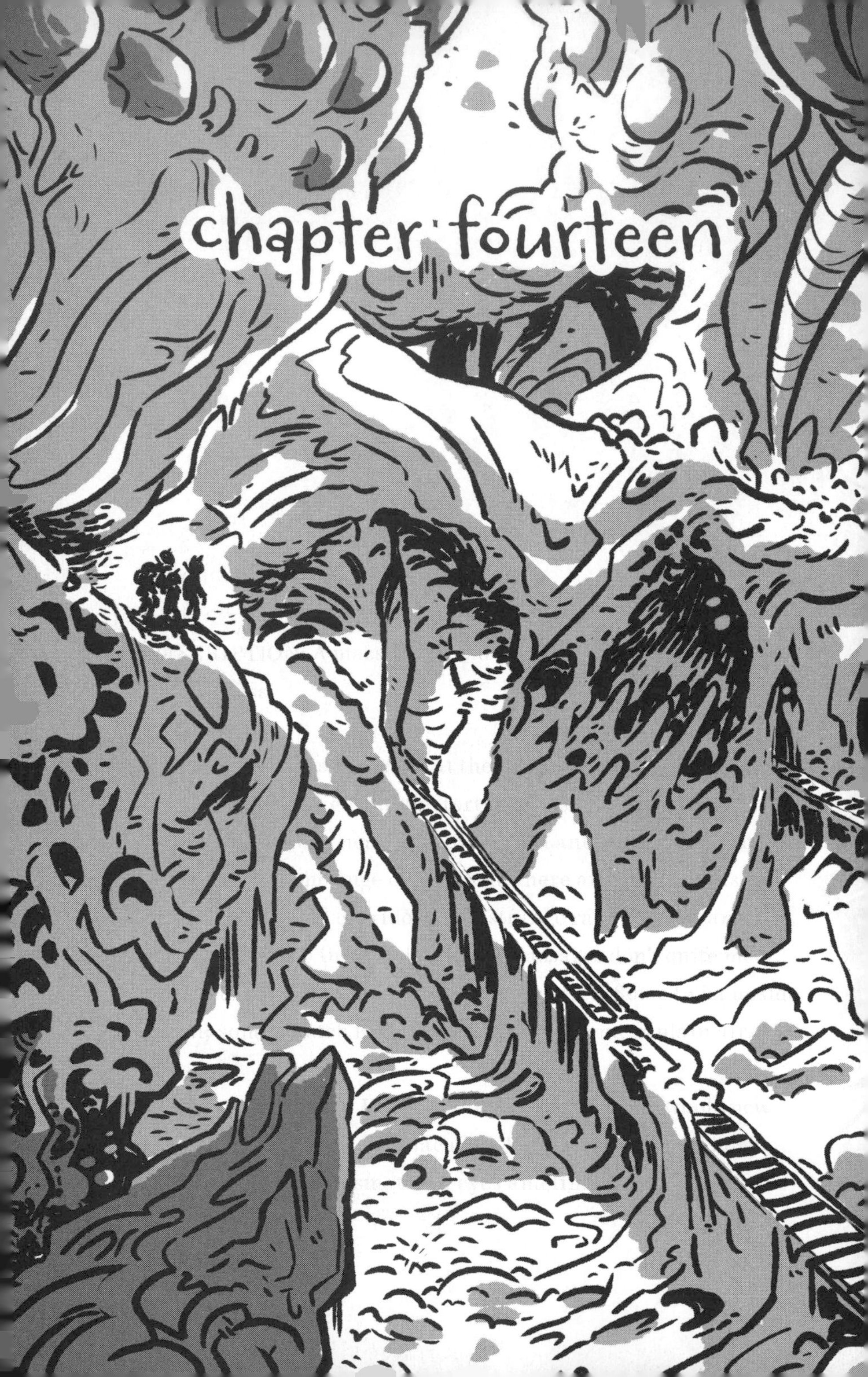

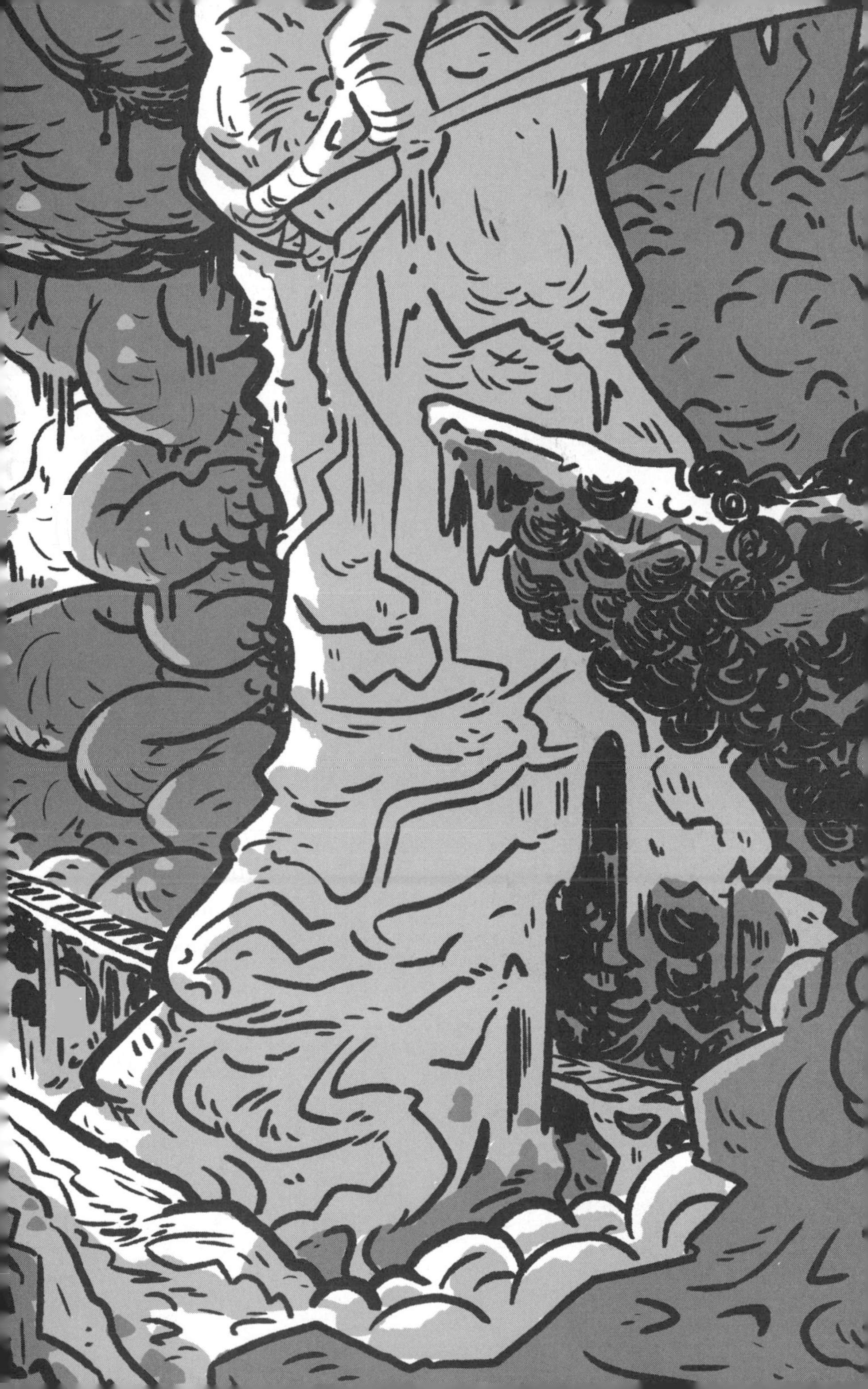

"Well. I didn't want to go home anyway," Dirk says, watching our human hamster ball drop into the swirling mist below.

"Just a minor setback," Quint says.

Yeah, I think. *And the moon landing was just a minor leap for mankind.*

The cavernous chamber reminds me of the inside of a hornet's nest. Only instead of hornets, this hive has monsters on monsters on monsters.

"It doesn't change anything. We've got a fortress to destroy," June says. Again, she thrusts her fist into the air—but this time, she whispers when she says, "Woo-hoo!"

A sloshing, screeching sound suddenly fills the air. I turn to see what looks like a horribly huge, grotesquely deformed caterpillar rocketing toward us, skittering along a thin track made of something like fingernails dipped in wax.

"Get back!" Dirk shouts, but it's too late.

The thing is upon us, and it's all we can do to jump. It's intended to be a jump *out of the way*.

But instead we're caught mid-leap, the speeding thing slamming into us with a tremendous—

We're knocked up and over the front, then sent sailing back, into the thing—

There is confusion—a dizzying scramble as we try to sit ourselves upright. Finally, we settle into position single file, like an Olympic bobsled team.

The Mind Cart suddenly veers away from the wall, carrying us out into the cavernous chamber. Dirk barks, "Quint, buddy, you gotta find that Directarium thing NOW!"

Quint doesn't waste breath responding. His eyes dart across the Maparatus screen while he swings the cannon, searching. He doesn't even blink when a gnarly bug splats against his cheek.

"Monsters!" Dirk shouts as the Mind Cart hurtles us into the next chamber. "Down below!"

But the monsters are not alive; not *real*.

They are statues.

Mammoth statues, carved from glowing stone. The stiff monstrosities rise up, piercing the neon mist below. Other effigies—cracked and crumbling—loom from the walls, gazing down upon us with hollow, lifeless eyes.

One of the horrible monuments—its two mouths stretched open in a frozen roar—reaches out. Arms sprout from its back like twisted growths—and they remind me of the Cosmic Hand and the way it continues creeping up my arm, growing, spreading like an infection.

Before the thought can fill me with further dread—and trust me, the last thing I need right now is *further dread*—I hear—

The Directarium! A faint signal! Another few moments, and I should have a full lock on its—

Quint is silenced as the Mind Cart dives downward, and—

"HELP!" I cry as I'm tossed out of my seat.

"CAN'T HELP! WE'RE BEING TOSSED, TOOOOOO!" June shouts.

I hang in the air for a horribly long moment, my stomach flipping and rolling, before—

SPLAT!

I land on the platform behind the cart, face-planting into what feels like a beanbag chair stuffed with bones. Pulling back, I see something like a . . . larva-sac? There's fluid inside—and floating in the fluid is a half-built monster. It looks unnatural, artificial—like it was cobbled together in a lab. And it's—

Oh no.

It's moving.

And there are more larva-sacs. Many more.

Recoiling in horror, I fall back onto the gummy, gluey platform.

> There's . . . monsters back here! In big larva-sac thingies. Like . . . about to be born. Or reborn. Hatched!

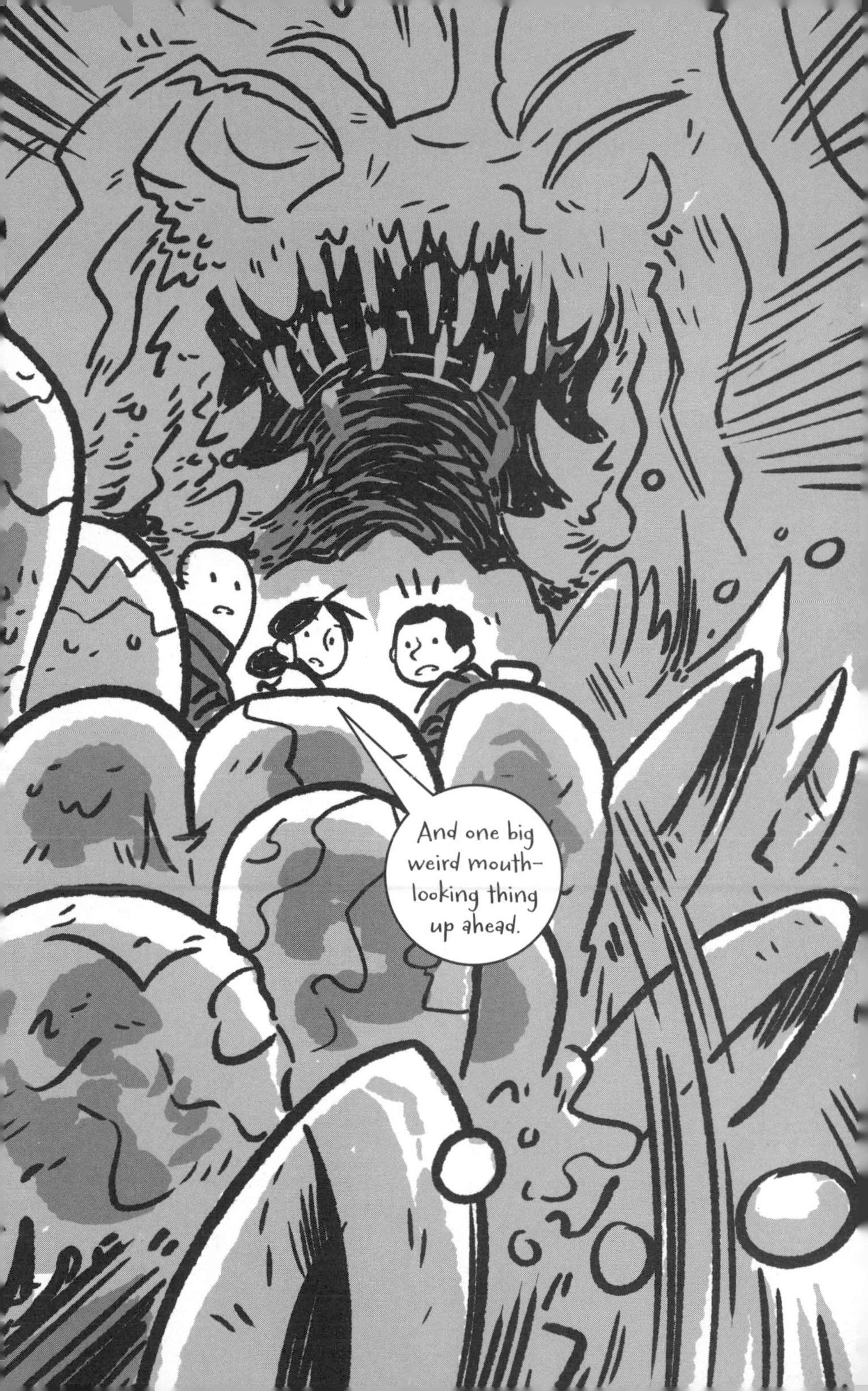
And one big weird mouth-looking thing up ahead.

Glancing up, I see what June's hollering about: the entrance to the next chamber of this twisted fun house. As we race toward it, a thousand eyes blink open, and I realize it *is* a mouth. A mouth that is *real* and *alive* and is *wide open* . . .

"I got a lock!" Quint suddenly exclaims. "The Directarium is somewhere down that way."

Unfortunately, "somewhere down that way" is not the direction we're heading. The shrieking, skittering sound of the Mind Cart grows louder as thousands of tiny pincers propel us toward the hungry mouth.

"The signal is getting colder!" Quint says. "We're losing it!"

With panic in her voice, June cries, "We need to get off . . . NOW!"

Suddenly, the larva-sac nearest me bulges— the half-built monster inside is waking. But the sac is soft and wet, and maybe, just maybe . . .

"Everyone, grab on to this larva-sac thing!" I shout, trying not to think too hard about the many awful implications of that sentence.

"Hang on, Drooler!" Dirk shouts as he dives onto the sac. I bear-hug the pod of fetal evil, then June and Quint pile on, too.

Up ahead, the horrible mouth yawns open just as—

"Overboard!" Dirk barks.

Gripping the larva-sac tight, we throw ourselves off the Mind Cart. The larva-sac's wet coating pours off in streams as it plummets downward, and there's nothing we can do but hang on . . .

chapter fifteen

Ick erupts as the sack explodes beneath us like
a water balloon dropped from thirty stories up.
The half-built creature inside breaks our fall—
and is flattened into a smear.

We all lie there for a moment, not quite able to
believe what just happened.

"Ugh, it's in my nose," June says finally.

"It's in my underwear," I say.

"It's in my *foot* underwear," Quint says.

"Just call 'em socks, Quint," Dirk says.

The ground is slippery from the gooey remains
of the shattered sac, and it takes us a comically
long time to stand. We've landed on the peak of
some peculiar structure—high-enough up that a
breeze whips over us.

As I finish scrubbing off, I hear June whisper,
"Uh, guys . . ."

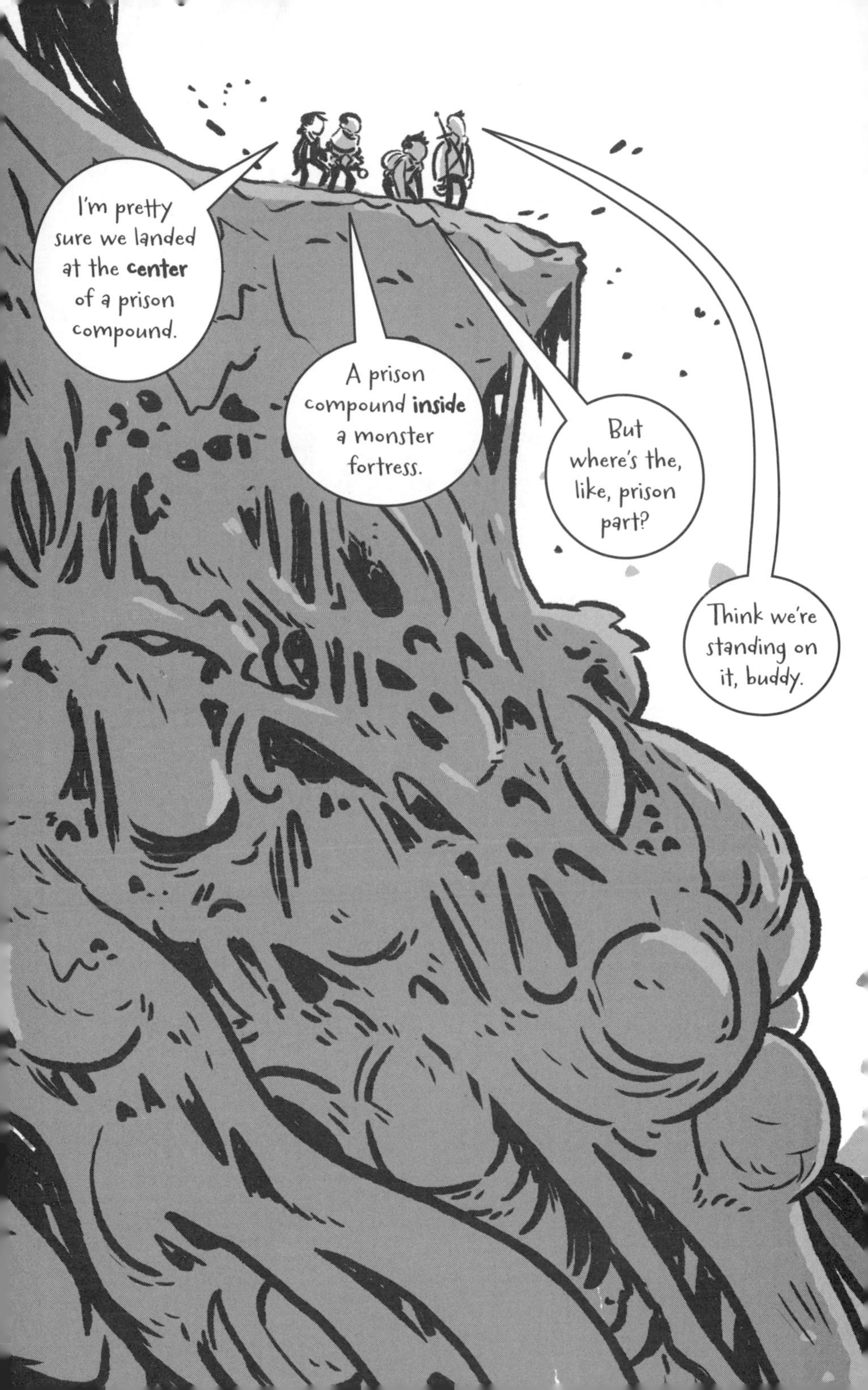
I'm pretty sure we landed at the **center** of a prison compound.
A prison compound **inside** a monster fortress.
But where's the, like, prison part?
Think we're standing on it, buddy.

"This is like a Russian nesting doll of lousiness," I say.

"The Maparatus is indicating that the Directarium is below us," Quint says. "Down there."

So down there is where we go . . .

There's a wet, floppy fissure at the platform's center—and we hurry to it. Squeezing through, we drop down into the spiraling prison. It's like a Jenga skyscraper—with some pieces missing, some only halfway inserted.

"This prison clearly wasn't built for human legs," Quint observes.

There are no steps—just a circular, endlessly winding tube, like a looping parking garage ramp. The tube is partly see-through—like it's made of plexiglass smeared with strawberry jam. It leads us past an endless string of prison cells—each one vacant.

As we continue down, we find ourselves— without meaning to—walking along the floor, then up the wall, across the ceiling, down the other wall, and finally back down to the floor. And then it repeats. Again. And again.

It's a long way down—er—up? Sideways, maybe.

"I never thought I'd miss trekking through the Forbidden Forest of Foreboding," Dirk says after nearly an hour of walking. "But I do."

"From our hero quest," Quint explains.

June laughs. "Oh, is that what you're calling it?"

"You bet," Dirk says. "'Cause that's what it was. Me and Quint even had statues erected in our honor. It was epic."

OK, seriously. Just how much stuff did I miss out on? I think, and my imagination runs wild . . .

-THE FOMO COLLAGE-

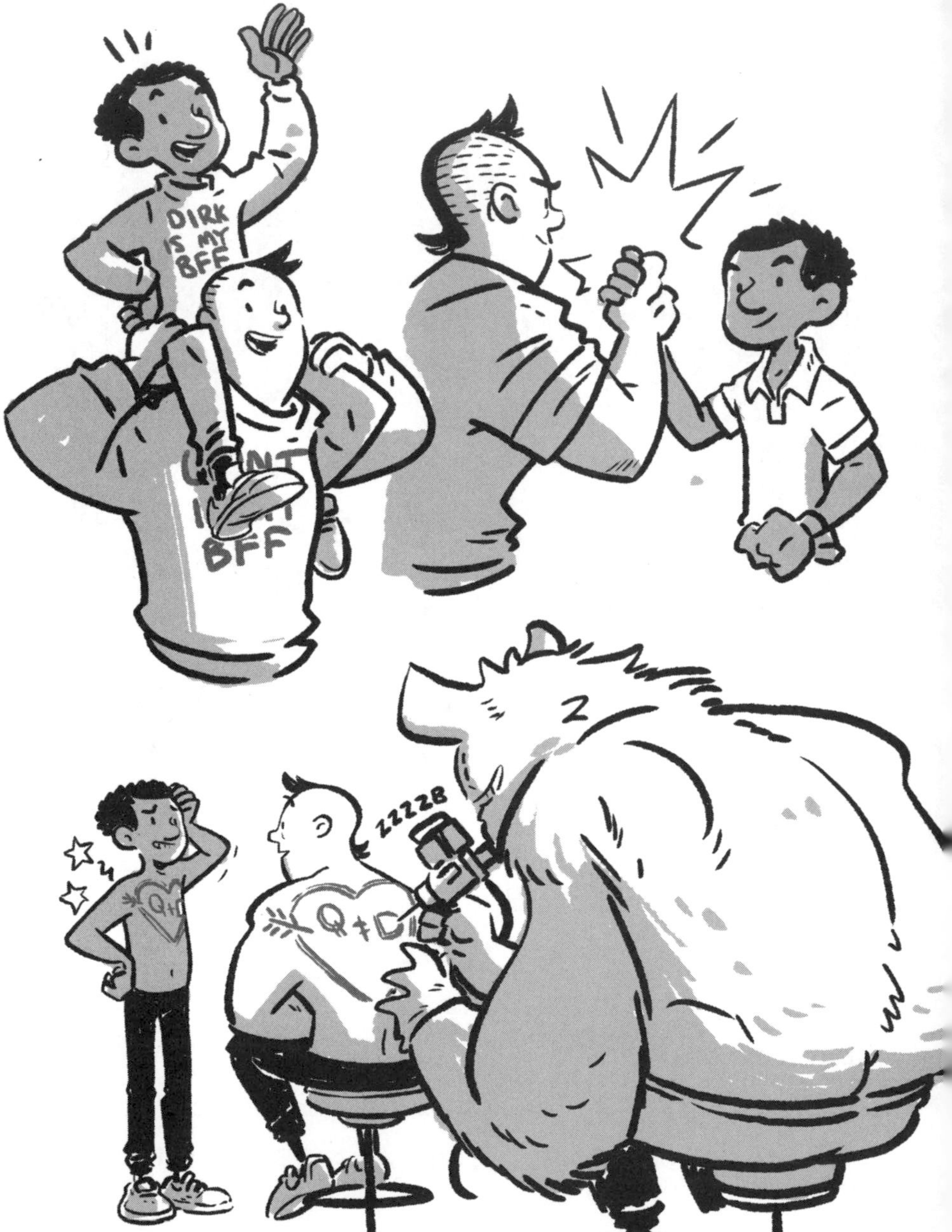
DIRK IS MY BFF
ZZZZB
Q+D

"Yeah, well," I start, my mouth quickly getting away from me. "Me and June had a hero quest, too. While you were gone. It was awesome. We, uh, we fought a Bone Halfer—"

"So did we," Dirk says, unimpressed. "But we fought the *front half.*"

"Yeah, well, we defeated Ŗeżżŏch and Thrull. Did I mention that? Yep, they're dead now. Also, we ran into a buncha zombie influencers and we all started a YouTube channel and already have a *ton* of followers."

I look to June to back me up.

But the only thing she backs up is the bus, right over me. "Nope, none of that happened. I already went on my own solo adventure; I don't need to join your fake imaginary one, Jack."

———◆———

I don't know how much time has passed when the never-ending tube finally spits us out on the ground floor—I just know I'm happy it's over.

We exit out into some sort of lobby. A single prison guard stands at a vending machine, angrily poking buttons.

We quickly tiptoe past . . .

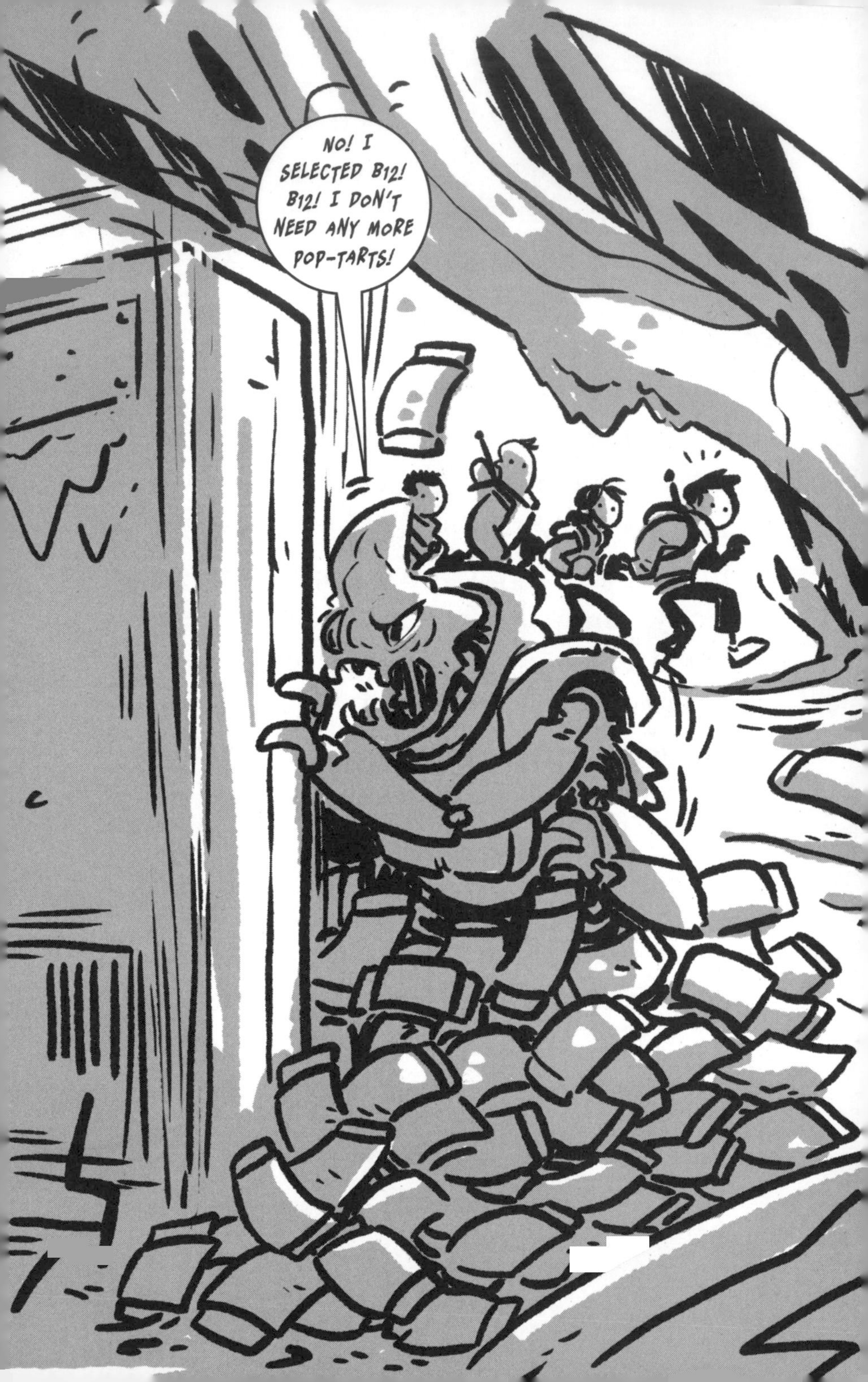
NO! I SELECTED B12! B12! I DON'T NEED ANY MORE POP-TARTS!

Ducking behind a row of overflowing garbage bins—*these monsters don't even recycle!*—we have a panoramic view of the prison compound. It's a smorgasbord for the senses. There's so *much*: movement, noise, odors.

This compound is the size of a small city. Structures are stacked on other structures, everything jammed together, almost squished: market stalls, taverns, and what appears to be a taco stand. Zigzagging beams and pathways crisscross this way and that.

The stench of evil wafts off *everything*.

In the distance, I spot what vaguely resembles a guard tower. But then I think, no, it *can't be a guard tower*—because it's *moving*. But then I realize *it can be a guard tower* because it's a *walking* guard tower: a huge, striding sentinel.

Nodding to the hub of activity in front of us, June says, "This must be the compound's, like, *market*."

"Evil prison guards gotta eat, too," Dirk says with a shrug.

The guards—along with other vile creatures—go about their business. But none are in much of a hurry—they look like they're on vacation. Benefits of being a prison guard at an empty prison, I guess . . .

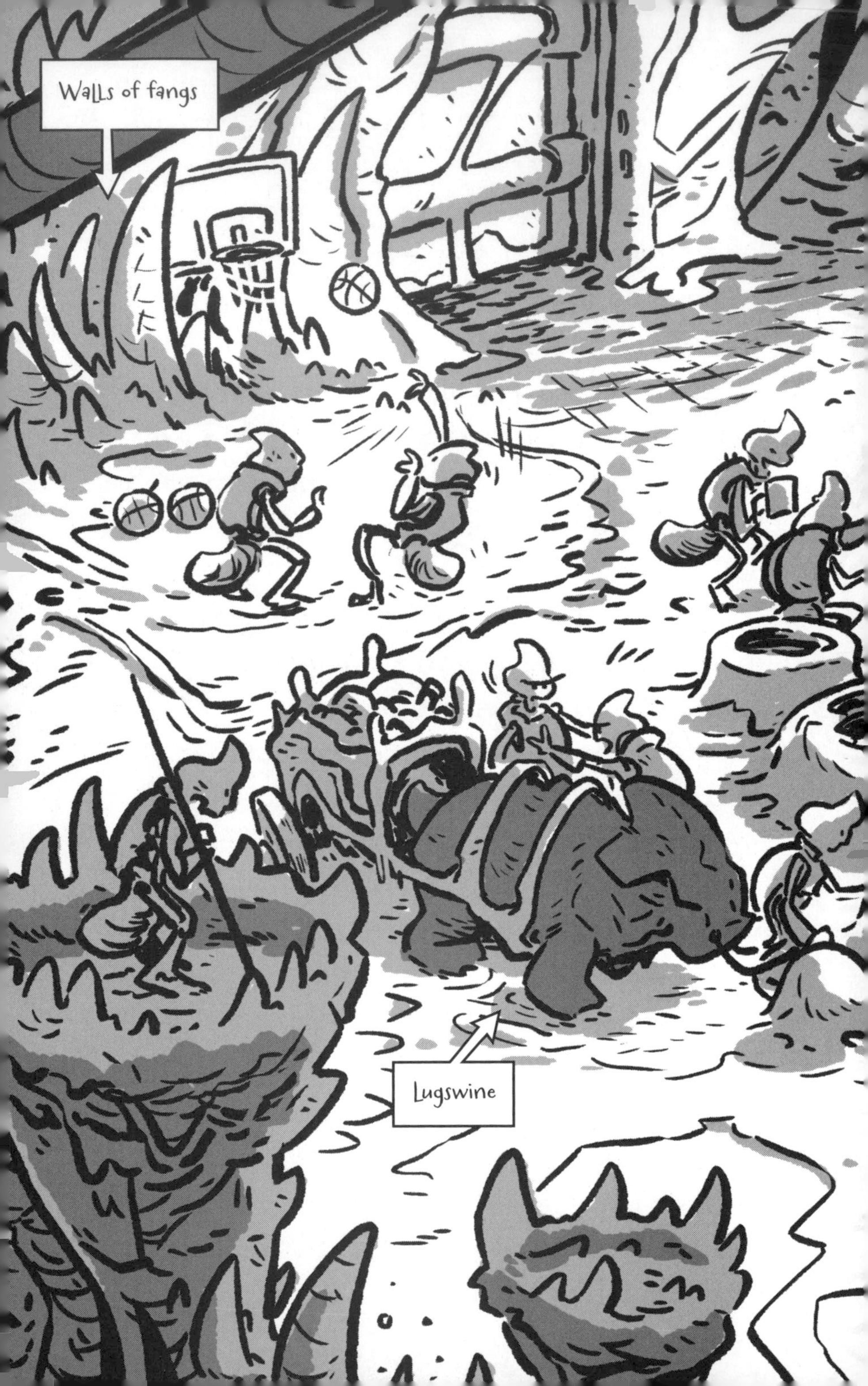
Walls of fangs
Lugswine

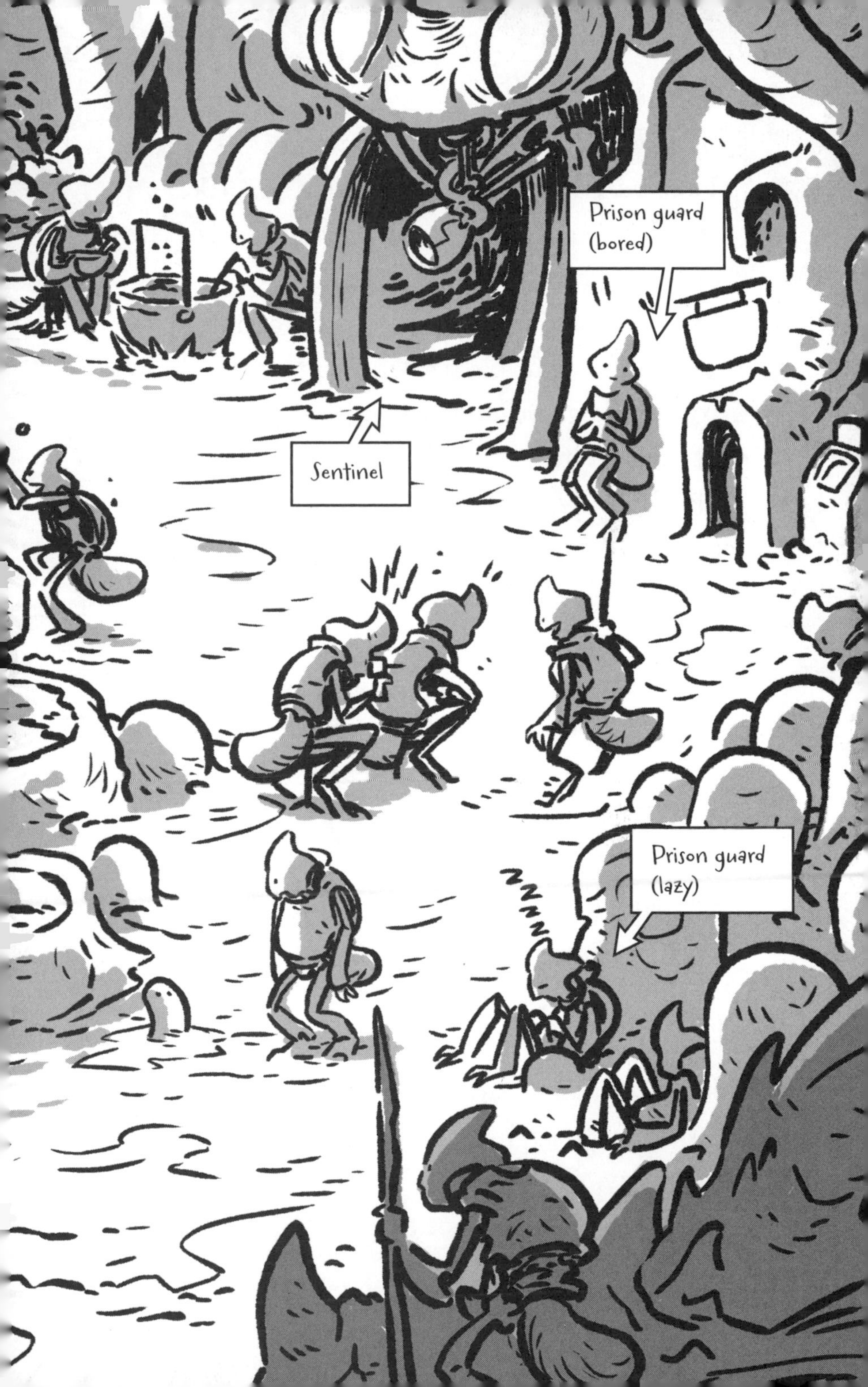
Prison guard
(bored)
Sentinel
Prison guard
(lazy)

Surrounding the entire compound is the prison wall: a series of jagged spikes, like thirty-foot-tall shark teeth, that jut out of the ground.

I squint, watching a lumbering beast—a guard barks at it, calling it a Lugswine—trudge through the guarded gate. The Lugswine tows a cart behind it.

"Probably laundry," Dirk says, nodding to the cart. "Prison movies always have laundry trucks coming and going."

"I don't think these monsters do laundry, dude," I say.

Suddenly, the Maparatus beeps—a ping.

"The Directarium," Quint announces. "Directly across the street."

June's eyebrows jump, and she rocks back on her knees, all fidgety anticipation.

Unfortunately, the Directarium's location is less than ideal. I hoped it would be, like, tucked away in a shadowy corner. Or in a sweet old lady's house. Any place where we could stealthily access it, get what we need, then be on our way.

But nope. It's right smack-dab in the middle of *everything* . . .

Quint clicks his tongue, thinking. "If we could get *above* the Directarium," he says, smiling deviously, "then I have just the thing to complete the job."

"For real?" I ask.

Quint nods, grinning proudly. "My role is Plan Man, and, as such, I have planned for every possible scenario, complete with accompanying gadgets!"

I can see Quint getting ready to launch into a long explanation of what he's built and how, exactly, it works—but Dirk cuts him short. "I'll get us there," Dirk says. "You just stick close."

"Huh?" I start, but Dirk is already on the move. And we're already following.

Way of the Muscle Ninja

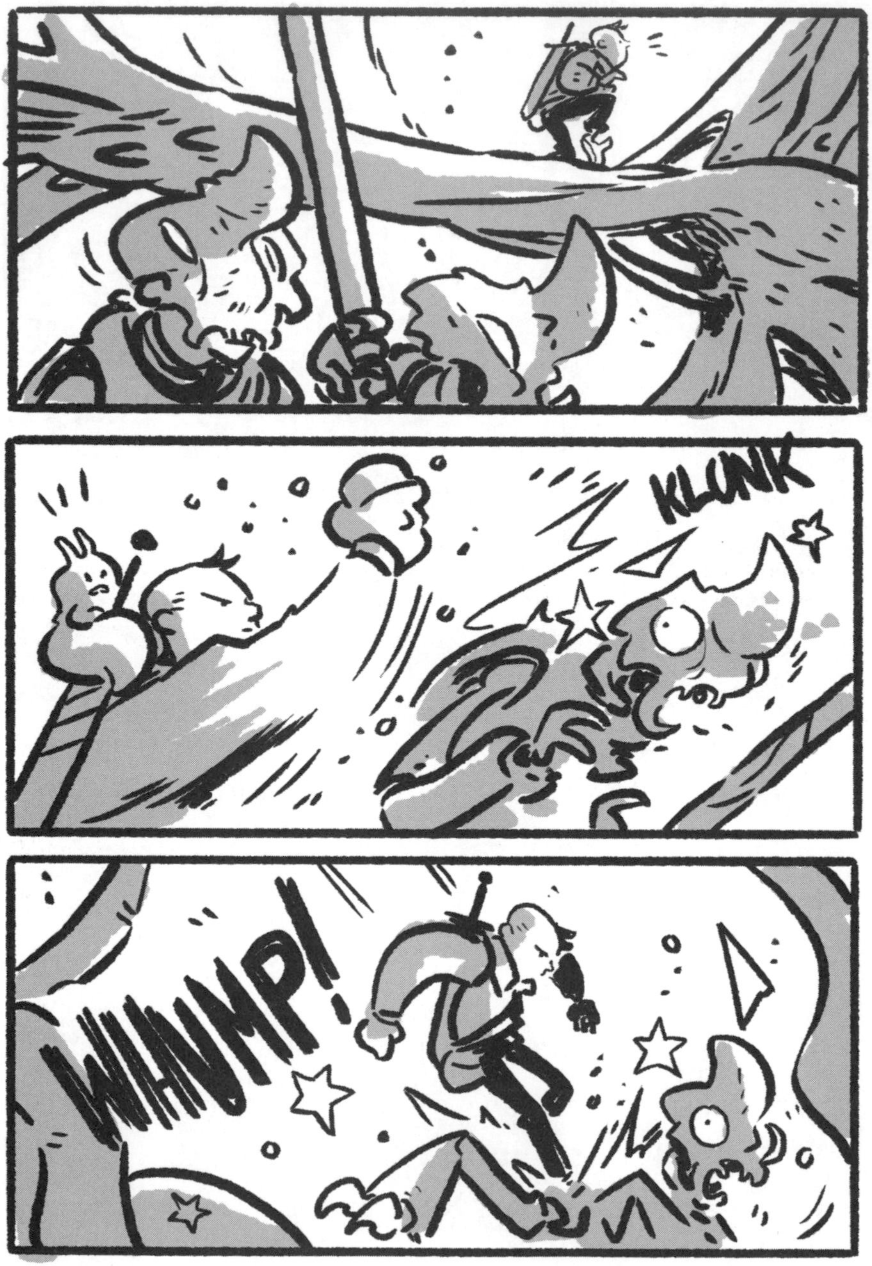
KLUNK
WHUMP!

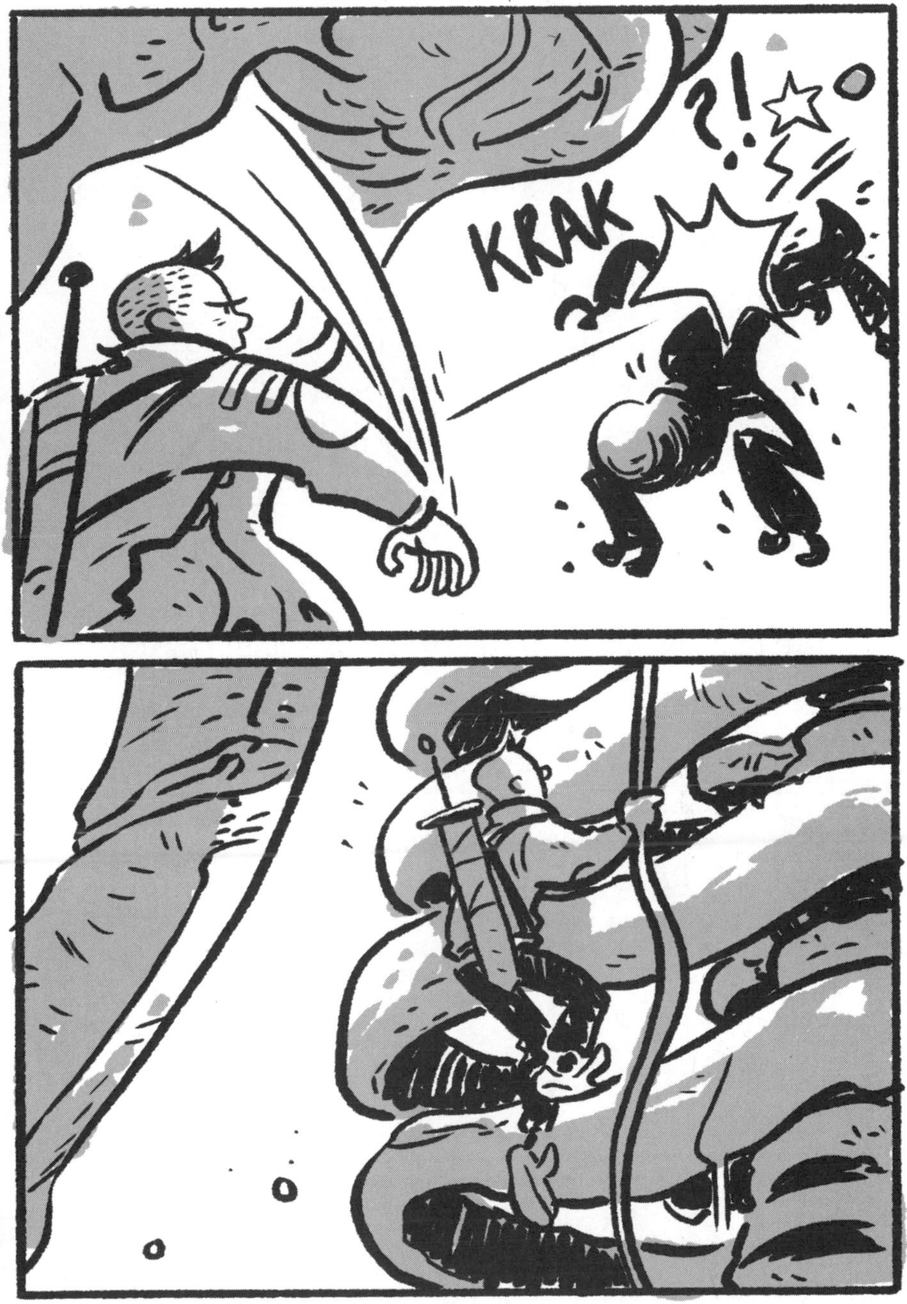
KRAK
?!

Dirk finally reaches an awning—made from what appears to be torn monster wings—directly above the bustling monster tavern. He flashes us a bunch of hand signals that we didn't discuss before the mission and have no need for because we're like two feet away from him. I guess he was just eager to do a hand-signal thing.

"Fantastic," Quint says as he peers over the side. "The Directarium is directly below us."

Unfortunately, happy hour just ended . . .

A door is loudly flung open, and monsters pour out of the tavern, gathering in the square. Screeching voices drift up. Most of it is in a language we can't understand, but some of it comes through, loud and clear . . .

I wish we could just sit up here, catch
our breath, listen to monsters ramble about
hoagies—but time is of the essence. Which
means . . .

"We need a way to distract these guards," I
start, but I'm cut short by—

"Drooler! Stop! *Get back here!*" Dirk orders in
a scolding whisper.

Something's got Drooler's attention; he's no
longer perched on Dirk's sword. Instead, he's
waddling toward the awning's edge.

"Can't look away for one second, can ya?" I
say.

Drooler glances back at us, *meeps* twice,
then—

SQUEESH

He hops over the side.

"NO!" Dirk says, scrambling toward the edge.

Drooler lands with a wet splat. We watch with
a mixture of fascination and dread as Drooler
totters out into the crowded square . . .

chapter sixteen

I immediately realize where Drooler is going—and why.

A group of guards are gathered around what appears to be a giant ball of squirming hair. They tear off pieces in wads, shoving them into their fang-filled mouths. Bits fall to the ground—and Drooler wanders that way.

"I think he's just hungry. Hey, what do you feed him anyway?" I ask, realizing I've never seen Drooler actually *eat*.

Dirk frowns. "Umm . . ."

"Dude, do you not feed Drooler?" June asks.

"He liked that spicy dough—" Dirk starts, before—

"GET A LOAD OF THIS LITTLE BUGGER!" a guard suddenly shouts.

"No, no, no!" Dirk says, inhaling sharply. "They're gonna beat him with pillowcases full of soap!"

But the evil monster jailers mostly just seem intrigued. One rips out a wad of hair and tosses it to Drooler, like some grandpa feeding stale bread to pigeons at the park. Drooler gulps it down.

"Guys," June says, realizing. "This is just the distraction we needed!"

"Drooler is *not* a distraction!" Dirk says.

"Hey," I say. "When opportunity knocks, you gotta answer."

Dirk glares at us all for a long moment, then growls, "Fine. Just be quick. If those jerks touch one drop of slime on Drooler's head, I can't be held responsible for what happens next."

Quint grins. "In that case, it is time I unveil . . ." he starts, reaching into his backpack for a big reveal. "The HAMMOCK HARNESS!"

"It's really only designed for one . . ." Quint says.

But I gesture to the guards below. "Who knows how long Drooler's hairwad-slurping antics are gonna keep those dudes busy. If anything goes wrong, you'll be dangling like a fish on a hook—*alone*."

Quint relents. Moments later, we're both crammed into the hammock harness while June and Dirk lower us down. But I'm quickly realizing I should have listened to Quint because—

The harness flips, spinning a dozen times, then—

Craning my neck, I'm just barely able to see the Directarium. It looks like an arcade machine made out of Jell-O and peanut shells.

Little nodules—that look unnervingly like belly buttons—cover its display screen. I shudder a little when Quint pokes one without hesitation.

He taps the Maparatus, and a short dongle arm extends. He presses the dongle against the Directarium's access port, frowns, flips it over, tries again, frowns again. No dice. He flips it once more—and the dongle slides in.

"Always on the third try," he mutters.

The Directarium flashes, then begins whirring as diagrams flash by at top speed.

Quint's got this covered, so I twist my head. I spot two gangly guards posing with Drooler. A squat guard tries to get into the picture—but they shove him away. "Speed it up, Quint," I whisper. "This could go south any second."

"Retrieving the full map of the fortress now," Quint replies.

There's a whirring sound as the Directarium transfers the information into the Maparatus. It only takes a few minutes—but it feels like an eternity. Thankfully—Drooler keeps the guards busy, hammin' it up for the crowd.

At last, the Maparatus beeps again—low and long. "Finished!" Quint says.

Finally, I think. *Now let's get outta here.*

I flash Dirk the "pull us up, *now*" signal—but Dirk doesn't see me. He's watching Drooler.

And at that moment, many things go wrong at once . . .

Drooler *meeps*—but it's not his usual *meep*. It's loud and *scared* and *confused*.

I turn—and gasp. "Those guards! They're playing . . . keep-away! With Drooler!"

Dirk lets go of the line—and without him anchoring it, June has no choice but to release us.

There's a twanging *ZIP* as the line whips over the side and the hammock harness drops.

Quint and I smash to the ground. I get the worst of it, facedown, nose buried in a warm puddle of I-don't-wanna-know-what.

Quint does a half-roll, throwing his weight so that we're both lying on our side.

Looking up, I see Dirk at the roof's edge, gripping his sword. Ultra-Slime drips down the blade, over his hand. His voice booms: "PUT. THE LITTLE DUDE. DOWN!"

Every guard turns toward Dirk. They shift, exchanging confused glances, and then—

SHINK!

Shockingly fast, the guards weaponize—their limbs morphing and stretching into needle-covered fists and jabby stick-arms. They all look tailor-made for inflicting pain via poking.

And then—

FLASH!

A searchlight floods everything as a Sentinel lumbers into the square, parking itself between us good guys and the monsters.

The Sentinel's head dips. Its eyes are spot-lights, bathing Dirk in neon light.

"All right, then, if that's how you want it," Dirk growls, taking a step back, out of sight.

"Where'd he go?" Quint asks.

Before I can offer an answer, I hear footsteps pounding the roof above, running fast, before—

"I'm a-comin', little buddy!" Dirk shouts, leaping off the roof, sailing over us, toward the Sentinel, and—

With a grunt, Dirk launches off the spotlight.

His feet slam into the largest guard's chest, knocking the monster on its back. Drooler squirts free, and Dirk snatches him out of the air like a pop fly.

"Quint, did he just do a Zorro?" I ask.

"Yep," Quint says. "He just did a Zorro."

Dirk's eyes are wide—not with fear or anger, but with what I can only guess is absolute shock that his chandelier-swinging swashbuckler move wasn't a total disaster.

Not yet, at least.

But maybe soon.

'Cause the Sentinel's cannon is aimed directly at Dirk and Drooler, and it's taking a heavy step forward . . .

chapter seventeen

"Jack, we've got to stand up!" Quint says. "Together!"

"Right!" I say. "On the count of—"

But Quint doesn't wait for *any* count, and I'm suddenly hoisted off my feet. My back is flat against Quint as he takes off running.

At that same moment, the Sentinel's heavy foot hits the ground—and lands on a puddle of Drooler's Ultra-Slime.

The Sentinel's foot slides, and the towering monster lurches sideways.

"It's going down!" June shouts.

I turn my head just as the Sentinel topples to the ground with a thundering crash—

The impact feels like a magnitude 7 earthquake. The force launches some guards off their feet and buckles the knees of others.

"Think it's your turn to be the legs, Jack!" Quint shouts as he stumbles over a discarded hairwad, falling sideways, and then it's my feet hitting the ground, my legs running.

I do my best to leap over a pair of toppled guards—but I'm not exactly Super Mario with Quint on my back, and we're about to fall when—

"Hey, guys, I gotcha!" June says, grabbing my arm, steadying me.

A screeching buzz builds around us. Then hundreds of footsteps—guards rising and running while more rush from the stalls and structures.

Suddenly, Dirk is running alongside us, cradling Drooler under his arm like a football. "This place is getting real crowded, real quick!"

"We need a way *out*," June says.

Laundry truck! I'm telling you—every prison-break movie has a laundry-truck scene. Trust me—

I can't believe we're talking about laundry trucks again. They're not laundry trucks!

What else would those carts be carrying?

LITERALLY ANYTHING!

"Although . . . There's really only one way to find out," June says, pointing down an alleyway as she skids to a sudden halt. "It went that way."

I stop short—*too short*. Quint flips over my back, feet hitting the ground while flipping me up, and now I'm the one being carried. I would very much like to get out of this death trap diaper.

We peel off down the alley, losing the guards for a moment. Running past an other-dimensional corndog stand—I jab my shoulder into the door, causing it to *schloop* open, as we continue past.

"Now they'll think we went in there!" I announce proudly.

As Quint turns the next corner, I spot pursuing guards pointing to the open door. "Told ya!"

"Laundry cart! Up ahead!" Dirk calls. I spot the Lugswine dragging a Dumpster-sized cart toward the gate.

We beat feet, and in moments, Dirk and June are climbing onto the cart. They grab Quint's hands, pulling us up, too. The hammock harness finally snaps—and Quint and I flop into the cart.

And guess what?

"Who had 'hiding in a cart full of guts' on their bingo card?" June asks. Happy to see she's keeping things light, even with a discarded pancreas on her head.

The Lugswine continues its lumbering path toward the gate, oblivious to the stowaways inside its cart.

"Quint," June says. "Please tell me that was all worth it."

Quint grins and flips open the Maparatus. It lights up the cart. "It certainly was! We now have—"

"SEARCH ALL EXITING MEAT CARTS!" a guard barks.

We all freeze.

The Lugswine snorts and begins to slow. We hear the chittering of approaching guards. Peeking through two slabs of monster meat, I see the prison fence's jagged gate looming over us. *So close.*

"Yep. This happens in every prison-escape movie, too," Dirk says. "Guards always check the laundry carts."

"Dirk . . ." June growls. "If Drooler wasn't here right now, so help me, I would—"

A guard's snarl silences her.

It's close.

We all freeze, locking eyes.

Footsteps crunch. A hiss whistles. And then—

SHINK!

The guard's jabby stick-arm suddenly bursts into the cart!

SKUTCH STAB

SPUT

Quick, Quint! Do a "These are not the meat carts you're looking for" Jedi mind trick hand-wave!

I can't do that.

You shouldn't have picked Obi-Wan if you weren't ready to do Jedi mind trick hand-waves!

"Will you two SHUT IT!" Dirk says, gently shifting to avoid the poking, prodding stick-arm.

Quint suddenly unzips his backpack, and—

"Ugh!" the guard cries, yanking his stick-arm out of the cart. "That odor! So foul!"

The cart suddenly jerks as the guard gives it a whack. "Get this one outta here!"

The Lugswine trudges ahead, and we're on the move again. No one says a word. Finally, we pass through the gate—leaving the compound behind.

We all exhale. "How did we get out of there??" I ask.

Quint grins, reaching into his bag. "Apparently, the guards do not appreciate the aroma of egg-salad sandwiches."

"You're *still* eating those things?" Dirk asks.

"Alas, no. But I was homesick for the smell," Quint says, revealing an egg-salad-sandwich *candle*. "Yursl crafted it for me."

Our jaws hang open.

Quint frowns. "OK, then, I guess I know what you *won't* be getting for Christmas this year."

"Please put the candle back in your bag immediately," June says. "And get back to telling us about the Directarium."

"Right!" Quint starts, twisting a dial on the Maparatus. "I understand now. Skaelka wasn't speaking poetically when she spoke about the *heart* of the fortress! She was being literal!"

Dirk grunts. "Say what?"

"The fleshy walls, the throbbing ground. This

189

fortress isn't just full of monsters," Quint says. "It *is* a monster! It's alive!"

I frown. "Quint, you sound awful excited about something that sounds only . . . awful."

"No, no," he says. "It's good!" He taps the Maparatus, and a diagram of the fortress is projected onto the wall of the cart.

The heart is where we place the Fortress Breaker. And using this map, we can get there!

And what's more . . . this map can get us out!

Drooler *meep*s. June starts to giggle. Is this what victory feels like? Or near victory?

"We're gonna do this!" June says. "We're gonna end the end of the world!"

"Sure are," I say, leaning back against something mushy, kicking my feet out. "The only thing that could make this moment better is an ice-cold orange soda."

"*Fountain* orange soda," June corrects. "The most refreshing."

The Lugswine lets out a long moo-howl, and the cart bounces to a rattling stop. Everything shifts—and that's when I spot the thin opening running the length of the cart floor. And hinges.

"Hey, guys," I say nervously. "Why would there be hinges on the *bottom* of the cart?"

And then we find out.

There's a *CLICK*, followed by a rusty creak as the floor of the cart swings open—and we're plunged downward . . .

chapter eighteen

We tumble down a long, curving tube—slimy
and slick—until finally, we're dumped out. The
ground is squishy and—

Oh. Hold up. This is no ground—

I'm face-to-face, nose-to-nose, with a bloated
husk of evil.

My hands push against the soft, fleshy coldness, and I start to tumble off the table, again crying out, "EVIL HALF—"

Dirk catches me before I hit the ground, throwing a hand over my mouth, silencing me.

"Everyone alive?" Dirk asks. My friends have landed all around me. I'm the only one unlucky enough to have been dumped out *on a cut-up monster*.

"Not everyone . . ." I say as the full extent of where we are slowly begins to dawn on me . . .

No wonder Skaelka didn't want to come back here, I think.

Monster bodies lie on tables; arms and tails and foot-long tongues dangle over the sides. Other monster corpses float inside glowing tube chambers, their limbs bobbing beside their bodies. Vials, syringes, and saws are scattered about. Monster parts are piled in a corner—a meat heap.

The air is humid; everything feels *moist*. And the stench doesn't just make my eyes water—it makes my pupils *burn*.

"It's OK! Everyone can relax!" June calls happily. She's on one knee, backpack open. "The Fortress Breaker is A-OK."

"June—" I start.

She shakes her head. "Nope. This is one room I will *not* read."

"Dirk, come look at this . . ." Quint says, eyeing a wall. "I think it's *him*! From Skaelka's memories."

"Enough gawkin'," Dirk says. "That guy's bad news. And now that we know where we gotta get to—let's get to it. *Pronto.*"

Uh-oh. Dirk's saying stuff like "pronto"—that means there's no arguing with him. Not that I'd argue anyway. I'll be happy to leave this place behind—and hopefully bury all memory of it in that corner of my brain saved for nightmares and really embarrassing memories, like that time I tried to slide down the railing at school and ended up just splitting my pants *and* my underwear.

We start toward the door—but Dirk holds up two fingers, halting us. He peeks his head out, gazing down the hallway beyond.

I stick my head out, too—then quickly yank it back. Two long, spindly monsters—wearing long robes, almost like nurses' gowns—are hurrying toward the morgueatory.

"OK, we need another way out of here," I say quickly.

"Isn't one," Dirk says. "First thing I checked. Just that door."

Which means we need the next best thing: a place to hide. Tool cabinet? Too small. Floaty

tube? Can't breathe underwater. Underground?
I'm not a gopher. There's nowhere to hide,
except, maybe—

The meat heap, I think.

A rotting, fetid lump of monster parts is piled
into a mound at the rear of the room. Most of
them unrecognizable as more than—*shudder*—
leftovers . . .

At the front of the heap is a bulging, round
monster husk—which I quickly dub Fly Guy. It's
got a head like a fly that was dunked in candle
wax, complete with dozens of softball-sized
eyes. A long gash splits its rippled belly down
the middle.

"Fly Guy," I mutter. "Has to be the Fly Guy."

"Absolutely not—" Quint starts, but then we
hear the nurses chittering back and forth.
They're close.

June's quick to get her hands dirty—dashing
toward the meat mound, grabbing hold of
Fly Guy, and heaving. And then . . . *yep—no
stopping this now, we're doing this, we're
climbing into the husk of a dead and bloated fly
monster.*

The nurses enter just as we yank the Fly-Guy's
eyeball-covered skin flap shut . . .

chapter nineteen

The Fly Guy's insides are rank and dark. There's just enough room for the four of us, plus Drooler. As I wiggle around, my elbow hits something soft and wet. Light starts to dribble in, shining like a prism through the Fly Guy's many eyes. His, heh, *flyballs*.

"This is a great view," I whisper. "If you really dig kaleidoscopes."

"No one really digs kaleidoscopes," Dirk grunts.

June scowls. With a tap, a metal spork-knife pops out of Blasty, and she cuts a slit in one of the flyballs. We have a clear view now—and I don't like what I see . . .

There are two nurses. The first has a head like an anglerfish, with a buzzing light dangling above its lone eyeball. The second nurse's face is splayed open, revealing a second, more horrific face underneath.

They scurry about, preparing the morgueatory for something . . .

–DIRE NURSES!–

OOH, THE NUMBERS LOOK GOOD. WRACKSAW WILL BE *SO* PLEASED.

DON'T BE SUCH A TRY-HARD, DEBRA.

We exchange confused glances. Split-Face's name is Debra? Monsters are weird . . .
Suddenly, we hear whistling. It comes from the corridor beyond, growing steadily louder.

"He's coming!" Debra says. "Look busy!"

"I *am* busy!" the other one shoots back. He plugs something like an other-dimensional oxygen tank into the fleshy walls, and it starts *ka-chug ka-chug*ging softly.

Debra grabs a flagpole-sized lever that juts out of the ground. She leans into the lever, until—

VRROOOOM

A large, circular section of the floor at the center of the morgueatory begins to slide open, revealing a pool of oil-goop underneath.

June shifts, pushing her head next to mine. "I really hope we didn't show up for evil bath time . . ." she says.

The whistling grows louder. It's a cheery little tune—the kind of melody Willy Wonka would hum right before faking a fall and feeding a bunch of bratty kids to a factory.

Wait! Crud. *We're a bunch of bratty kids!*

"He's here!" Eye-Bulb hisses, smoothing his scrubs.

The nurses quickly stand at attention.

And then he enters.

The monster of the hour. The employee of the month for the last four hundred months . . .

-WRACKSAW!-

Armacles

Skin like a mood ring. Current mood: annoyed

Tentacle-legs

My skin turns all goosebumpy as Quint says, "That whistling . . . it appears to be air passing between the thin tendons connecting his head to his body."

Debra makes a gleeful *tchk-tchk-tchk* sound. "Wracksaw, sir," she says. "Your calculations were correct. The pool has further softened the subject's tissue."

"Of course my calculations were correct," Wracksaw says, drawing out each *s*. "My calculations are never less than perfect."

One of Wracksaw's armacles reaches out, tugging a thick cord that hangs from the ceiling.

The pool starts to bubble, like he's getting ready to boil a Blarg-sized helping of Kraft mac and cheese. Then something begins to rise from the liquid darkness . . .

Drooler *meeps*. "Aww, you want a better look?" Dirk asks softly, gently releasing the little guy and setting him on the floor.

Wracksaw slithers toward the pool. Spongy pods on the surface lock together, creating a bridge, allowing Wracksaw to cross to the center. Goop sloshes over the shape that breaks the surface.

I know who—*what*—that is.

We all do.

GHAZT! DEAD!

chapter twenty

My Cosmic Hand pulses again, and for a second,
I feel strangely . . . alone.

He's dead. He's really dead.

I'm *not* sad that Ghazt is gone . . . but a part
of me feels—weirdly empty? Like something's
missing. I wouldn't have the hand without him—
and the hand is filling me with monstrous fear.
But I wouldn't be able to command my Zombie
Squad without him, either—and I do love those
guys. My insides are totally mixed up right now.

"I find myself strangely sympathetic," Quint
whispers, breaking the quiet.

Dirk scowls. "Uh, breaking news? He's evil."

"*Was*," I point out.

HERE LIES
GHAZT
BORN:
10/08/6,102,616,110
DIED:YES
WAS EVIL

A loud *SNAP* brings our attention back to Wracksaw. He's putting surgical gloves—or, like, surgical *mitts*?—on his four armacles.

Most of the oil-goop has finished dripping from Ghazt's fur now. The tips of Wracksaw's armacles rub together like evil, twisty hands.

One armacle ensnares Ghazt's head, then tugs, wrenching the body upward. Wracksaw hums as he forces open Ghazt's eyes and mouth.

Finally, Wracksaw releases Ghazt, and the massive body crashes back down to the slab.

"No more tests," Wracksaw announces. "The subject is ready for knowledge-extraction."

Wracksaw swirls back toward the nurses. Colors flash across Wracksaw's face, blending and flickering. They finally settle on an expression: horrible pleasure.

"Now," Wracksaw says. "It is time for Ąäðđűḷ to fully awaken."

"Ooh, I love this part!" Debra squeaks.

"I think he's talking about the fortress," Quint whispers.

Wracksaw looks upward to the laboratory's jagged, curved ceiling. His body expands like a marshmallow in a microwave, filling up the space around Ghazt's body.

"Lying on this slab is Ghazt the General, a Cosmic Terror from the Cosmic Beyond! Which means . . . I HAVE A <u>GOD</u> ON MY TABLE! And this night . . . I operate on a GOD!" Wracksaw says as his armacles extend outward, stiffening. "And that makes ME a GOD! Sorta."

His armacles suddenly jab upward, stabbing into four glowing holes that dot the laboratory's ceiling. The armacles enter with a *schlurp*, then twist, locking into place. The morgueatory trembles in response.

Wracksaw's body begins to *glow*. His eyes shut, his head sinks into his body, and then—

A harsh, grinding groan comes from all around us. The morgueatory's trembling builds to a rumbling. Bursts of warm, putrid air blow from cracks and fissures.

Eye-Bulb elbows Debra excitedly.

Colors and patterns flare across Wracksaw's skin as, finally, he extracts his armacles from the morgueatory ceiling.

The fortress trembles hard once more—then settles into a soft, steady shuddering.

"By nightfall, Ą̈äðđűį will be fully awake."
Wracksaw says. "Then I will perform the
knowledge-extraction."

Wracksaw suddenly whirls around. "Now . . .
retrieve my revitalizing smoothie from the
shared refrigerator, posthaste!"

Debra trembles. "Oh, um . . . I didn't realize
that was yours, sir. And I was so very parched
that I—"

Wracksaw cracks an armacle against a tank, jostling the floating corpse inside. "It sure sounds like someone—*Debra*—wants to take a trip to the carcass pit. Is that right, Debra? Do you want to take a trip to the carcass pit?"

"No, my leader," Debra says, avoiding Wracksaw's gaze.

Wracksaw runs an armacle across his bulbous head. "I'm at a high stress level right now, OK?! Which means I *must have* my revitalizing smoothies! Is that so much to—"

Wracksaw suddenly goes silent. "And would someone tell me—"

Drooler! We looked away for like TWO seconds, and now he's playing peek-a-boo with evil!

We all stare at Dirk. He mutters, "OK, fine, I'll get a toddler leash."

"Eye-Bulb? Does that belong to you?" Wracksaw asks, snapping around. "Did I miss the memo that today is Bring Your Child to Frontal Lobe Excavation Day?"

Huh, his name *is* Eye-Bulb. Good guess.

While Wracksaw is busy berating the nurse, Dirk quickly reaches out, grabs Drooler, and—

YOINK!

MEEP.

"Phew," Dirk says. "That was a close one."

We all glare.

"What, you think the big guy noticed?"

"YES DIRK I THINK HE NOTICED!" June says.

Suddenly, the light flooding Fly Guy is blotted out. With incredible speed, Wracksaw snakes toward us. Two armacles slither underneath Fly Guy, and then—

VOOSH!

The entire carcass is flipped backward.

I feel like I just got caught dumping an entire bowl of Halloween candy into my candy sack when the sign clearly said TAKE ONE.

Uh, hi. Do you take expired coupons for the mad–scientist laboratory tour?

Jack, why would he take **expired** coupons?

"Would you like me to examine the coupon, sir?" Eye-Bulb calls.

"IF I WANT YOU TO EXAMINE A COUPON, EYE-BULB, I WILL ASK YOU TO EXAMINE A COUPON!" Wracksaw roars. His body swells, his mottled skin flashes like a cracked iPad, and then—

SKNIKT!

Scalpel blades—tools of Wracksaw's terrible trade—erupt from his armacles! An angry slash of neon crosses his face.

"You three chose the wrong evil monster fortress to go snooping about . . ." Wracksaw says.

You three? I think.

That's when I realize Dirk and Drooler aren't here. Dirk must have clung to the carcass as Wracksaw flipped it! And suddenly—

Wracksaw recoils, but more out of surprise than any real fear.

With that brief moment of opportunity, we all *rush* from our hiding spot, like roaches scattering when the lights come on.

"SEIZE THEM!" Wracksaw shouts as Quint and June dart free.

"You want them to seize us, sir?" Eye-Bulb asks.

"No, Eye-Bulb! I want *YOU* to seize *THEM*!" Wracksaw looks like his balloon head might just pop off and explode from pure anger.

"I knew what you meant, sir!" Debra says as she hurries to block Quint and June's path to the exit.

Beside me, Dirk's sword glistens as it cuts through the air. "Cover your eyes, Drooler!" he says as—

SCHWOCK!
SLAM!

Two of Wracksaw's armacles are sliced in half, the severed tips flopping to the ground.

Whoa. *Whoa.*

But Wracksaw simply grins.

We are in *way* over our heads here.

Wracksaw lashes out with one of his newly regrown limbs, grabbing Dirk and hurling him into Quint and June. Together, they crash into Debra and Eye-Bulb.

In a flash, all of my friends are locked in combat with the two Dire Nurses.

I gulp. Just me and Wracksaw now.

And that's a fight I want no part of.

I try to bolt past, but Wracksaw thrusts an armacle at me.

It snakes around me, lifting me off my feet until I'm dangling in the air, face-to-face with the hideous villain.

Wracksaw studies me like I'm one of his specimens. He appears ready to discard me—another body for the meat heap—until his eyes lock on the Cosmic Hand.

A whistling snarl passes through his neck tendons.

"Now, this is interesting . . ." Wracksaw says as one armacle slithers up my forearm, snaking around the Cosmic Hand.

I wince as the armacle tightens.

THIS LABORATORY IS WHERE I BUILD MONSTERS. BUT YOU WON'T NEED TO BE BUILT. YOU ARE WELL ON YOUR WAY TO BECOMING A MONSTROSITY YOURSELF—WITHOUT MY HELP.

"That's not true," I manage to say.

"You would like to believe that, wouldn't you?" Wracksaw says.

Loud clangs and crashes fill the morgueatory as Quint, Dirk, and June battle the Dire Nurses. But I don't even look their way—I'm too full-up with fear and rage.

A cruel grin appears on Wracksaw's face, and I *roar—*

THAT'S NOT TRUE!

"It is very true," Wracksaw says, his voice softening. "Unless . . ."

That last word hangs in the air. He doesn't finish the sentence. Because I know he wants me to ask. And . . .

I want to ask, too.

"Unless what?" I finally say. The words come out in a quivering almost-snarl that sounds more desperate than I want it to.

"Your monstrous transformation is not inevitable," Wracksaw says. "I could remove it from you. That is within my capabilities."

And . . . my head goes to a place I thought it never would. Never *could*. Across the room, I see the horribly monstrous nurses looming over my friends. My memory flashes back to the guards on the train. I was terrified they'd hurt June. But when all was said and done, I was the one who caused June pain. With this monstrous hand.

And . . . I think, maybe . . . I should consider Wracksaw's offer . . .

No. What am I saying? I could never—

I open my mouth, about to ask him what *exactly* he means. But before the words are out, a shock of force shoots through the Cosmic Hand and my mouth clamps shut. My jacket sleeve bulges and splits as energy explodes out.

ZZZ-KRAK!

Wracksaw's armacles snap open, and I'm dropped to the floor.

"Your appendage . . ." Wracksaw says, with a cruel laugh. "It didn't give you a choice, did it?"

I don't respond.

"Oh yes," he says. "You will be one of us soon . . ."

I swallow down a throatful of terror and manage to stand. I shakily grip the Slicer, but—

KRAK!

Wracksaw smacks me across the room like a rag doll. I slam into a tank, bounce off it, then tumble directly into the fight.

A fight that is not going well . . .

Both Dire Nurses smile. They've got surgical saws at our throats.

But then—

WHUP! SCHLOOP! BLOOSH!

Something bursts through the wall behind us. Bands tighten around us, squashing the air right out of my lungs. What the Flamin' Hot Cheetos is going on?!

Thick, fleshy heat envelops us, and everything goes dark as we're hauled back—into and *through* the wall!

In the distance, Wracksaw roars . . .

chapter twenty-one

We've been rescued! I think for a half-second

But, no, being rescued shouldn't be this *painful*.

We're being hauled off like sacks of potatoes. I can't see anything, and all I can hear are stomping feet. Something sharp stabs at my gut, over and over, until—

OOF!

Whoever's abducted us has—not so gently— dropped us to the ground.

My eyes blink open.

A fine web of flesh and tendon is draped across the ceiling, beaming fluorescent green. Looming over us, almost glowing in the light, three figures come into focus. Three of the most mind-bogglingly *bizarre* creatures I've ever seen . . .

Goons. A . . . platoon of 'em.

"Please tell me you're good guys . . ." I say.

-The Goon Platoon-

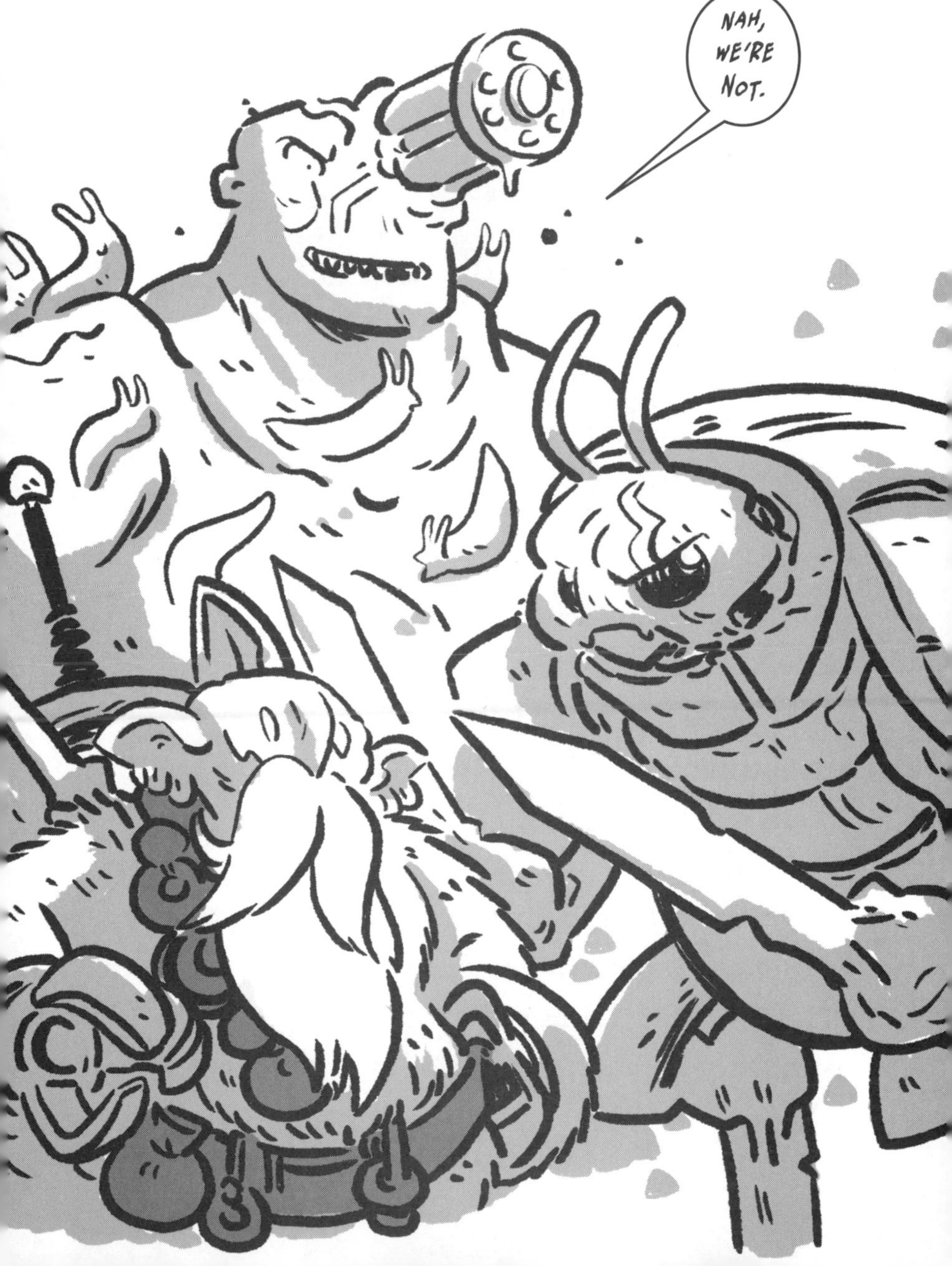
NAH, WE'RE NOT.

"Cool," Dirk deadpans.

A stomach gurgling noise—like flat soda sloshing around a warm bottle—comes from the creature that looks like a sleepy Care Bear.

But there's another sound coming from a few feet away.

Something familiar.

Something monstrous—but not *evil*.

It's funny, you hear so many weird, unexpected sounds during the Monster Apocalypse, they sorta start to blend together.

But this sound stands out because—

No.

It can't be.

It's a soft, questioning growl that builds to a yipping, yapping, eager bark.

My heart races as I stand.

The monster with the cannon head shoves out a meaty arm to stop me—but I duck underneath.

My eyes start to blur a bit.

Something *big* moves behind the Goon Platoon. Then a high-pitched, happy yip and suddenly the monster trio is knocked aside as—

I want to believe it with every last stupid fiber of my stupid being, but . . .

If this apocalypse has taught me anything, it's that nothing and no one can be trusted. I've seen too many weird visions, had monsters in my head showing me things that aren't real.

And I want this to be real so, so bad that I'm afraid that it's a trick. It doesn't seem possible otherwise, it—

Rover licks my face. It's the same messy, slobbery lick he gave me when we first met— what feels like forever ago—on the streets of Wakefield.

I jam my fingers into his fur, now thick, overgrown, and matted with ooze and dirt.

Rover keeps lapping at my face until I flop onto my back and he collapses on top of me—his head resting on my belly.

I look up at my friends.

"Guys . . . ? It's real, right?"

Quint smiles. "It's real, friend."

But . . . if it's real, why aren't my friends rushing over to join in the hugging and reuniting?

Oh right. The Goon Platoon.

They still loom over us.

Rover hops up and looks toward the Goon Platoon with wide eyes, swishing his tail back and forth, like he's trying to tell these guys that I'm A-OK. That we're all A-OK—and definitely not the sort of creatures that should or would make a good meal.

But Rover's swishing tail hits June, knocking her to the side, and her backpack opens as she tumbles back.

We watch, frozen, as the Fortress Breaker slips out, sliding across the floor toward the Goon Platoon . . .

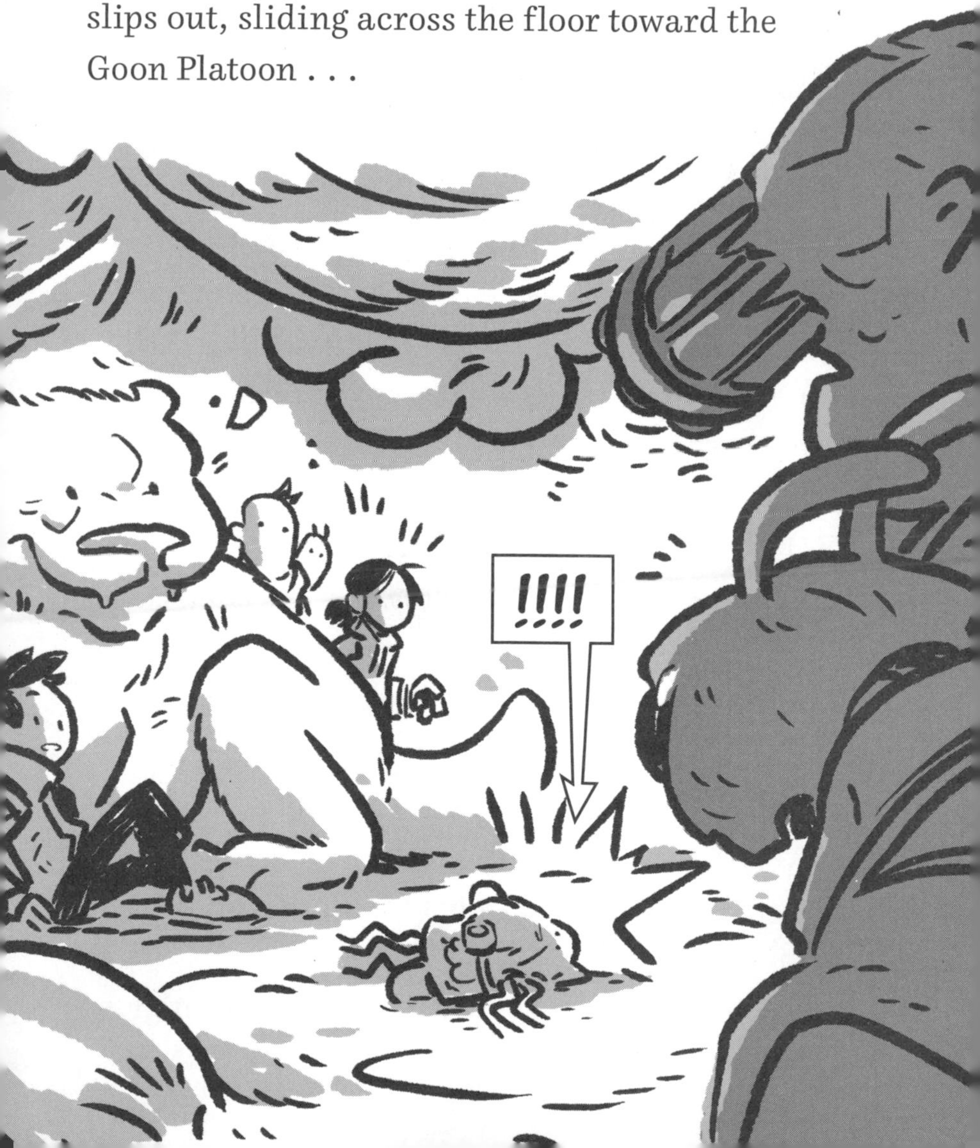
!!!!

Dirk inhales sharply. I can practically hear June's fingers digging into the hard ground.

The Goon Platoon moves toward the Fortress Breaker.

The beetle-looking creature with sword appendages gives it a gentle push with its leg. And then a poke at the seam. Sparkly flecks of glitter sprinkle out.

"Don't!" June shouts, holding out a hand. "That's our . . ."

"Wait? Hold up. Thrull?!" I exclaim. I suddenly realize I've never actually *seen* the finished Fortress Breaker. "It's inside a *Thrull* stuffie?? Dirk, that's what you were sewing up? *Really?!*"

Dirk scrunches his brow and shrugs.

"Not now, Jack," June says.

The Goon Platoon turns toward us. Then they look back to the Fortress Breaker. The beetle-looking one gently slides a blade-arm through it, lifting it up like a little baby. A little baby that could blow us all into next Thursday . . .

And that's when June shouts—

"DON'T! BOMB! It's a bomb. Stop, stop. It's a bomb."

The beetle-creature lifts its appendages higher.

BOMB?
WE LOVE
BOMB!

June lets out a titanic-sized sigh of relief, and behind her, Quint, Dirk, and I are her backup sighers.

"Me too, buddy. Me too!" June says, jumping to her feet and throwing an arm around the monster. "BIIIIG bomb! Packed with big bomb stuff—plus glitter!"

"Glitter for your enemies!" crows the beetle-looking monster. "It will never come off! You are a diabolical GENIUS!"

"We're taking that bomb and placing it at the heart of this fortress!" June says. "We're gonna blow this joint sky-high before the bad guys do *worse* bad guy stuff! And then . . . no more torture factory, no more Tower Schematics, just one big KA-BLOOEY!"

June's beaming—waiting for them to reciprocate her excitement. But then we watch, shocked, as the beetle-monster *schlorps* the bomb into her belly, and—

chapter twenty-two

June erupts. "WHADDYA MEAN WE CAN'T USE IT?? We're not gonna blow *you* up. We didn't know you were here!"

Quint nods. "Our intel said this place was empty of non-bad guys."

Dirk looks toward the Goon Platoon. "You can just come with us when we leave. I bet you're good in a fight, on account of all that . . . uh . . ." Dirk pauses, eyeing their many bizarre appendages and attachments. "All your *stuff.*"

"We cannot come with you," the beetle-lady says. I get the sense she's the leader of this weird trio. "We must remain here."

I glance down at Rover, tempted to whisper something in his ear like, "Hey, buddy, your new friends are kinda jerks." But I resist.

"Hold up," Dirk says, and I hear him drop his voice a notch deeper, getting gravelly. "Let's try and keep this sociable. Like friends. And friends got names."

With a few head nods, Dirk introduces us.
Nothing fancy, no rad backstories, just the facts.
Then he stares at the Goon Platoon, waiting.

Rover looks up at the beetle-lady, happily
panting. She finally says, "The sounds of our
native tongue will fry your insides twice over.
For simplicity, you may call us . . .

Before we can ask why they'd need to remain here, and—more importantly—why we can't use the Fortress Breaker, a stomach-churning *YOWL* rings out.

"ALARM!" Peaches barks.

In a flash, the Goon Platoon goes into lockdown mode. Cannonhead gets behind us, shoving us along.

Ahead of us, a door spirals open with a *schlurp*. We hurry into a huge, weird, wet cavern as the door revolves, sealing us in.

Peaches scrapes a long claw-finger over a fleshy nodule on the side of what now appears to be an other-dimensional freight elevator. We begin to move down the shaft, and I hold on a little tighter to Rover. Suddenly, the lift stops, and the darkness is cut by a sliver of red light as the wall opens up behind us, revealing something I did *not* expect to see . . .

"Is that . . ." June starts, then pauses, like she's not sure she can believe what she's seeing. "A fast-food joint from the monster realm?"

And that's not even the weirdest part. There are monsters. *Creatures. Critters. Everywhere.*

I recognize a few from Quint's bestiary, back in the day. But this room is like a monster menagerie . . .

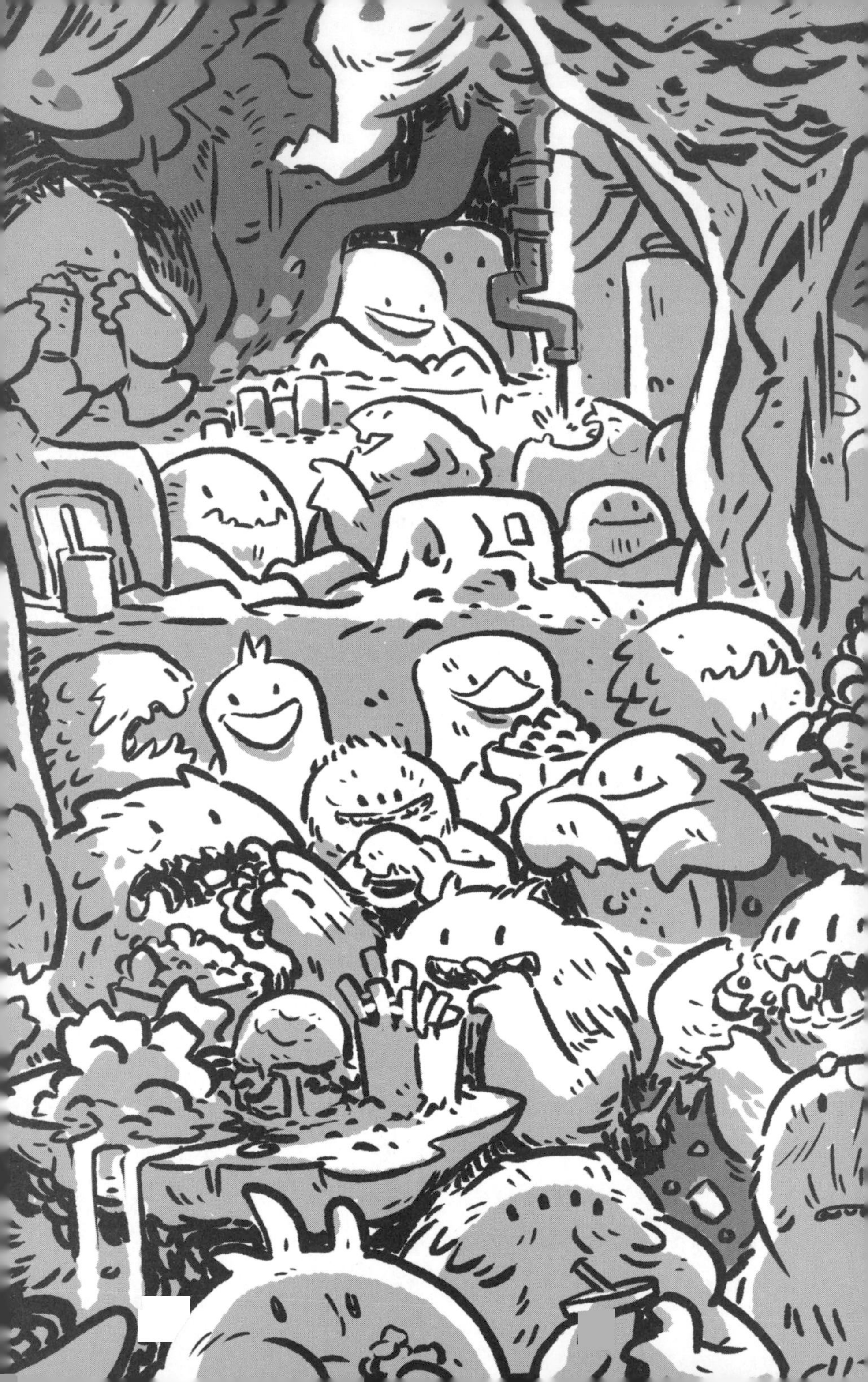

"What is all this?" Quint asks.

"The Grub Bonanza," Cannonhead Johnson says. "Best honkin' food in any dimension. Decent milk shakes, too."

"Think he meant these creatures," Dirk says.

"Survivors," Peaches says. "Like us."

"It's the cutest thing I've ever seen," June says. Then Rover looks up at June with big, wide eyes. "Except you, cutie pants, duh," she quickly adds.

It appears we're safe, for the moment. So I drop to one knee and give Rover another big hug. "I missed you, buddy," I say. "I missed you more than I knew I could miss anything."

I never had much to begin with. But then I moved to Wakefield and met Quint, and finally I understood what it meant to have a *best friend*. Then, after the world ended, I found Rover. And that was the start of this weird *family* of ours.

My chest hitches. I run an arm across my eyes, and the sleeve comes away wet. "What happened after you and Skaelka got separated?" I finally manage to ask.

Rover stiffens, at attention, then lets out a string of barks in quick succession. It's a very Lassie moment . . .

"OK . . ." I say. "Think I got most of that. And you've been here ever since?"

Rover woofs.

"Hey, buddy," Dirk says, as Drooler waddles toward Rover. "Somebody wants to say hello."

Rover licks Drooler toe to head, flipping the little guy up into the air. When Drooler lands, he *meep*s and licks Rover back.

June kneels down. "Hey, Rover," she says quietly. "Have you seen a young Winged Wretch around with—with no wings?"

She's asking about Neon, the creature she buddied up with while she was lost in the wilds.

June's face falls when Rover barks and shakes his head. I know that face: half relief, half disappointment. This would be a bad place to find someone you love, but . . . at least then they'd be found.

A sudden *DING* gets my attention.

"Ooh, yes, here comes the Chow Canal!" the monster named Dave says. He reminds me of a sloth—slow and tired. But he's clearly excited for some grub.

"Uh, we didn't schedule 'lunch' into our Mission Operation agenda," I start.

But Peaches holds up a sword-hand, calling for quiet. Through the walls, we hear Wracksaw's guards rushing about, calling to each other with updates.

"No humans in this quadrant!" one calls.

"Search it again!" another voice shouts back. "They have to be *somewhere*!"

Dirk reaches for his sword, but Dave sets a gentle hand on Dirk's wrist. "Chill out, amigo. You're safe here."

Peaches nods. "It's the ideal hideout, because this . . ." She pauses, trying to figure out how to explain it. "This area of the fortress serves no purpose to the larger entity."

"Like a vestigial organ!" Quint says. "Akin to the human appendix. Although, technically, the appendix is not—"

"We got it," Dirk says, slinging an arm around Quint's shoulder. Then: "Well, if we're stuck sittin' and waitin'—might as well be sittin' and waitin' and eatin'."

So, with no other choice, we plop our butts down. The Grub Bonanza is like an other-dimensional McDonald's—complete with a fun center. A pair of penguin-looking creatures climb up the slide, zip down, then scramble up to do it again.

There's another *DING*, and right then, a single stream of pinkish liquid gushes from above, like the ceiling just sprung a leak.

"Chow Canal," Dirk grunts. "Neat."

The stream changes directions, arcing and curving through the chamber. It's like rainwater rushing through a gutter—only there *is* no gutter. The liquid simply flows, suspended—ignoring gravity and physics.

"Eat, consume, imbibe," Peaches says like a concerned grandma as the canal surges past us, carrying endless Happy Meal–type boxes. I pluck one from the gooey liquid.

"OK, so . . . who are you guys?" June says, opening a box and tossing a handful of beads into her mouth. As soon as they hit her tongue, they burst to full size, and her cheeks puff out like a squirrel.

"Rifters are the worst," Dirk says.

"You meatballs fought Rifters?" Cannonhead Johnson asks, clearly not believing us.

"Whole bunch of 'em," I say.

"Ṛeżżŏcħ's servants sent us to this fortress. Wracksaw required test subjects . . ." Peaches says. "And then came the torture. Experimentation. Unspeakable alteration."

Only then do I realize all the things about the Goon Platoon—the things that make them seem less naturally monstrous than other creatures we've encountered—are the result of Wracksaw. The howitzer-sized hunk of artillery jutting out of Cannonhead Johnson's skull. Peach's sword-arms and sword-legs. Dave's pincer-hands and bony wings.

I pull Rover closer.

"We were in the fortress when Ṛeżżŏcħ opened the portals," Peaches says, gently running one of her blades over the fur of a purring cat-creature. "And we fell through with it. Here."

"It was a wild ride, man," Dave says. He's got a worm in his mouth, doing a Lady-and-the-Tramp thing with something like a mutant baboon.

"Hold up," Dirk says. "If you can sneak around this joint, poppin' in and out of walls . . . how come you haven't just up and ditched?"

Peaches leans back thoughtfully. Her belly opens with a wet *schloop*, and she pulls out the Fortress Breaker, setting it on the table with a plop. "For the same reason we cannot allow you to use this . . ."

The creatures . . . You can't leave . . . 'cause you'd have to abandon all these guys to Wracksaw.

AND THERE'S ABOUT A KAJILLION, SO IF WE EVEN, LIKE, TRIED AN ESCAPE—THE GUARDS WOULD BE ALL OVER US.

AND YOU CANNOT DESTROY THIS FORTRESS WHILE THESE INNOCENT CREATURES ARE SHELTERED HERE.

"I'd ditch these fuzzballs in a second," Cannonhead Johnson says, scooping a fistful of soup into his mouth. He reminds me of a pro wrestler who took a few too many hard hits. "But Dave says it's *not cool.*"

"Where did they all come from?" Dirk asks as he attempts to unstick Drooler from one of the furry creatures.

"Some were already here when the fortress fell through the portal," Dave says. He stands, yawning, and waddles toward the playset. "Others were grabbed by Wracksaw's sentries after the fortress landed."

Like Skaelka, I think. *And Rover.*

"We have rescued them from the prison," Peaches says. "Brought them here."

From the safety of the hollow cavern, I hear scurrying guards searching for us. Yet, somehow, *we're* the ones who found what we didn't even know we were looking for: unexpected allies. *Maybe.*

But time is short. Any moment, the fortress will awaken—and Wracksaw will get to splitting open Ghazt's brain and sucking out the Tower Schematics.

And with this Goon Platoon and these creatures, our plan has become *way* more complicated.

"I have a question," Quint says. "If you were already prisoners when the fortress fell through—how did you get *here*?" He gestures to the surrounding room.

"When the fortress was sucked through the portal—there was chaos," Peaches explains. "During that chaos, we saw our opportunity to escape the prison—and we seized upon it."

Looking down at June's Fortress Breaker, an idea starts to form inside my head . . .

"So, what if . . ." I start. "What if we could create some *more* chaos?"

Cannonhead Johnson grins. "This funny-lookin' kid is good at thinkin'. I *love* creatin' chaos. Almost as much as I love makin' mayhem."

Peaches taps a blade-hand against the Fortress Breaker thoughtfully. "Your 'Fortress Breaker' . . . You expected—what were the words?—*one big KA-BLOOEY*. But the fortress is alive. Its destruction will not be instantaneous. Once the heart is destroyed, there will be a chain reaction as the body begins to shut down, crumbling in upon itself, until it is finally a mass of smoldering energy. And *then* . . ."

"Ka-blooey?" June asks eagerly.

Peaches nods. "Ka-blooey."

At once, excited chatter fills the room: my friends and the Goon Platoon going back and forth, rapid fire. Everyone is hashing out some sort of double-distraction plan—except for Dave, who might as well be on Mars.

I spot him lounging in a pile of huge, fluffy critters. His eyes are shut. A small bird-looking creature eats crumbs off his chest.

It's only then I notice that he looks a bit like Bardle. Like, they could be ninth cousins, twice removed.

I stand up, walking over to him, about to tell him he reminds me of a friend. But he yawns and speaks first, "I always zone out during the 'big plan' stuff."

His eyelids open halfway, and he sits up, leaning against some sort of giant, fluffy kangaroo-creature. He looks me over—pausing to eye the Cosmic Hand.

I jam my hand into my pocket, but he keeps on staring like he knows what I'm hiding. Finally, sounding very sage but also very sleepy, he says, "I've seen some *weird* stuff in my day. You mind if I give you some advice?"

Rover nuzzles up against my leg. "Uh, sure," I say, even though unsolicited advice is always the worst.

I gulp.

I don't love the way that sounds: "*the other side on you.*"

And . . . er—lean into it? What does that even mean? Lean into becoming a monster? Or giving Skaelka the thrill of her life by letting her chop off the Cosmic Hand? I want to ask, but—

A groan echoes through the fortress. The salmon-pink walls turn blood-red. On the ceiling, globs of goo start to churn, bubbling like a cold, frosty glass of root beer.

"Guys!" Quint shouts. "The map—it's changing again!"

"Well," Dave says with an apathetic sigh. "The fortress is awake."

"GUARDS!"

The voice is like thunder, pumped through the fortress, carried by the arteries and veins, surrounding us completely.

It's Wracksaw.

"Guards!" he repeats. "Report to the Operating Theater. No dillying or dallying! Anyone caught dillying or dallying will be disintegrated. THAT MEANS YOU, DEBRA! I repeat, report to—"

Guess my conversation with Dave will have to wait.

My friends are out of their seats, packing up their gear. June's pulling her backpack straps tight, Fortress Breaker secured inside. Looks like they've got a real-deal plan.

So, things are still in motion. Sure, we hit a detour. But what was it George Washington said? Or maybe it was Bruce Lee.

"Life is a highway."

And sometimes, it seems, detours turn out to be shortcuts.

chapter
twenty-three

A door slithers open—and a tunnel maze, leading to the Operating Theater, lies beyond. As we enter, Cannonhead Johnson shouts like a drill sergeant, "Move, maggots!"

Dirk starts to tell Cannonhead to take it down a notch—when we realize he's talking to *actual* maggots. Or, slugs, maybe. A parade of slugs steadily slithers up his neck and into the cannon that juts out of his head.

"Gotta load up the ol' noggin musket," he says.

"Of course," Dirk says, like that's a normal thing. "Well, good luck. We'll see you on the outside."

SQUITCH WIGGLE!

DON'T NEED LUCK, MEATBALL. I GOT A CANNON ON MY HEAD.

Fair point.

Moments later, we're speeding through a maze of curving, splitting tubes and tunnels. They're slick and angled at a steep incline— but we surf *up* them with incredible speed, propelled by some weird reverse gravity.

The tunnels warp around us—expanding, bulging, then tightening.

"Rerouting!" Quint says for the third time, watching the Maparatus. "The fully awake fortress's body is changing! It seems to be shutting down nonessential organs and redirecting all energy to the Operating Theater!"

It's a good thing we tapped into the Directarium—otherwise we'd be squished to a pulp right now.

"That'll get Wracksaw's attention," Dirk says. "Enough to clear some guards outta the theater."

"Which," June says, "should allow us to place the Fortress Breaker. And detonate it! Setting off that chain reaction Peaches was talking about."

"Left!" Quint shouts, leaning at an impossible angle. We zip through the mouth of the forking tunnel. "It will be chaos! The guards won't know what's up and what's down anymore!"

"Yes, not knowing what's up and what's down sure will be awful for them," I say dryly as I watch the gravity-defying floor rush beneath my feet.

"And in that chaos, the Goon Platoon and the creatures complete their escape," Quint says.

"And we do, too," Dirk continues.

"It's the perfect double distraction!" June says.

Glancing down at the Maparatus, Quint says, "Ready yourselves—we're about to arrive!"

An instant later, we're out of the ever-tightening passage, sliding and skidding into a massive arena-like venue. Thankfully, we enter at the rear-rear-rear mezzanine, back row—the cheapest of the cheap seats.

"Forget Operating Theater," June whispers, eyes wide. "This thing is as big as an *opera* theater."

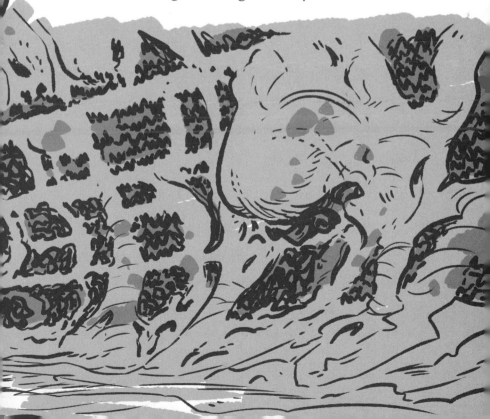

The stadium's many rows are filled with guards. There are no seats or benches—instead, the guards kneel, their insect-like legs folded and twisted beneath them.

Thankfully, their eyes—or rather, the dents where their eyes *should* be—are fixed on the preparation happening below.

On Ghazt . . .

His body lies on a floating slab: the operating table. Though it reminds me more of an altar.

The acoustics in this place are rock-and-roll good—we're at least one hundred feet above the operating floor, but the clanging of tools and the chittering of the Dire Nurses carries up.

Debra tightens the restraints around Ghazt's body. Eye-Bulb carries a long hose.

And looming over them all is Wracksaw.

"IT IS TIME!" His voice echoes through the theater.

"This thing is about to get underway," I say. "We gotta place the Fortress Breaker *now*."

"But where is the *heart*?" June says.

"It appears we're on top of it . . ." Quint says, eyeing the Maparatus as he twists it around.

While Quint searches, I watch the action down below. Wracksaw extends his armacles, calling for his tools.

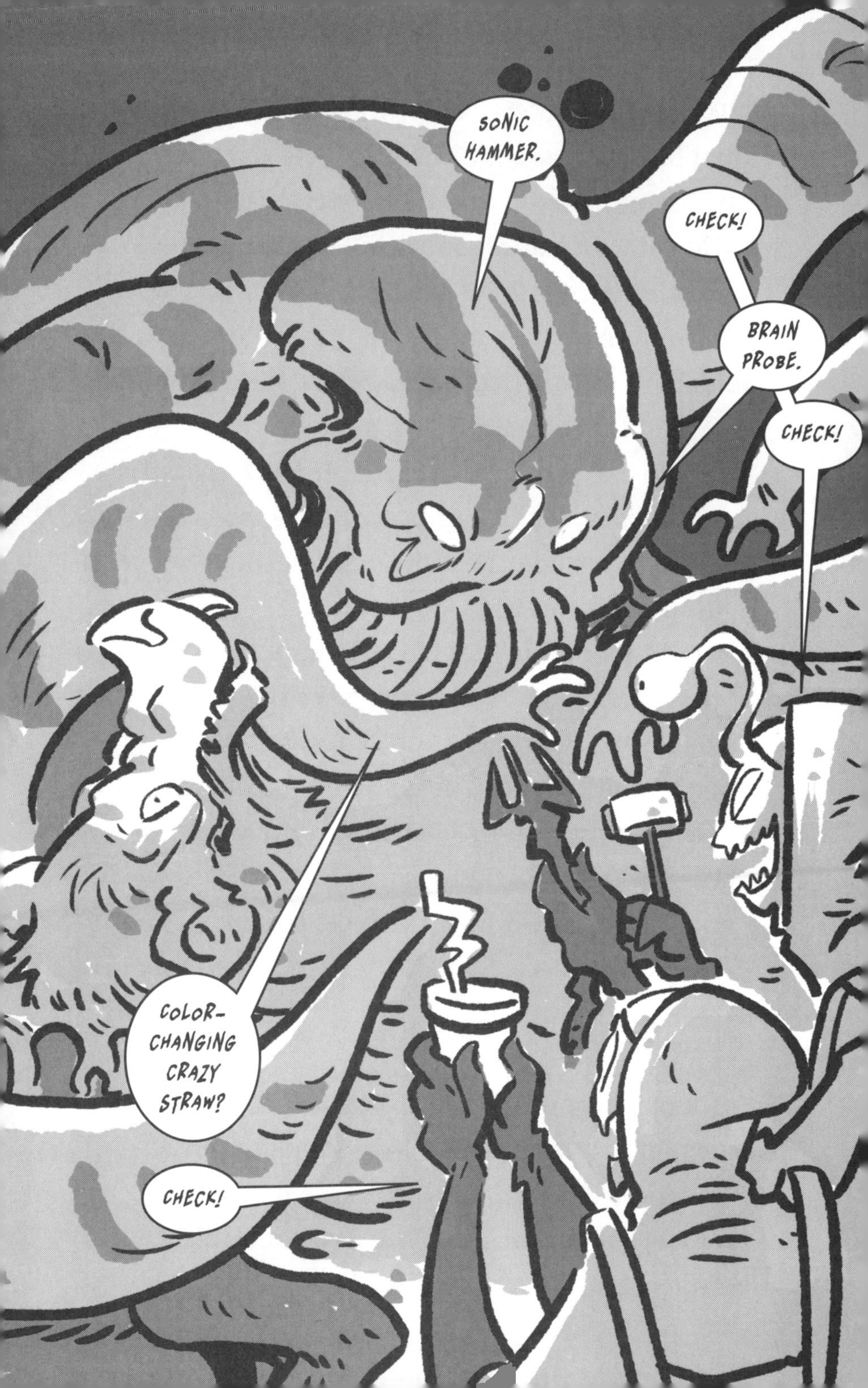
SONIC HAMMER.
CHECK!
BRAIN PROBE.
CHECK!
COLOR-CHANGING CRAZY STRAW?
CHECK!

Wracksaw slides and slithers around the slab until he stands over Ghazt's head. "Our patient is a Cosmic Terror who has lived for many millennia. His mind contains nearly infinite neuro-bytes of knowledge and memory."

"This is gonna be a toughie," Eye-Bulb says. He holds out a bottle of Neat-O Buzz, straw bobbing in Wracksaw's face. "Soda, sir?"

"No procedure is a 'toughie' for my skilled armacles!" Wracksaw snaps. But he does take a long slurp of soda. His lips smack, then—

"Sonic hammer!"

Debra hands the device to him, and the tip of his armacle coils around it. With a swirl, Wracksaw raises the sonic hammer, holding it outstretched for his audience of guards to gaze upon. They click wildly at the sight.

Wracksaw swings the sonic hammer down. It knocks against Ghazt's skull with a horrifying *CRACK*.

"We're almost out of time . . ." I say, glancing at Quint.

He has lowered the Maparatus—and is now looking up, toward the very peak of the Operating Theater. He sucks in a deep breath. "We weren't on top of it," he says, realizing. "It's on top of us."

The heart is high above the theater—positioned like a jumbotron in a basketball arena. It looks like a red jewel, set within the fleshy circular ceiling. A half-dozen arcing bones, like a ribcage, lead up to it.

"BRAIN PROBE!" Wracksaw calls, thrusting out another armacle.

Eye-Bulb sweeps in, handing Wracksaw what looks like a meat thermometer.

Oh no . . . I think.

Wracksaw plunges the probe into the center of Ghazt's skull with a sickening *POP!* My stomach wants to hork up that monster lunch. I stuff a fist in my mouth to keep barf from bubbling up.

The guards click and hiss excitedly. Their applause sounds like somebody knocked over a crate of crickets.

Wracksaw twists and grinds the probe around like he's trying to find an outlet to plug it into.

"There!" Wracksaw calls.

And then something truly bonkers happens . . .

Holographic images—the information and knowledge and all the awfulness within Ghazt's mind—are suddenly projected into the air.

My jaw drops. I can't believe what I'm seeing.

The memory it extracts is . . . wow.

"I need *the schematics*!" Wracksaw snarls. He wrenches the probe, and the image flickers away. "Not these nonsense residual memories with a human woman!"

He pushes the probe deeper. Images flash by: a blur of bizarre symbols, runes, and characters.

"It's almost like Kimmy and Skaelka," Quint says. "But those were memories. These are—*thoughts*. Knowledge. Information."

As Wracksaw continues probing, the images become clearer, taking form.

He's *close*.

"June, give me the backpack," I say. "I'm gonna climb up there and place the Fortress Breaker. We can't wait for the Goon Platoon."

"What? No way, that's *my* job," June says, clutching the straps.

But before I can argue—

SMOOOOOOSH!

The Operating Theater wall behind us starts to jiggle—and move . . .

It slowly spirals open, and—for one brief moment—we see the world outside. And then we see something else. Something big, something alive, something approaching the fortress.

It’s, like, a . . .

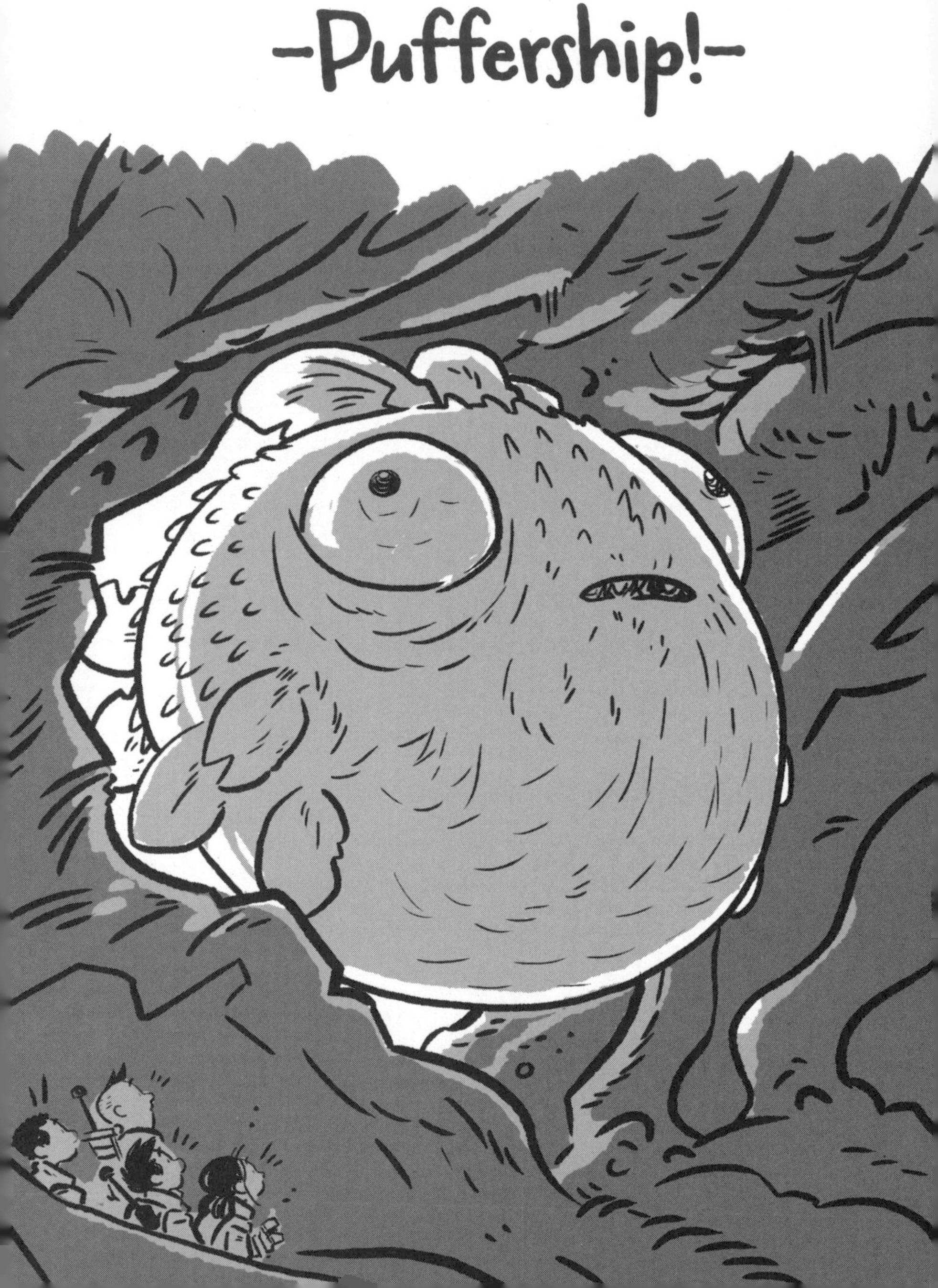
-Puffership!-

The Puffership's glazed eyes blink slowly, light pouring through them as the ship glides into the fortress.

I slide down the wall and hit the ground.

June's eyes are perfect circles. "What . . ."

"Is . . ." Quint continues.

"That?" Dirk finishes.

"It ain't the Goodyear Blimp, that's for sure," I say.

Wracksaw gazes up—he appears to be just as surprised by this thing's sudden appearance as we are. I watch him slither back, his body flickering and flashing, probably in shock.

We watch the Puffership drift through the chamber, slowly descending down to the Operating Theater's floor. It's a soft, gentle landing—surprising, considering what comes next.

The Puffership's wide mouth opens, the jaw touching down on the floor with a soft thump. A tongue unfurls, tumbling out of the mouth like the world's strangest Fruit Roll-Up. It hits the ground with a soft, wet smack. And then, out he steps.

The least soft, least gentle villain this side
of anywhere.

chapter twenty-four

"Ooh, you invited Thrull?" Debra squeals. "How exciting!"

"NO! I DIDN'T!" Wracksaw snaps. "Did you?"

"No."

"Eye-Bulb?"

"Not me."

"You're *both* going in the carcass pit later," Wracksaw growls, then shuts up as Thrull marches down the ship's tongue-ramp. The Dire Nurses quickly attempt to look busy. Debra flicks gunk off the table. Eye-Bulb polishes his eye-bulb.

Thrull's voice booms. "I hope I am not interrupting you, Wracksaw. But I have grown tired of waiting."

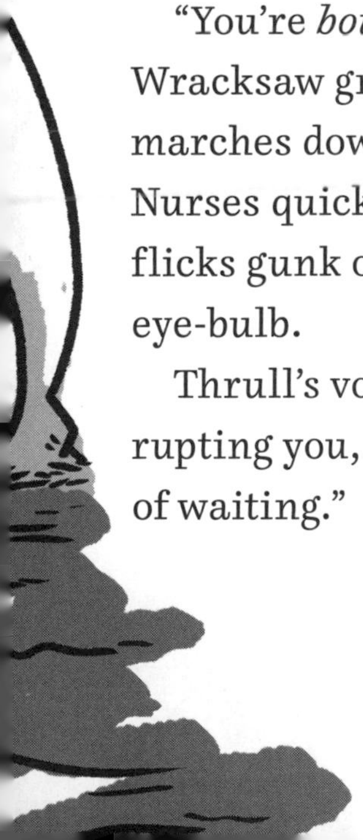

Wracksaw attempts to look calm, but the patterns along his armacles tell the truth: tiny, helpless polka dots, like goose bumps. He sinks into a sad little bow. "You could never interrupt me, Thrull. I am, after all, your humble servant."

Thrull's presence sends a nervous chitter through the guards. And a nervous chill through me.

The last time I saw Thrull, he'd just speared Ghazt like a cocktail wiener—then disappeared like a thief in the night.

Wracksaw regains his composure. "Your timing could not be more perfect. The Tower Schematics are nearly found."

"So get on with it," Thrull orders.

"Of course, my lord," Wracksaw says.

He returns to his work—angrily wrenching the probe back and forth. Electronic hissing echoes through the theater. And then—

Something like a holographic cross section of a nightmare is projected.

"There!" Thrull cries in a voice that borders on actual joy. "At long last . . ."

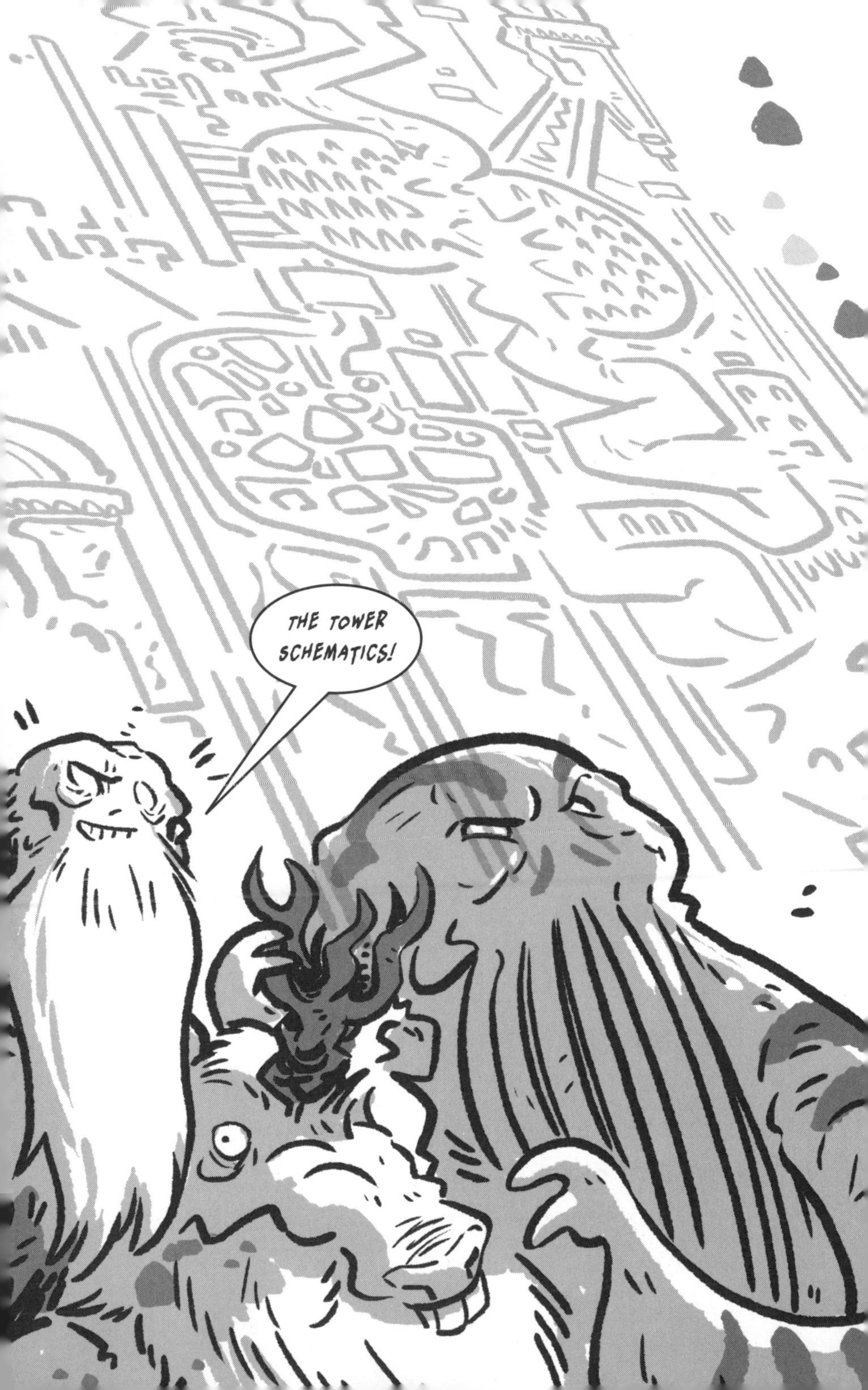
THE TOWER SCHEMATICS!

I look to my friends. Nervous glances pass between us. Rover and Drooler are frowning.

"What do we do?" Dirk whispers.

I don't respond. I don't shake my head. I don't move an inch. Because I truly, truly do not know.

"The bio-vac tube, Debra. Now!" Wracksaw snaps. "It is time to extract and transfer the information."

Debra hands Wracksaw what looks like a pool noodle made of worm skin. I spy a toggle switch on one end. Wracksaw yanks out the probe and drops it onto the slab. The schematics flicker away.

Wracksaw raises the bio-vac tube high above Ghazt's cranium. He looks like he's about to stake a sleeping vampire through the heart. "Placing the extractor-end . . . NOW!" he says, jamming it into Ghazt.

Once it's secure, he turns to Thrull. "The honor is all yours, my leader," Wracksaw says, offering him the tube.

Thrull's long fingers—all bone and vine—wrap around it. He lifts it up and presses it against his face. No. Actually—*into* his face.

We watch in horror as Thrull's head *splits*, opening in a vertical seam down the center. His forehead opens, his cheekbones crack, his eyes shudder sideways.

Thrull forces the tube into his wide, horrifically open visage like he's inserting a gas pump nozzle into a car's gas tank.

"DELIVER THE SCHEMATICS TO ME!" Thrull roars.

Eye-Bulb reaches for the toggle, but Wracksaw slaps his hand away. He flicks the toggle—and Ghazt's head jerks.

The tube snaps to life—and I realize it's like a *vacuum hose*. It pulls and pulls until, with a sickening *schlorp*—

POP!

The crucial piece of brain-knowledge—the Tower Schematics—are suctioned out of Ghazt's brain. The tube bulges as the information is carried toward Thrull, and then finally into Thrull.

The rush of information is so powerful it lifts Thrull's body off the floor as he cries out—

With each neuro-byte of information, Thrull's body spasms. It looks like this process might tear him apart, rip him open. But we don't get that lucky . . .

There's one last, long tremble—then Thrull crashes back down to his feet.

With a squelch, Thrull removes the tube from his head. It hangs limply in his hand for a moment, then drops to the floor.

Thrull's face re-forms.

"All is clear to me. Soon the Tower will be completed. Soon comes the activation. Soon Ṛeżżőcħ will be ushered into this dimension."

Thrull flicks out his tongue, and it snakes upward, licking a single droplet that drips between his eyes. He smiles in satisfaction.

"Wracksaw," Thrull says, finally, "you performed . . . adequately. Ṛeżżőcħ will know your name when he arrives."

Wracksaw manages to maintain his composure despite the not-quite-compliment and nods his appreciation. The Dire Nurses exchange giddy glances.

Without another word, Thrull turns—his cape snapping in the air. He strides back to the Puffership. The ship's tongue coils up behind him as he marches inside, then the mouth closes.

The Puffership silently lifts into the air.

"ADEQUATELY?! *ADEQUATELY?!*"

Wracksaw's skin pulsates—first red rings, then midnight blue. Scalpels and calipers clatter across the floor as his armacles lash out. A scream whistles through the fleshy cords that connect his head to his body. "I would like to know how *he* would have improved upon my technique!"

But Wracksaw's rage doesn't matter—not now.

The Puffership glides back through the window, gone—and with it, all our hopes of stopping Thrull.

A cosmic gut punch hits us all at the same time. Dirk comforts Drooler—or maybe it's the other way around. Quint clings to his conjurer's cannon and tries not to hyperventilate.

And June stares at the Fortress Breaker—now useless—in her hands.

My mouth flaps around. I want to say a lot of things, all at the same time.

We didn't just fail a little. We failed a lot. We lost all the marbles, in one shot, and it's stupid how hopeful we felt.

Thrull has the schematics. The Tower will be
completed and activated. Ṛeżżőch *will* come.
We're *not* gonna save the day. We're just a bunch
of kids who got lucky a couple times—

"*FOOL.*"

"Huh?" I glance up. "Who said that?"

"*Jack, you fool!*"

The voice seems to come from inside my head.
Then buzzing. Then boisterous humming.

My hand is throbbing and thumping, and my vision goes cloudy.

I finally blink open my eyes.

I must have been out for a few seconds because now . . . stuff is happening. The fortress's heart is beating so fast that the blood pumping through the walls creates a *thud-thudding* alarm.

"Must be the Goon Platoon's distraction!" Quint says.

"Just a smidge too late," June spits out angrily.

The chaos has begun. Hundreds of guards are skittering across the operating floor and funneling through the exit.

Wracksaw is mid-tantrum. "What is the cause?" he roars, snapping an armacle at a trembling Splotcher. "Is it the humans?"

"No. Creatures. On the loose. Lots of them."

"I AM NOT ENJOYING THIS DAY THE WAY I HOPED TO ENJOY THIS DAY!" Wracksaw shrieks.

I take a tiny bit of satisfaction in the fact that Wracksaw is super not pleased.

"Debra, Eye-Bulb—follow me," Wracksaw snaps. With that, he slithers out of the theater, leaving a skeleton crew of guards behind. (Not literally. Literal skeleton crews are Thrull's bag.)

Silence again. And then, once more, from inside my head—

JACK, YOU
DIM-WITTED
BUFFOON!

"You guys didn't hear that, did you?" I ask, a sick feeling rising in my stomach, because I already know the answer.

June's eyebrows raise. There's pity in that look, but also—I think—fear. Like, *Uh-oh, this is the day that broke Jack. He just cracked like an egg—fried. Kids, this is your brain on **defeat**.*

My Cosmic Hand pulses. I stare at it, thick and alien, alive like never before. The strange, monstrous thing that is filled with so much *unknown*—that has filled me with terror and dread and confusion . . .

And then it hits me, like that line from so many horror movies: "The call is coming from inside the house!"

It's the Cosmic Hand.

An impulse shoots through me: *go see Ghazt.*

Which makes no sense. I've been looking at his corpse off and on all day!

The pulse quickens, turning into a buzz. Just like it did when I climbed the cliff. Like . . . it knows something. Like—

"Hey, Jack," June says softly. "Remember . . . back when we were about to jump on the train, you were gonna tell me something? It was about your hand, wasn't it?"

I glance up. "How did you—"

June shrugs. A half smile crosses her face. "Intuition?"

I swallow. And then I start . . .

I tell them all about how, at first, I *thought* I had controlled the zombies with my *mind*. But I didn't. It was the Cosmic Hand. And how, since then, the Cosmic Hand has been changing.

Finally, I take off my jacket, roll up my shirt-sleeve, and show them—

"And yeah," I say, wrapping things up. "That's everything there is to know about my rapidly changing and not-at-all-frightening hand!"

But, of course, it is totally frightening.

And, of course *again*, that's not *everything* there is to know . . .

I swallow. "Actually, there's one other thing . . ." My head feels like it weighs about two tons as I lift it up. "June, I hurt you."

"Did you say I *heart* you??" Dirk asks.

"He did! I heard it!" Quint says.

"He totally did!" Dirk says. "Quint heard it, too! Jack said it! Ooooh, he said it!"

I look at June. Part of me wants to step toward her, throw my arms around her. Another part of me wants to turn and run so that I can never hurt her again.

"June was cornered. And I . . . I was so scared. I reached out, just wanting to do *something*, and . . . the Comic Hand did *more* than *something*. It turned into, like, a spear. And it . . ."

June reaches up to touch her cheek. Exactly where I cut her. Everybody's quiet. Then Dirk breaks the silence . . .

Kill him! Kill him with fire! No one's safe while he's alive!

Rover bolts up, placing his body between me and Dirk.

"Whoops, sorry, Rover . . ." Dirk says, rubbing his scruff. He looks up at me. "I'm just messing around, Jack. Whatever you're going through, we're with ya."

Quint simply shrugs. "You're my best friend, Jack," he says. "A weird arm doesn't change that! Nothing could change that."

June's eyes find mine.

"June? It's gonna be OK?" I ask.

"Obviously," she says. "Obviously times twelve."

"JACK! YOU IMBECILE! ENOUGH WITH THE FOOLISH EMOTIONAL NONSENSE!"

The voice again. I stare at the hand.

Before, I didn't know what you were capable of—and that made things bad. Then, when I saw June in danger, I felt real fear—and you reacted. And you hurt her. But . . . we wouldn't have made it inside this fortress without you. So this time . . .

"I'm gonna trust this thing," I say. "For better. For worse. Till death do us part. I'm gonna lean into it . . ."

With that, the hand *jerks*—and I'm no longer in control.

chapter
twenty-five

"Something's happening!" I call as the hand literally *drags* me away. "I gotta follow the hand."

"Where??" June shouts.

"To Ghazt, I think!"

"WHAT?" June shouts. "WHY?"

"I DON'T KNOW!" Rover darts alongside me, and I glance back, catching Quint's eye.

"We'll be there when you need us," Quint says.

Dirk nods. "We'll all be the Muscle."

With that, I'm yanked around the corner—and flipped up onto Rover as his snout catches my legs. I feel at home on his back. "Missed you, buddy," I say.

Rover growls softly as he dashes down a steep, slick ramp toward the Operating Theater floor— and the remaining guards. I hope whatever's telling my hand to visit Ghazt isn't also gonna tell the guards to turn around and punch me in my nose.

We reach the floor. I count a dozen guards, all with their backs to us. They look even more vile than the ones at the prison. Jagged helmets are fused to their thin, mantis-like heads.

And there is Ghazt, in the center of the room. Lying lifeless on the slab.

The Cosmic Hand pulses—sending a burning shiver up my arm, into my skull.

The burning fades to warmth, though, as I remember what I said I'd do once Rover and I were back together: play fetch.

I take a deep breath, and step out into the light.

Expecting the guards to turn at once—a big, dramatic, villain-packed greeting—I'm surprised when—

None of them notice us. One is scratching his eyeball. Another sucks on a frog leg like it's a Popsicle. A few others stare at their feet.

I stand there for an awkward moment, then clear my throat. "Ahem," I say, coughing into my hand.

That gets them. The guards turn to face us.

Not sure why, but I give them a little wave. A weird sensation comes over me suddenly, like I'm back at one of the dozen schools I attended before the apocalypse—a constant

rotation of first days, teachers, and classfuls of
strangers . . .

Weapons pop from the guards' arms,
shoulders, heads, kneecaps, elbows, and . . .
yeah, it's just a whole lot of weapon-popping.

"Looks like they mind," I say to Rover.

The guards spread out, forming a barricade around Ghazt's body and the operating table . . .

I scrub my hands into Rover's fur. He lifts his head. "Hey, buddy. Those guards look pretty cool, huh? With their shiny helmet-heads?"

With a growl, Rover stretches out, arching his spine. At first, I think he's begging for an underbelly scratch. But no. He's coiling up, a spring, ready to unload.

His head turns, tongue hanging out, waiting. Then—

I've waited *so* long to say this again . . . "ROVER . . . FETCH, BOY!"

Rover charges into the theater like he's been shot out of a cannon! He bounds toward one guard, then another, and another . . .

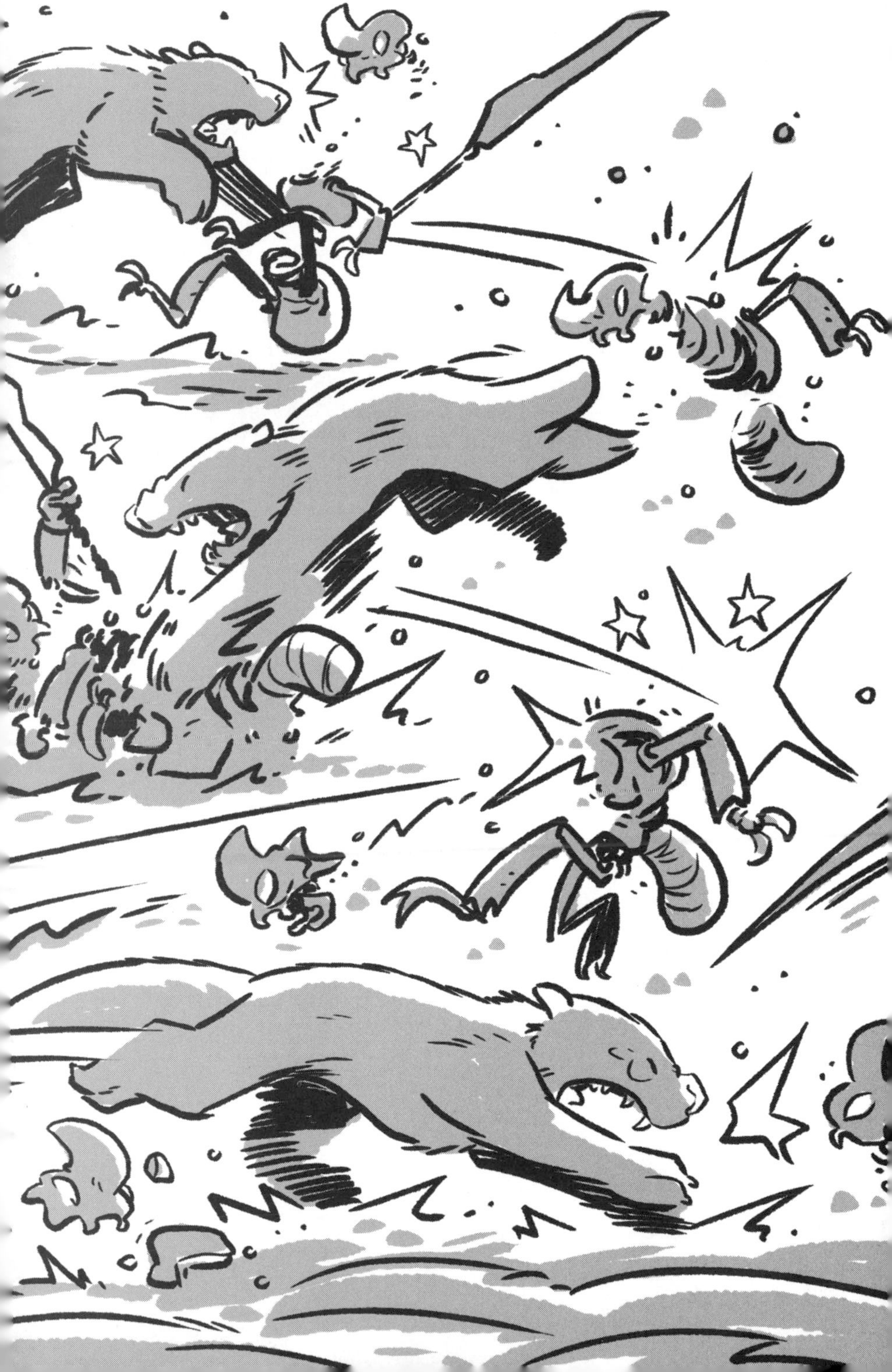

It's nineteen seconds of dashing, gnashing speed. Like all of Rover's pent-up anger toward Wracksaw is being unleashed in a magnificent display of giddy energy.

And then—after every last helmet has been ripped off its respective guard—Rover comes trotting back to me, carrying a single slobber-covered hunk of metal.

The guards totter on wobbly knees, tiny showers of sparks erupting from their heads.

Rover drops the helmet at my feet with a *CLANK*. And then come a dozen *THUNK*S: the guards collapsing, one by one, like dominoes. They lie on the ground, mumbling softly.

"Wow," I say, giving Rover a hard scratch behind his ear. "Guess you were eager to play fetch, too . . ."

I quick-walk toward the operating table, eyes darting around the theater—expecting more guards to pop out at any moment.

But the floor is empty except for me, Rover, and *him* . . .

Ghazt.

I stand over his lifeless body. His eyes are dull. The bio-vac tube still sticks out of his head, one end draped across his body.

No response.

If this was supposed to be some sort of big, grand-finale, mano-a-rato showdown . . . it doesn't look like it's gonna live up to the hype.

It's nothing like our first showdown. The anger and rage and fury in those beady eyes after I sliced off one of his whiskers is gone . . .

So . . . What now?

Why did I come all this way?

Stupid mysterious Cosmic Hand, why can't you just make clear what I'm supposed to do?

But the hand is still. It doesn't pulse or throb or turn into a giant foam #1 Fan hand or *anything*.

Until it does.

Not the #1 Fan thing.

But it twitches.

Then—wait. Was that? One of Ghazt's whiskers twitches at the very same moment. The exact one I sliced off when we first fought. It's regrown. Which makes me realize how long it's been since then.

I swallow . . .

"Ghazt?" I say softly. "Were you talking to me? Through the hand?"

Nothing. But then—

His head lolls to the side, and a low grumble comes from the depths of his throat . . .

JJJJJJJJAAAAAAAAAACKKKKKKK . . .

chapter
twenty-six

I leap back. Way back. I might have just created a new Olympic event: the *backward* long jump.

I stammer. "You said that, right? That came from your mouth? It wasn't delivered through the hand, or, like, from *within* my own brain? I mean, I saw your mouth move—but I wanna clarify, because—"

"Yes . . ." Ghazt says.

A shiver runs through Rover, and he nuzzles into me. I inch forward. "So, you're . . . alive?"

"Not for long."

"Hey . . ." I start. "That sounds like something *I* should be saying to *you*. Like a cool hero quip just before we square off or something."

"There will be no more 'squaring off' between you and me." His voice is rough, like he's been eating rusty nails and washing them down with bubbling acid. Which is actually not out of the realm of possibility in this nightmare fortress.

"But . . . you were dead."

Ghazt's whiskers flick again. "No. I was only . . . dying. It is a slow process for a Cosmic Terror."

Hope soars through me, and I clutch the table.

You tricked Wracksaw, didn't you?? That stuff he took from your brain wasn't **really** the secret to finishing the Tower, was it?

Ghazt, you ol' rascal, you.

I pat myself on the back—we didn't lose at all! We can still win, still *gonna* win, still—

"The Tower Schematics were real, Jack," Ghazt says. "The Tower was *my* weapon! But now . . . it is Thrull's. He has all he needs to complete and activate the Tower."

Well, shoot. Talk about whiplash. "Then what . . . I don't understand . . . What am I doing here??"

"Come closer," Ghazt says, and it feels like a trick. Suddenly, it seems like *all* of this has been a trick . . .

I take a step forward—but the ground rumbles beneath my feet. Behind Ghazt, a section of the floor is cracking open like an egg. Something is *forcing* its way up through the floor.

Some creature . . .

I gasp.

One of the Sentinels—but different.

This one has been horribly augmented and brutally altered by Wracksaw. It's like . . .

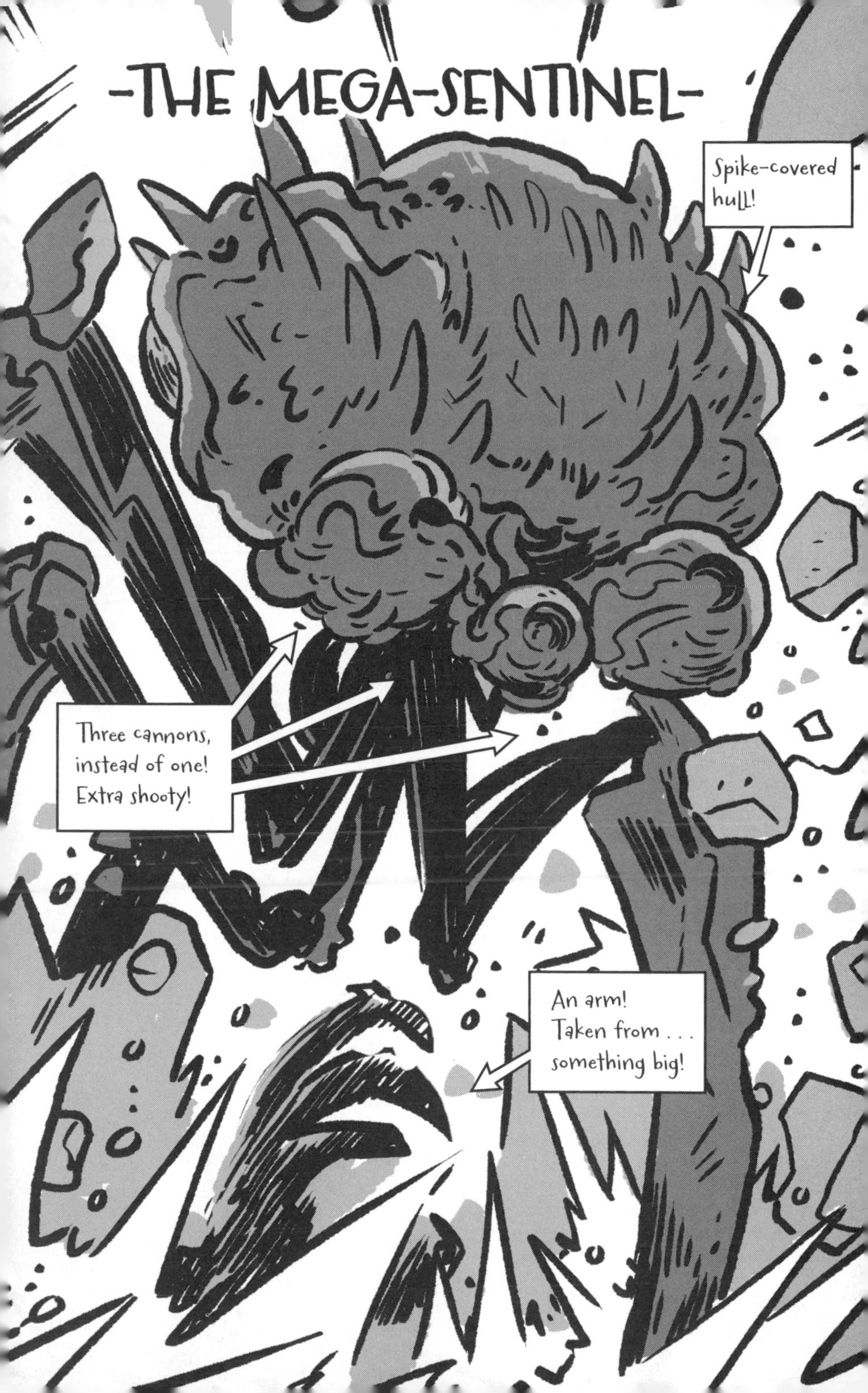
-THE MEGA-SENTINEL-
Spike-covered hull!
Three cannons, instead of one! Extra shooty!
An arm! Taken from . . . something big!

A sound that is simultaneously gooey-wet and razor-sharp blares through the theater.

Another searchlight lowers—this one covered in a hundred jagged spikes and blades. Dirk won't be doing any swashbuckling swings off of that one . . .

The light flashes over us.

Whatever Ghazt and I are supposed to talk over, hash out, work through—we can't do it now. Because the Mega-Sentinel is stalking forward, about to—

"MUSCLE BUDDIES!"

Three figures suddenly burst from the shadows, appearing at the bottom row of stadium seats surrounding the operating floor.

My friends leap from the overhang, sailing and crashing onto the Mega-Sentinel. The monster makes a creaking sound as it staggers to the side.

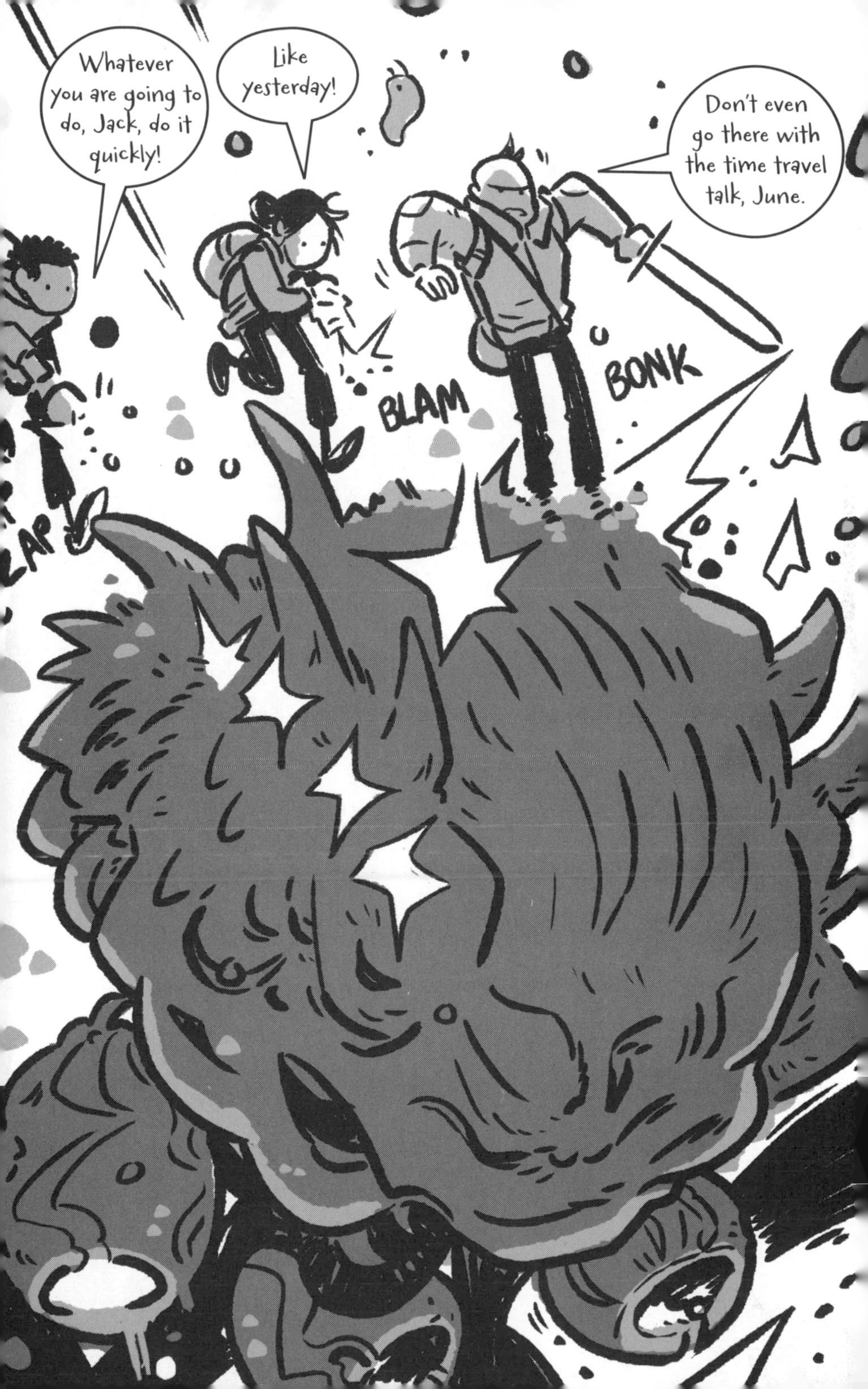
Whatever you are going to do, Jack, do it quickly!
Like yesterday!
Don't even go there with the time travel talk, June.
BLAM
BONK

Rover snarls and gets low, eager to leap into the fight—but I grab him by the scruff. "No, Rover. Stay by my side for this . . . Please, buddy. I'm . . . scared."

Behind us, the Mega-Sentinel screeches. I hear Dirk's sword clang to the floor.

"OK, my friends and I gotta move. It's escape time," I say to Ghazt, trying to catch my breath. "But we'll bring you. Somehow . . ."

"NO!" Ghazt roars, crashing against his restraints. The fury in Ghazt's voice causes me and Rover to jerk back. A dying Cosmic Terror is *still* a Cosmic Terror.

One of Ghazt's mangy paws shoots up, grabbing me, pulling me close. His eyes are cloudy—but they flash with urgency. Like he has a lot to tell me but there's not enough time to tell it all.

His paw tightens, balling around my coat collar. "Jack, you think stopping the construction of the Tower will end this," Ghazt says. He doesn't quite smile—but there's something almost taunting in his voice. Like "look how much I know and how much you don't."

"But you are wrong," Ghazt says. "The Tower will be completed—"

I sink back—not sure if it's because the ground is quaking or because my head is spinning. But Ghazt's grip is tight.

"Wait . . . What? Your zombie-controlling powers?" I ask. "You're saying I have to let Ṛeżżőch through because of the power in the Cosmic Hand? Also, technically, me and my buddies only sliced off your tail—it was Thrull who stole your powers, but then I took them from him; it was a whole thing, and—"

"SILENCE!" Ghazt roars. "Had you and your friends not severed my tail, the Tower's construction never would have begun."

"OK, well, I didn't know that, so, not my fault," I say quickly. "Also don't go around telling people that, OK?"

"Things are going to happen very quickly now. The power that is in your blade, and in your hand . . . it is MIGHTY."

Yeah, no kidding, I think. *I've been noticing.*

"It is mighty, but—"

"COMIN' THROUGH!"

Ghazt is interrupted by Dirk, who is suddenly on Ghazt's belly, then flopping off onto the floor. Dirk's covered in monster goo—along with blood, bruises, and cuts.

"Wrap it up, Jack!" Dirk barks as he dashes back to continue battling the terrible tripod.

Ghazt's stomach swells as he breathes. "It is mighty . . ." he says again. "But you . . . you treat my power as if it were a plaything. You do what? Control *three* zombies? When you have *my* power . . . the power of A GENERAL?"

Ghazt's lip curls in disgust. I'm not sure who's more annoyed with who right now. Actually, he's dying, so, yeah, he's got dibs on most annoyed.

"With that power, you can make Thrull pay!"

"I don't *care* about making Thrull pay!" I shout. "I need to save my dimension! My friends need to find their families! There are people out there who need saving! A big list of them! Who cares if we defeat Thrull? Ṛeżżőch's still coming, and if he gets here, my world will be lost!"

June suddenly slides beneath the table, then pops up before vaulting back over it, launching off Ghazt's belly. "FASTER, JACK!" she shouts. Mini explosions rock the Operating Theater as she fires off a triple-blast of bottle rockets at the Mega-Sentinel.

Ghazt takes a thin, shuddering breath. "If another one of your idiot friends steps on me . . ."

"So speed it up, dude!" I say.

His eyes catch mine—penetrating. "During every battle, there is a moment—a moment when everything balances on a razor's edge. That moment when a *leader* can swing defeat to victory, or fumble victory into failure . . ."

Leader. I hate that word. It's not what I am. It's not who I . . .

"That moment *will* be there during the Battle of the Tower," Ghazt says. "Now . . . grab the remains of my tail."

I gulp. What if I grab that tail and we trade bodies and it's, like, the *freakiest Friday*!

Suddenly, my friends are tossed onto Ghazt. Dirk's head bounces off Ghazt's leg. Drooler flops onto Ghazt's head—then tumbles off.

Light shines over us—the Mega-Sentinel.

Dirk sits up, raising his sword above his head. With a mighty heave—

He hurls his sword! It sails end over end, and then—

SQUANCH!

It slams into the Mega-Sentinel. The monster staggers back, then roars.

My friends bound off the table.

"I'm only half listening over here," Dirk says, grabbing one of the guard's slobber-soaked helmets off the floor and whipping it, Captain America–style, at the Mega-Sentinel. "But you had better not be about to trust Ghazt to help us!"

Rover nudges his head up, pushing my hand aside—like he's also telling me, "Don't trust Ghazt!"

I look down at Ghazt. Then I grab a fistful of his thin fur. "Do you care what happens to my dimension?" I demand.

For the first time, Ghazt pulls himself nearly upright, until his face is almost pressed against mine. "You heard Wracksaw's words: a *god* on his table. Yet he still cut me to pieces. I despise your dimension, Jack. I despise you. But I *hate* Wracksaw. And Thrull . . . There is no word in your language strong enough."

"Not even a four-letter one?" I ask.

"Not even a four-letter one."

Another George Washington quote jumps into my head. Or maybe it was Ryan Seacrest. Yeah, probably Seacrest—

"The enemy of my enemy is my friend."

And with Ryan Seacrest's wise words in my head, I reach out with the Cosmic Hand and grab hold of Ghazt's tail nub.

chapter twenty-seven

Ghazt's body vibrates, and I get the same sensation in the Cosmic Hand. We're connected. Two puzzle pieces—separated by Skaelka's ax, rejoined in a living monster fortress.

The world is weird, man.

"BEAR WITNESS!" Ghazt roars. "BEAR WITNESS TO THE INDOMITABLE POWER OF A COSMIC TERROR!"

Ghazt's body begins to shudder. Tiny sparks of electricity dance across his fur. I brace myself for the biggest, most epic display of interdimensional cosmic power in history as—

Ghazt falls back to the slab with a thud.

Power? What am I supposed to do? Ask if
anyone has any spare AA batteries?

I glance across the room.

Dirk and Quint are on either side of the Mega-
Sentinel, trying their best to give the beast the
business. Probably using a bunch of cool attacks
they worked out together during their buddy-

302

buddy hero quest. But I'm not even jealous this time . . . even if they did become best friends with that break-dancing Drakkor guy.

But June's not with them. My eyes search the floor, and then I zero in on a figure soaring across the room.

It's June, flailing in midair like a crumb that's been flicked by a monstrous finger.

She bounces off the wall, her fall cushioned by her backpack. And inside that backpack—

"June! The Fortress Breaker!"

Despite her crash landing—the words "Fortress Breaker" quickly have her springing back to her feet.

"We're gonna use it?" she asks. "Ooooh, YES!"

She's not gonna like what I have to say next.

"Give it to Ghazt."

"Ooh, NOPE!" she responds.

She eyes me like I'm not the Jack Sullivan she knows. And maybe I'm not anymore. But something in me says this is the *only* move.

June scans the room, the destruction, the battle still waging, and then, reluctantly, she slides the backpack off her shoulder.

Pulling the device out, she runs toward me and Ghazt.

In a flash, June is by my side—plonking the Fortress Breaker down onto Ghazt's chest. He smirks. "Ha. Thrull. Perfect."

"It's full of potential energy," June warns. "Detonating the bomb with all of us huddled around it would *not* be smart!"

Ghazt chuckles. "Oh, there was a time when nothing would have delighted me more. But not now. I will be the bomb's conduit—and together, Jack, you and I will send a beacon to the world. You will *understand*, Jack—after it is done. You will truly appreciate what it is to be a general."

I stand at the end of the table, the Cosmic Hand wrapped around Ghazt's nub.

June stands to his left. She no longer looks eager. Rover is between us.

"BEAR WITNESS—" Ghazt starts.

"JUST GET ON WITH IT! WE KNOW WE'RE BEARING WITNESS TO SOME EPIC OTHER-DIMENSIONAL GOD STUFF!" I shout.

Ghazt glares. "So do it," he says.

June and I lock eyes. Her finger hovers over the detonator affixed to Blasty.

I nod.

Here we go . . .

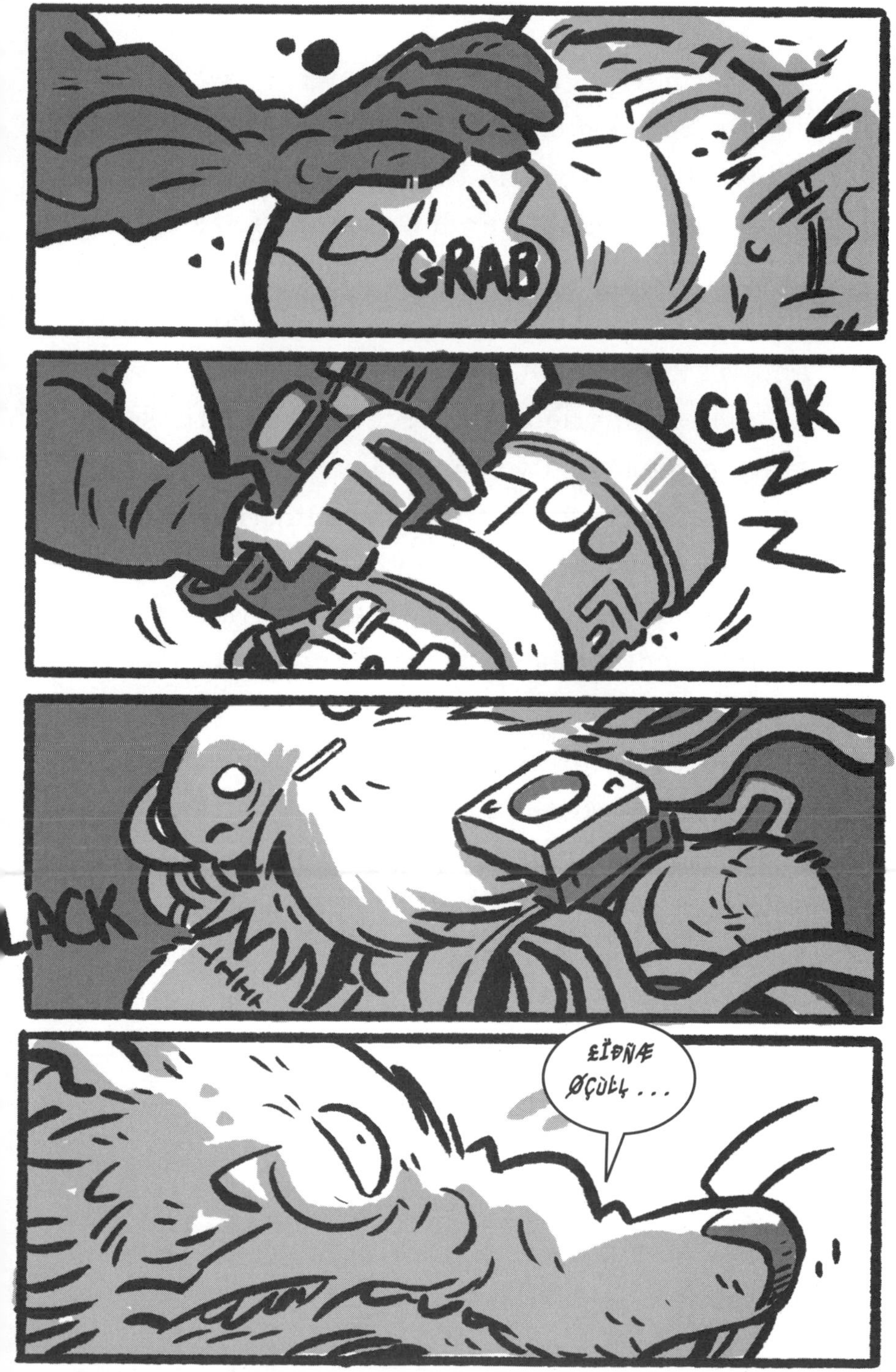
GRAB
CLIK
LACK
£ÏÐÑÆ
ØÇÙĿĻ . . .

Rover buries his head between his paws.

June leaps back.

I want to join her, but I can't—I couldn't let go of Ghazt's tail-nub even if I wanted to. It's like holding on to a live wire.

But the explosion is small—quickly contained and absorbed by Ghazt.

Rays of light flood from the Fortress Breaker, like a disco ball. Two beams blast through the Thrull stuffie's eyes—then through every part of him, until he has melted away to nothing.

And that same light begins to pour from Ghazt's body as the power and energy of the Fortress Breaker is funneled through him.

Ghazt's back arches violently—but his arms stay wrapped, python-tight, around the Fortress Breaker. And my hand's grip on Ghazt's tail-nub is unbreakable—even as my feet lift off the floor.

The full power of the Cosmic Terror drives through me. I feel like I'm being turned inside out! It's like my entire being—every molecule, every atom—is being pulled apart.

And then—

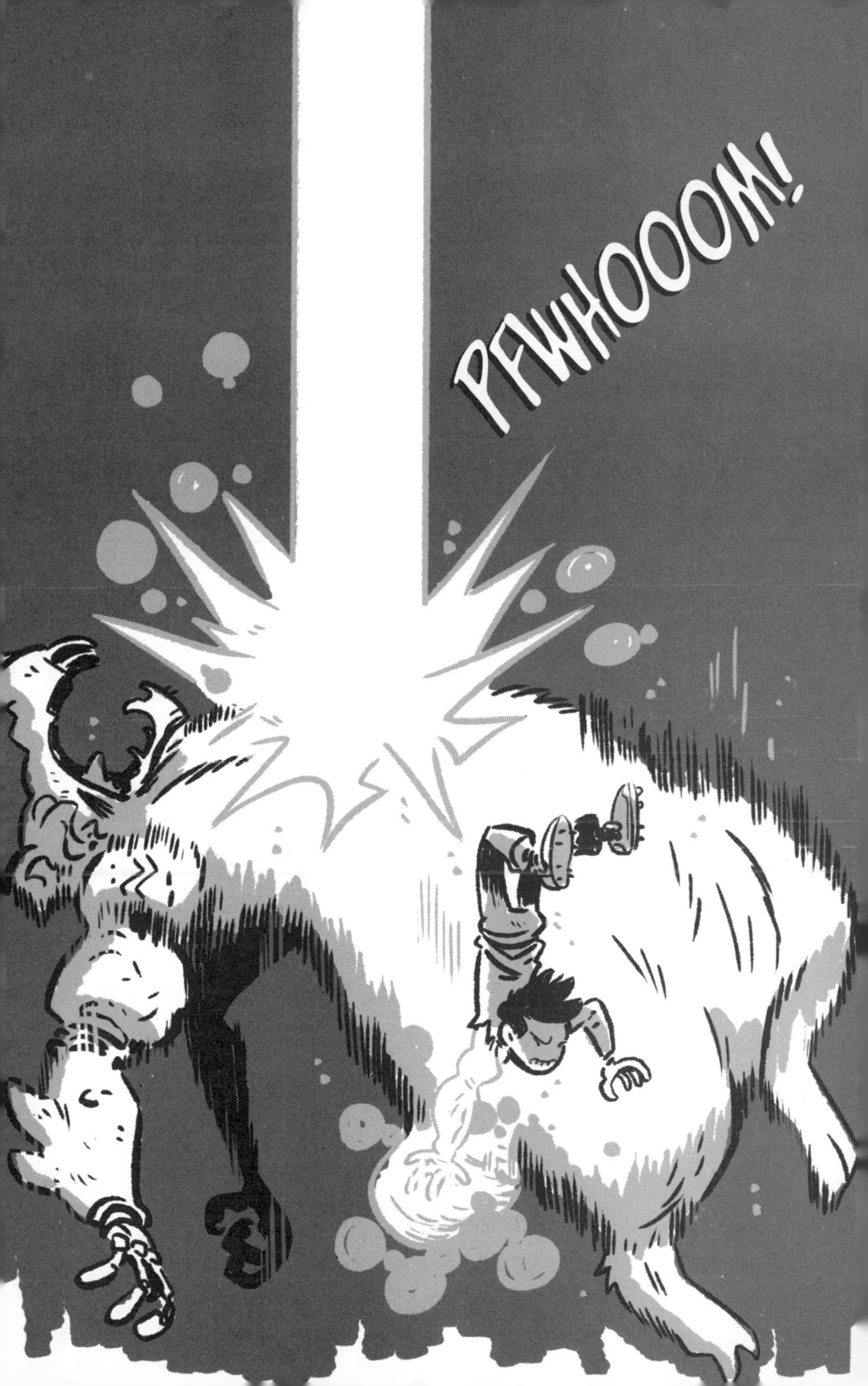
PFWHOOOM!

The pillar of other-dimensional energy that erupts from Ghazt's body blasts a perfect circle through the heart of the fortress, then continues upward.

The burning turns to broiling. My hand is on fire—my bones are going to melt! Or, no, my skin is going to melt, and then my bones are going to just fall to the ground because they've got no more skin encasement to call home!

I hear myself screaming. Ghazt screaming.

And then . . . it ends.

Darkness drops around us.

My toes barely touch the floor before I collapse. Catching myself on the extraction table, I wobble, but I don't hit the ground.

"Is that it?" June asks. "Did we just break the fortress?"

"A chain reaction has begun . . ." Ghazt says. "It will now begin to collapse in on itself."

June starts to scream out in joy—but stops when she spots me clinging to the extraction table.

"JACK!" June cries. "Are you okay?"

"June . . . I think you used . . . too much . . . glitter . . ."

It feels like somebody took a melon baller and scraped my insides out—another carcass for some other kid to hide in at the end of the world.

I smell burnt hair. I look down: Ghazt's tail-
nub has vanished. And my hand . . . my *arm* . . .

It's a ghastly, grisly horror. An abomination.
Dense. Primal. With every beat of my heart, I
can *feel* my blood rushing through my body, into
my arm, into the hand.

And with every beat, the blood is flooding and
filling me with something monstrous.

WHAT
DID YOU
DO?

"With my final command," Ghazt roars, "the army of the undead now marches toward the Tower!"

"But my hand . . . It's monstrous!"

Ghazt wheezes a laugh. "Yes, it is. *Now* you are the general, Jack. Bear witness!"

"Say 'bear witness' one more time, so help me—"

"BEHOLD!" Ghazt cries.

I mutter. "That's better, I guess."

We all look up, because what else are you going to do when somebody says *behold*. And *whoa*. We behold, all right.

Through the gaping hole at the peak of the fortress—where the remains of the fortress's heart slowly pulse—we see . . .

The fortress shudders. The shattered heart quivers, still pumping, just barely, but not for long.

The Operating Theater seems to take a deep breath, rising and sinking. The walls suck in. The pressure changes. It's like slurping all the air out of a juice box.

Ghazt closes his eyes. There's a thin smile on his face. "That portal will devour the fortress. And it will take my remains with it. Home."

This is the first time I've seen an open portal since the day the monster-zombie apocalypse began. It's like a storm turned inside out. I half expect it to start spitting out monsters like baby teeth.

But the portal spits nothing down.

Instead, the portal begins to suck everything *up*. It pulls and draws and *inhales*.

I feel the fortress beginning to break apart around us.

Ghazt's eyes flicker open. "You're still here?"

"Um. Yes?"

"Be less of an idiot, Jack Sullivan!" Ghazt wheezes. "I didn't do all of this for *nothing*. RUN!"

"Yes, let's!" June says.

The floor tilts. The fortress quakes. Wind shrieks through the theater. A chain reaction is happening, that's for sure—just not exactly like Peaches promised.

"Oh, uh—one last tiny thing before I go," I say. "How *exactly* do I control all the zombies now? Do you have, like, an instruction manual, or . . ."

But Ghazt's eyes are closed. Never to open again . . .

"GUYS!" Dirk barks. "MOVE IT!"

The guards are ripped off the floor, pulled through the hole at the peak of the theater.

The Mega-Sentinel hangs in the air, one leg snared by something that looks like uncoiling fortress intestine.

I feel myself being lifted off my feet.

The fortress heaves again. It sounds like somebody squeezing an elephant through a garlic press.

The howling wind and the shattering, splintering bits of *everything* build to a deafening scream.

Just when I think it can't get any louder, it does.

Like thunder, except it doesn't fade away. In fact, it's building . . .

It's a sound like . . . like stampeding feet and hooves.

And then—

chapter twenty-eight

"Double distraction, still happenin'!" Cannonhead Johnson barks as the Goon Platoon, along with the entire creature-brigade, charges into the theater!

And in a flash, they're scooping us up for a getaway.

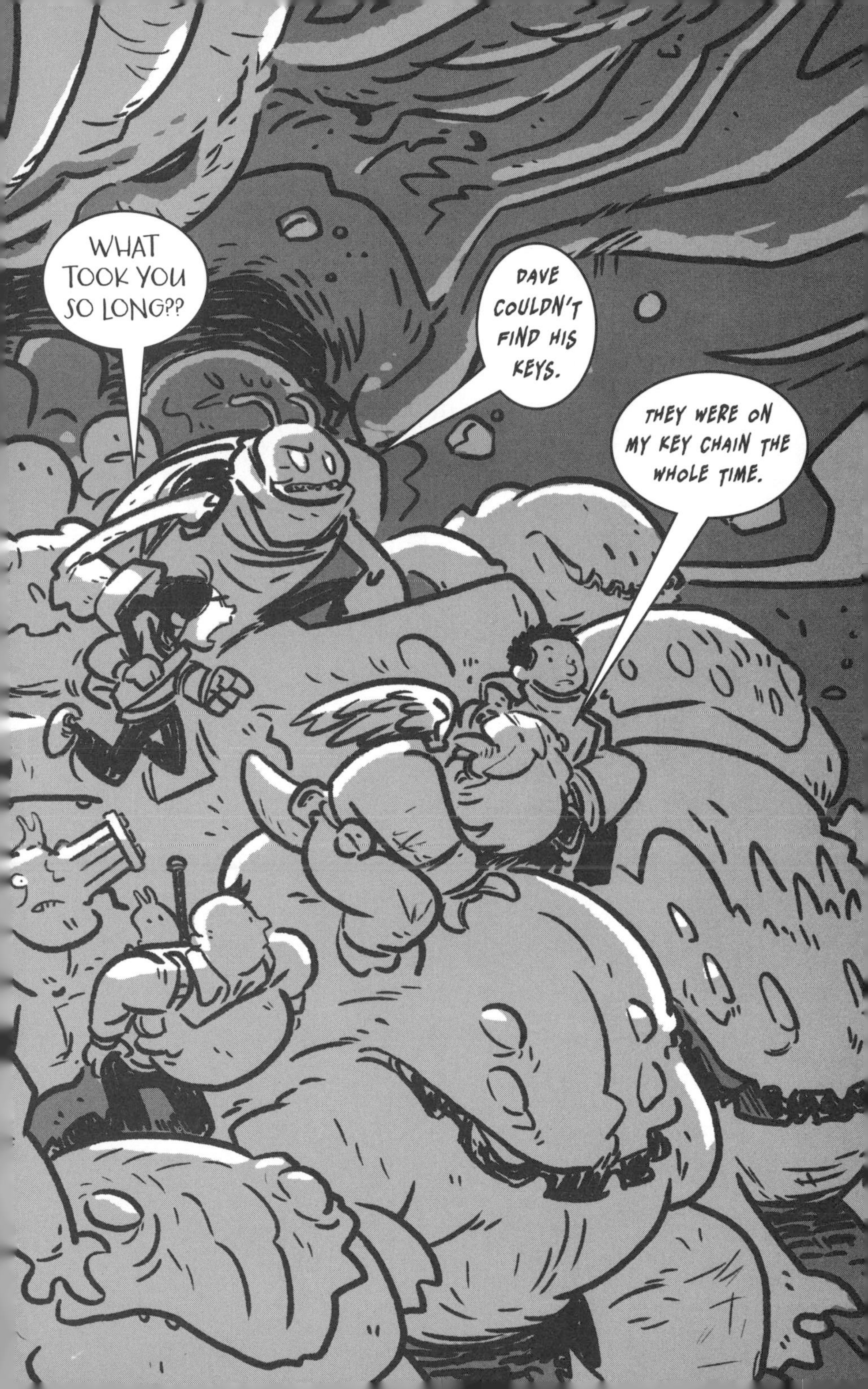
WHAT TOOK YOU SO LONG??
DAVE COULDN'T FIND HIS KEYS.
THEY WERE ON MY KEY CHAIN THE WHOLE TIME.

"Think it's time to go, Rover," I say, hopping up onto his back.

Everything is quaking, breaking, toppling—and then being yanked toward the sky. Theater benches are torn loose. Operating equipment flashes as it spins and sails skyward.

"That way!" Quint shouts as an entire wall is torn in two like it's nothing but a cardboard diorama.

But the Mega-Sentinel blocks the way . . .

One of its long legs is still ensnared, preventing it—for the moment—from being sucked into the portal.

Its body glows with rage, like little supernovas of anger are exploding inside it. Light flashes over us, its cannons bobbing and jerking as the Mega-Sentinel struggles to resist the pull of the portal.

The triple-cannon bulges like it's about to cough up something—and I'm guessing that whatever it hocks up is gonna be served with a side of smoldering death.

But still, we speed toward it. I wince, about to shut my eyes.

"Whatsa matter?" Cannonhead Johnson asks. "You guys couldn't handle that thing? Well . . ."

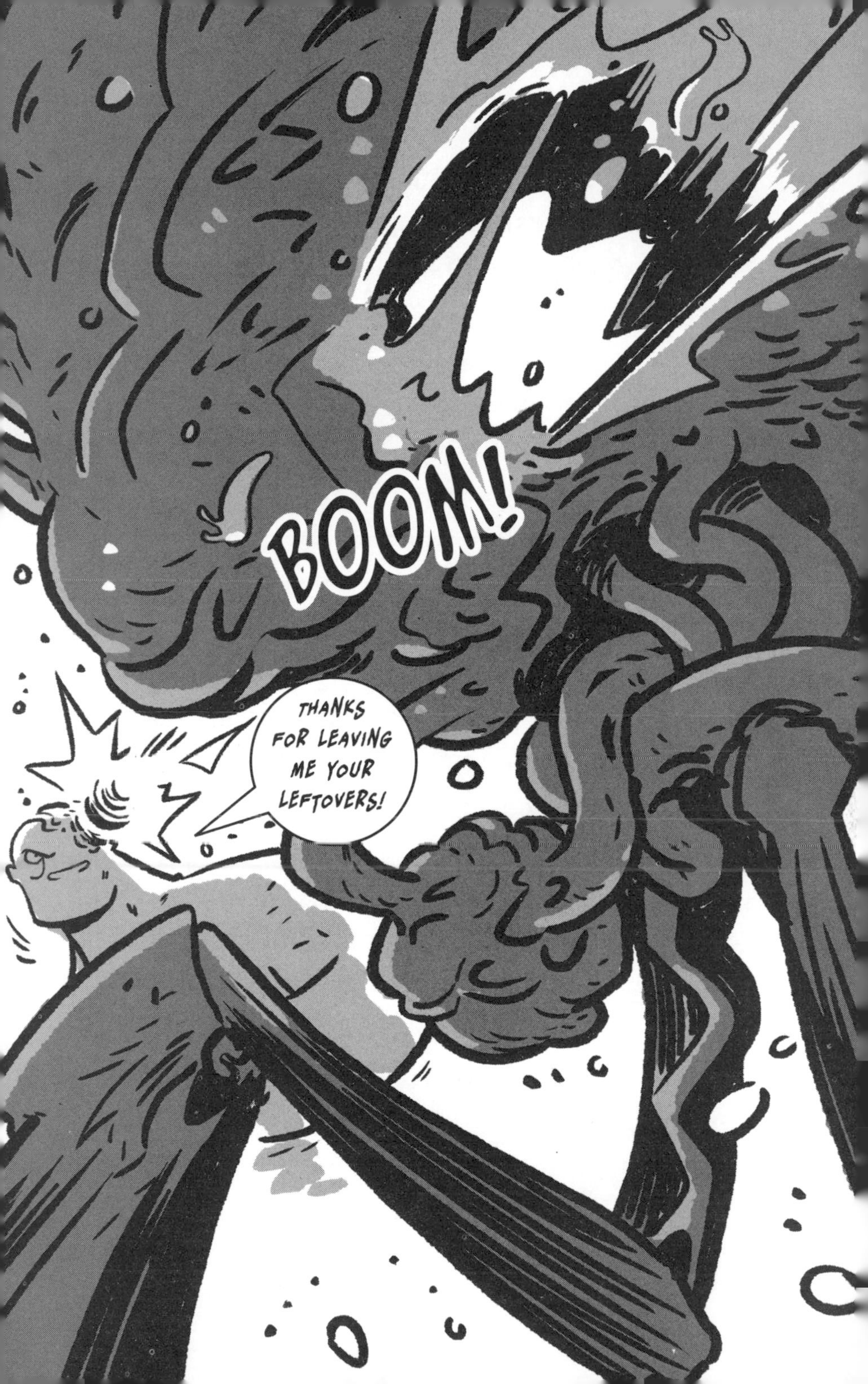
BOOM!
THANKS FOR LEAVING ME YOUR LEFTOVERS!

Ooze-soaked chunks splatter the floor as we speed beneath the smoking Mega-Sentinel, toward the Operating Theater's gaping exit.

"Just so you don't misunderstand—I don't like leftovers when it's food," Cannonhead says. "Just when it's stuff that needs exploding."

As we speed through the exit, I throw one final glance back at Ghazt. His body lies still.

What did you do to me, Ghazt?

"HEADS UP!" Dirk shouts. "Everything's comin' apart at the seams!"

Dirk's voice snaps me back to our speeding escape. Ahead of us, the fortress is opening up, wide, as entire chunks of other-dimensional drywall are pulled up into the portal.

We race through the rapidly disintegrating fortress. Some walls close around us, others open.

The path beneath our feet is crumbling—but Rover's paws somehow manage to find solid ground. Even if that ground doesn't stay solid for long. The only thing keeping us all from being plucked upward is our steady, speedy movement *forward*.

"Oh yay, back in that weirdo hall of statues,"

I say as we burst into the chamber we passed through during our Mind Cart ride. The creature-brigade leaps from horrible statue to horrible statue, crossing the ghastly room.

I see the same statue I noticed before—the one that reminded me of *myself*—with the awful tendril arms reaching up.

With an ear-shattering *CRACK*, the statue's arms snap off—shooting up and smashing into the fleshy ceiling. Then the entire ceiling explodes, suctioned up by the portal's centripetal pull.

I look away . . .

We burst out into some new, awful chamber, and gravity flips—we're suddenly flung sky-high.

I crane my neck *down* so that I can look *up* and see the prison tower we descended. It has broken in two—leaving one long section of it wedged between two jutting, unmoving crags of fortress.

The creatures slam into it, feetfirst, and we're suddenly speeding across it—upside down. The Directarium flashes in front of my face as it ricochets off the prison. *See ya later, evil directory. We already got what we need out of you. I think . . .*

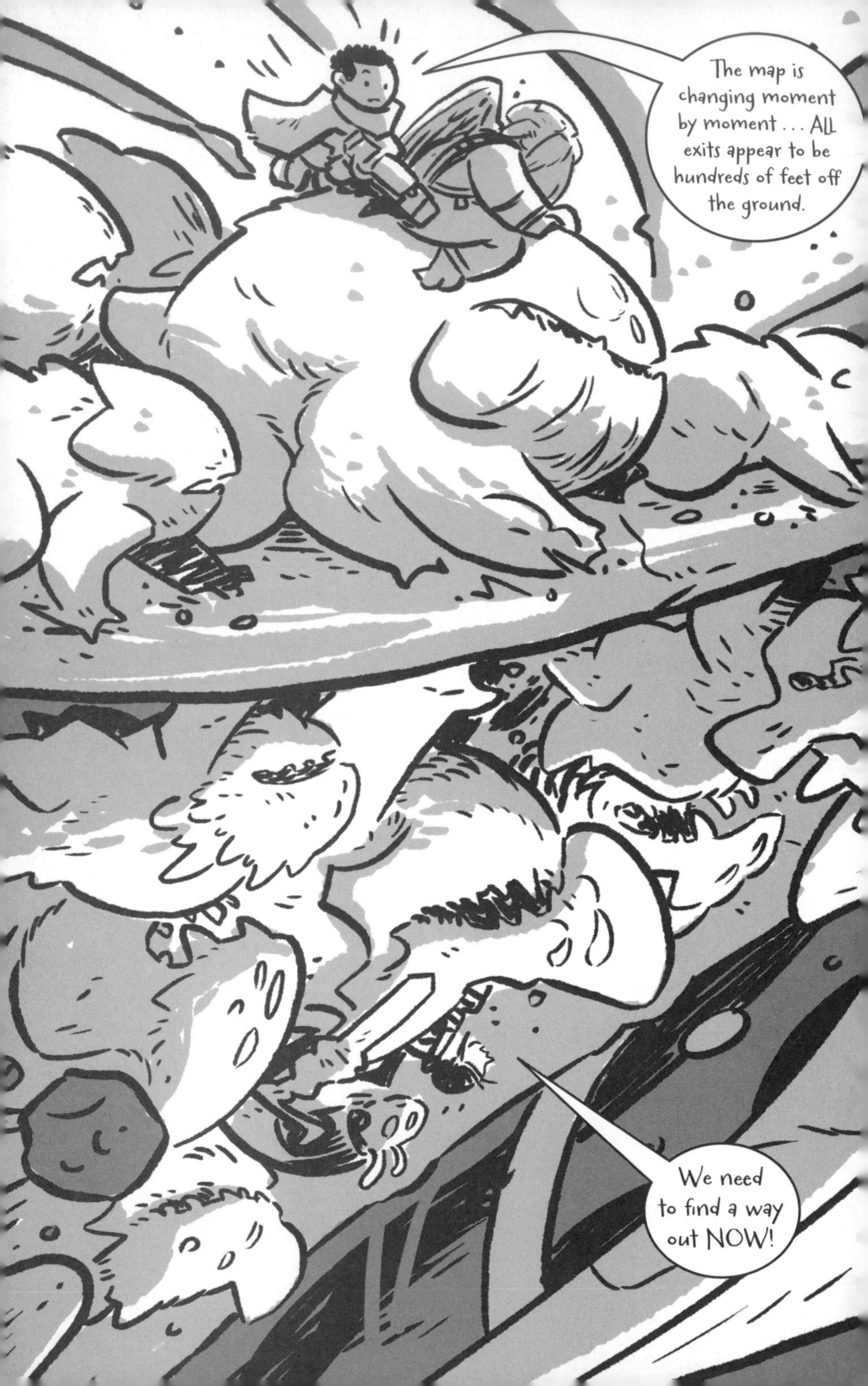
The map is changing moment by moment . . . ALL exits appear to be hundreds of feet off the ground.
We need to find a way out NOW!

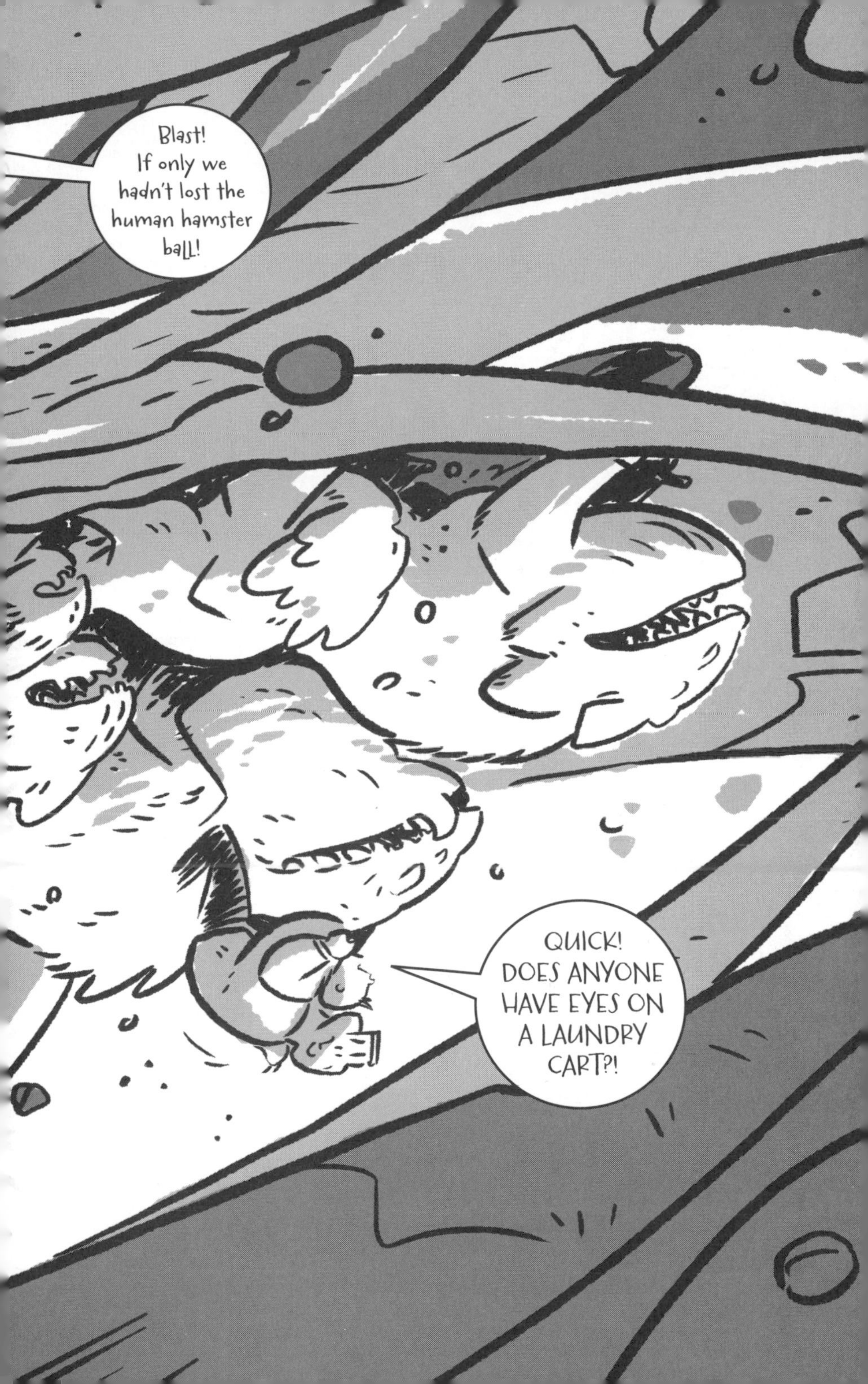
Blast! If only we hadn't lost the human hamster baLL!
QUICK! DOES ANYONE HAVE EYES ON A LAUNDRY CART?!

At that very moment—

"HEAVEN ALMIGHTY, I HATE THAT THING!"
Dirk cries as the ball ricochets off his face and
skims along the surface of the prison tower.

As we reach the structure's end, we're
funneled into a tunnel, right side up again.

We burst out of the tunnel—speeding through
every foul, awful corner of the fortress.

I suddenly gasp.

Up ahead, a swarm of Razorkaws fights to
stay aloft, talons slashing and gnashing.

Oh crud, I think, *am I gonna get an eyeball*

pecked out now? I specifically wanted that to *not* happen. But then . . .

"Ooh, yeah," Cannonball Johnson says, jerking his creature to the right. "It's maggot time."

In the fluttering remains of horrible feathers, something materializes . . . An idea! But June is one step ahead of me . . .

"JACK!" she cries out. "THE BIRD! Remember?"

Wheeling around, I shout, "And the train tracks! They're at least a hundred feet off the ground at the point where they connect with the fortress. We could ride down 'em right on out of here!"

"On it!" Quint says. But as we burst out of the tunnel, we're greeted by a vat as big as a tanker truck tumbling toward us. One of Wracksaw's horrible experiments spills out, its limp body immediately yanked upward through the roof.

Our getaway caravan swerves, and—

"Stupid, ugly, good-for-nothin' . . ." Cannonball Johnson mutters as his creature topples, tossing him off. I see Cannonhead Johnson soaring backward—before being snagged by Dave.

Cannonhead growls. "Dave . . . Why am I always rescued by stinkin' Dave . . ."

And Quint is thrown loose, too.

Rover lunges to the side, grabbing him by his robe. I reach out, hoisting Quint up—setting him in front of me. And the entire time, Quint barely takes his eyes off the Maparatus.

A moment later, Quint exclaims, "Back through Wracksaw's morgueatory! It's the only way!"

Ugh. Of course.

Rover knows the way—and I hate that he does. He veers right, galloping over a disintegrating path that crosses a bubbling marsh.

Rover dives down—through a spot in the ground that's spiraling open—and we careen through darkness, gravity flipping again, before erupting up through the morgueatory's oil-black pool.

The place is already halfway disintegrated, bits of it swirling up like dust particles. The meat heap ascends into the sky. Man, somebody on the other side of that dimension is in for a big, weird surprise . . .

It's one endless blur of wreckage until—

"The train depot," June shouts. "I see it!"

It has mixed and merged with the fortress. Jagged walls jut out of the ground, looming over the track. Trains lie scattered about, rattling in place, about to be pulled up.

"And the tracks are still there!" I shout. They're still holding strong—maybe because they're connected to our world outside.

There's no more bird-exploding door for us to worry about, either. The fortress entrance that the track passes through has split wide open. Chunks of dismantled fortress float in the air.

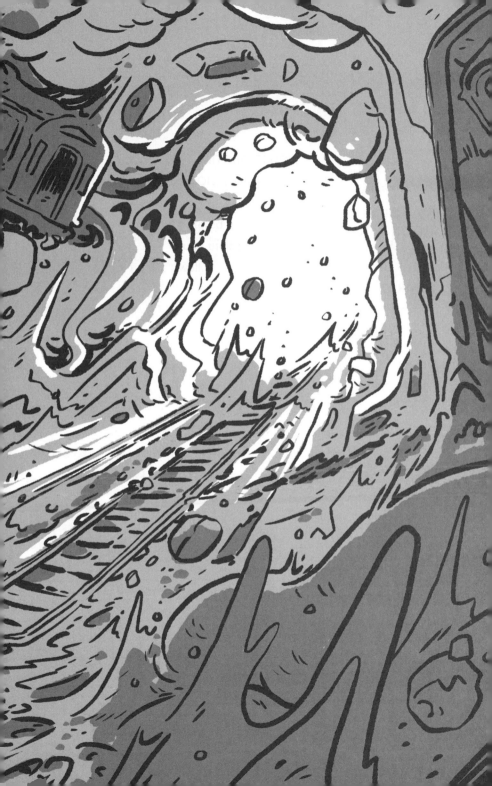

We're almost out. We're almost free. We're . . .
Oh no.

Something flashes in the air, and—

WHACK!

Wracksaw seems to appear out of nowhere, one armacle snapping out, smashing into my chest. It feels like I just got hit with a paintball the size of Milwaukee.

I'm knocked clean off Rover.

With a whistled *HA!* Wracksaw flings another armacle out, and—

YELP!

Rover is snatched off his paws.

The creature-brigade reels up, skidding and rolling and sliding to one big stop.

Wracksaw's tentacle-legs wrap around a crag of fortress—one that's still holding strong to the earth below.

DUN DUN DUN!
LOOKS LIKE I'M GOING HOME . . . BUT I'LL BE TAKING YOUR PET WITH ME.
I NEVER GOT THE CHANCE TO HAVE ANY FUN WITH IT. TO SEE WHAT I COULD CREATE. I'M GOING TO MAKE SURE IT SUFFERS.

Sword in hand, Dirk shoots a look down the line—landing on me. Everyone knows we're not leaving without Rover.

"And you three," Wracksaw says, eyes fixing on the Goon Platoon. "Look at you! You look *so incredibly rad*! I made you that way! And how do you repay me? By being a confounding annoyance for so very long."

Suddenly, there's a vicious rumble—the biggest yet. It feels like the entire fortress has suddenly shifted 19 degrees sideways. But Wracksaw, bobbing on his tentacle-legs, handles the unexpected tilt with ease.

"And the humans . . ." Wracksaw says, raising one razor-covered armacle. "Who have left me SO VERY PEEVED on what was to be my greatest day!"

"Jack's good at that," June says. "Peeving."

It's her way of buying time.

I ball my monstrously changed Cosmic Hand into a horribly heavy fist. I don't know what's gonna happen—can't guess what it's gonna do. I just know I'm gonna throw a haymaker at Wracksaw—and it's gonna hit *hard*.

"Put Rover down," I say, "And—"

"And what? No one gets hurt? Is that one of those sad little human expressions of yours?"

"Oh no," I say. "You're still gonna hurt."

"I suppose people tell you you're funny, Jack Sullivan. Alas, they lied."

"Last chance," I say.

"No . . . it is *your* last chance," Wracksaw says. He points one long armacle at my monstrous hand. "I can still help you . . ."

"I don't want your help."

"You will," Wracksaw says, cackling. Then he surges, gliding back from me. Rover dangles in the air, his paws scratching at nothing. Cracks jag through the walls, oozing blue ichor.

"You know what I think?" Wracksaw asks as he brings the glistening armacle slicing down—

Wracksaw's armacle slices through the track, shearing it in two! I hear the howl and crunch of metal as the severed track is torn apart by the portal's unstoppable pull.

Chunks of track hang in the air. Some clatter down. Others are vacuumed up.

"No . . ." June gasps.

With one brutal chop, Wracksaw has removed our escape route.

"I will see you . . . on the other side," he says, with a fiendish smile.

Wracksaw's tentacle-legs push off the ground, and he drifts upward, still clutching Rover tight.

Rover's tail snaps helplessly.

His eyes, wide and desperate, find mine.

Before I can react, a harsh voice growls from behind us—

"*You cannot leave yet, Wracksaw,*" the voice calls. "*You have unfinished business here.*"

Suddenly, a sharp whistle pierces the air. Not the whistling of Wracksaw's stringy neck tendons. This is a wind-crashing sound: an ax slicing through the air. A brutal *THUNK* rings out as the blade slams into the villain's chest.

And then—

The sudden force of the ax shocks Wracksaw.
His tentacles flail out—and Rover is released.
Rover hovers for a moment, the portal's force
like a magnet, pulling him away. But before
he rises any further, his hind legs slam into
Wracksaw, launching off.

Rover sails toward me.

Barrels into me.

I throw my arms around him, pulling him down. And I whirl around to see—

I PROMISED YOU, JACK. I PROMISED I WOULD PROTECT ROVER.

OK, rad, cool entrance. I'm thankful—but confused? Where did she come from? There's no way *out* anymore. We're hundreds of feet high.

But then—through the broken wall—I see. And
I realize . . .

That last tremendous rumble we felt wasn't
the fortress breaking. It was—

"Johnny Steve to the rescue!" June exclaims, and her whole face lights up.

Peaches jabs a sword-arm at the opening in the fortress wall. "Creatures! Go forth! The time to escape is now!" she orders.

She delivers the commands in a hard bark—but I see something like triumph on her face. Peaches, along with Dave and Cannonhead Johnson, risked life and limb—*very strange limb*—to rescue those creatures and keep them safe and hidden.

And those creatures are finally breaking out of this foul place. In a flash, they're stampeding past us, dashing toward freedom! They reach the open wall and leap to the safety of the Mallusk—and the world beyond.

The Goon Platoon's mission is complete.

But *our* mission is anything but a done deal.

Wracksaw was jostled for a hot second, but he's quickly recovering. His tentacle-legs stab into the ground—pulling him down.

"Skaelka . . ." Wracksaw snarls. "The one who got away. It seems we *both* have unfinished business here."

Skaelka pulls another ax from behind her back and marches toward Wracksaw. "Then let us complete it."

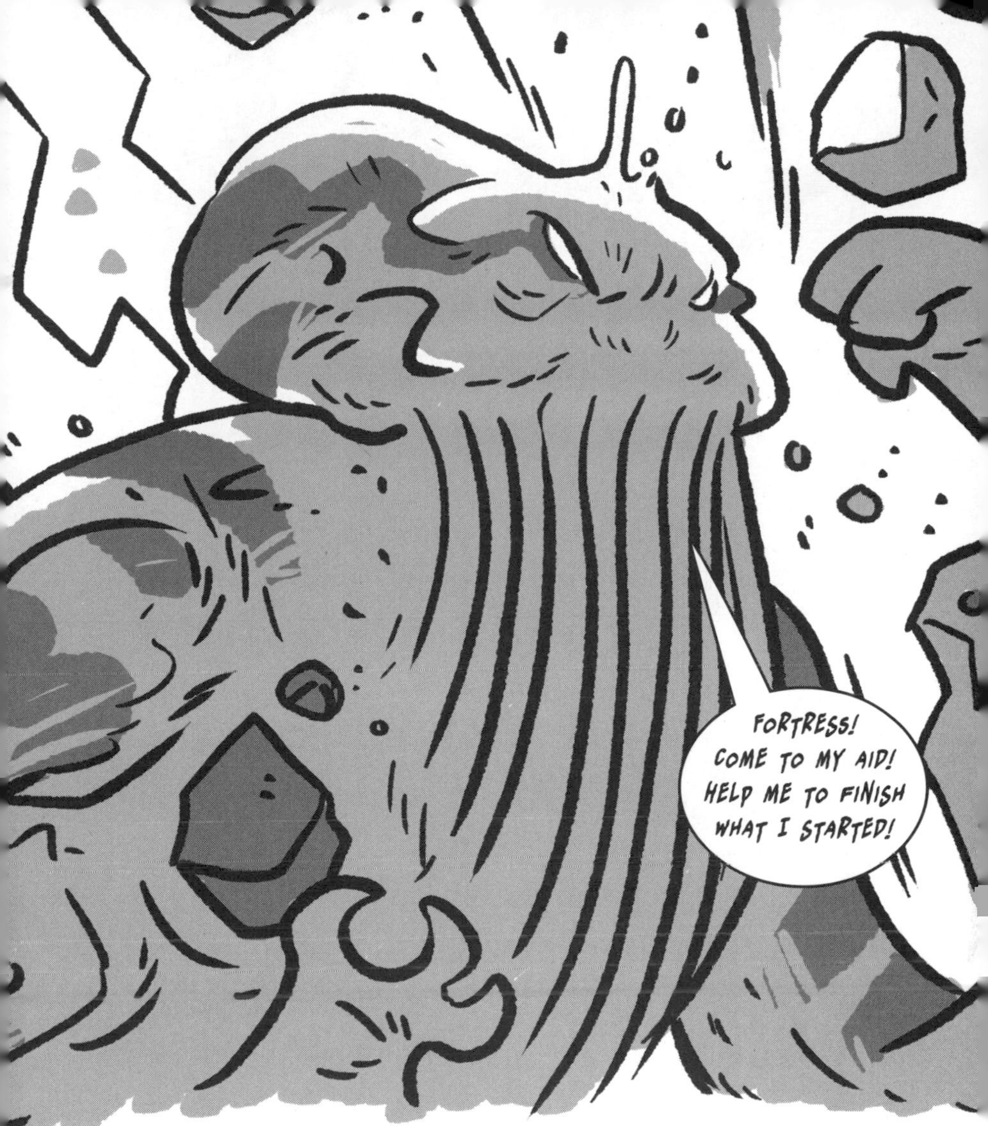
FORTRESS! COME TO MY AID! HELP ME TO FINISH WHAT I STARTED!

Even in the throes of death—the fortress helps its master.

The floor erupts, arcing and curving around Skaelka. Jagged weapons of flesh and bone surround her. But Skaelka strides through them, a monster possessed, all her previous fear funneled into a focused fury . . .

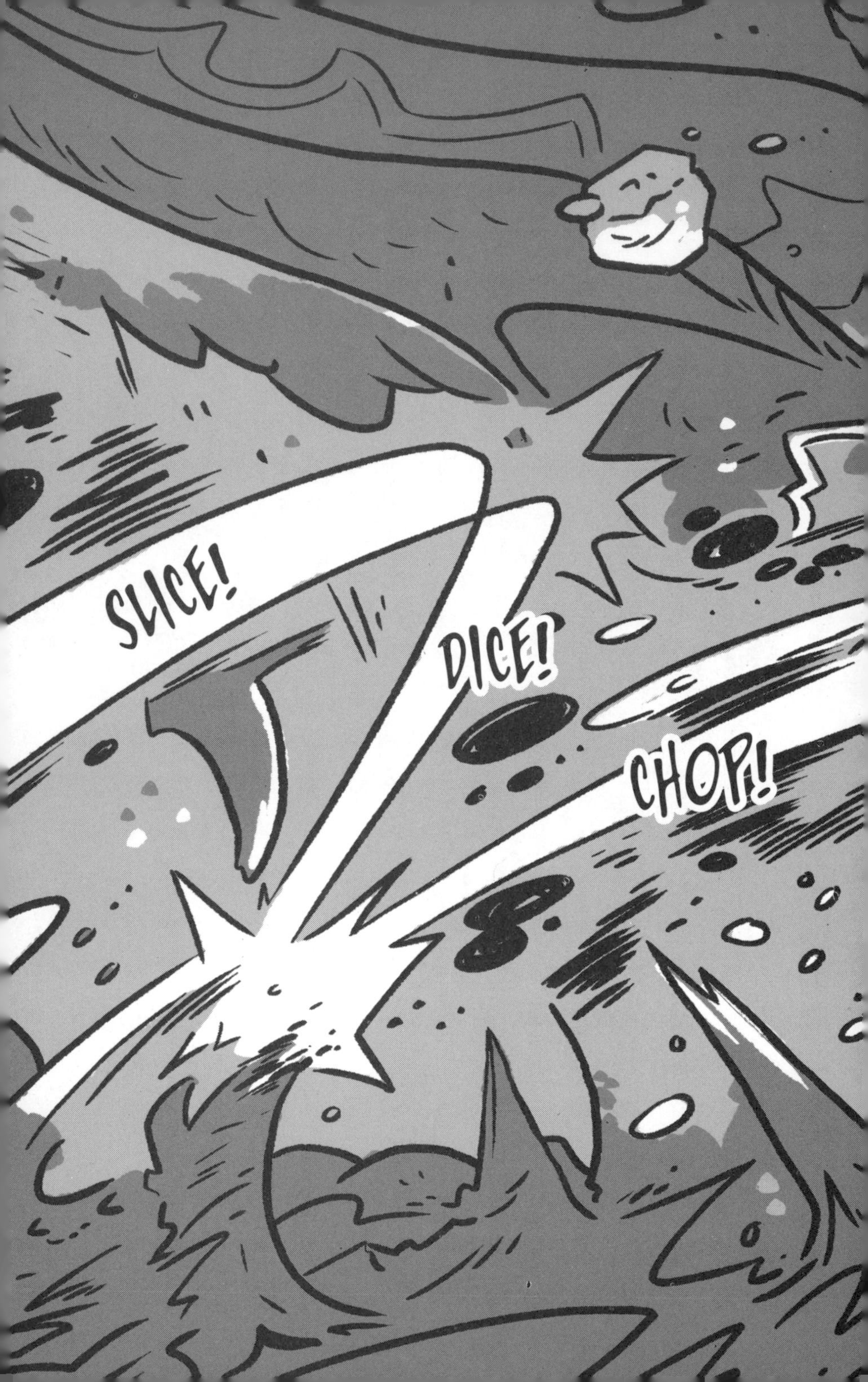
SLICE!
DICE!
CHOP!

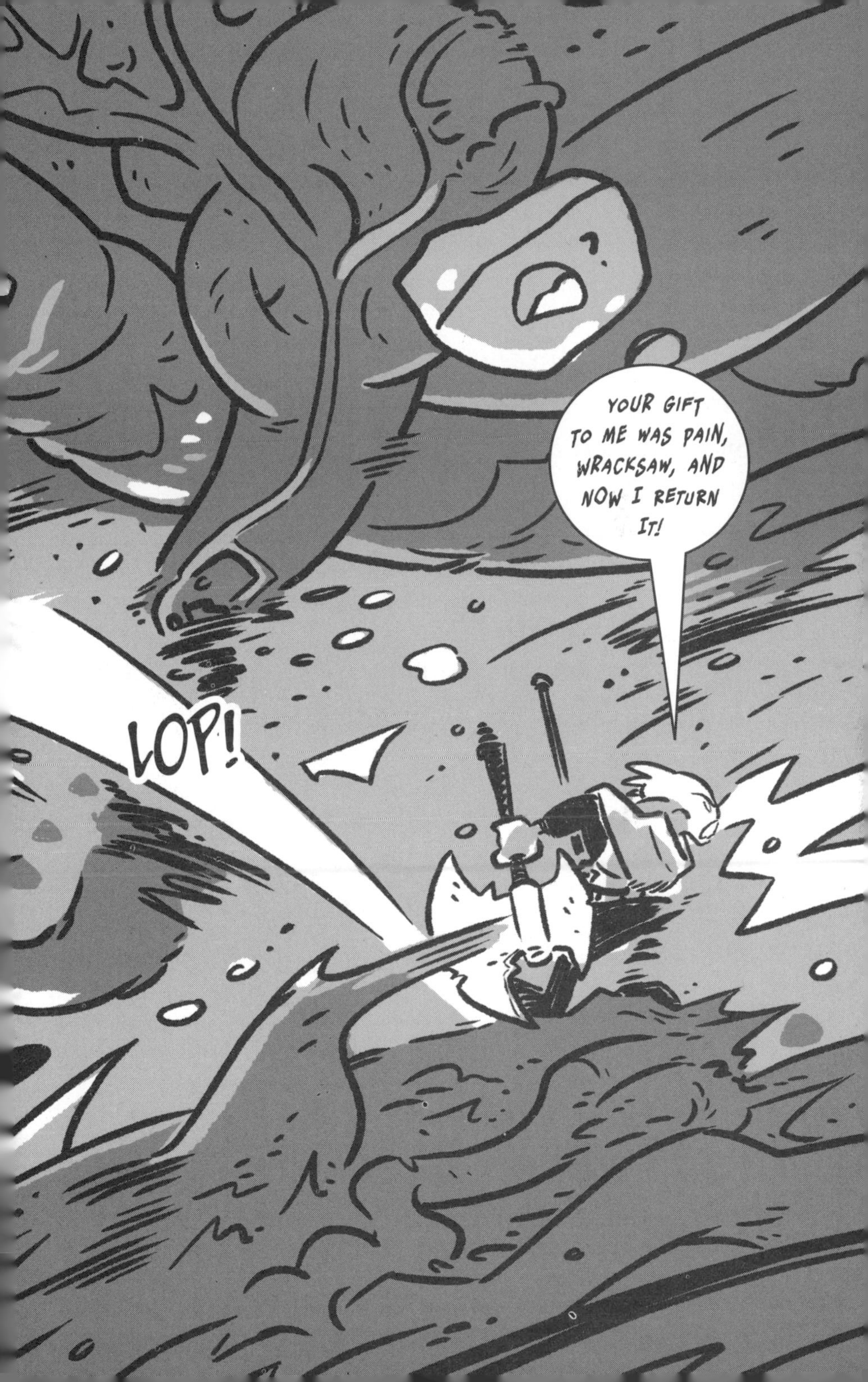
YOUR GIFT TO ME WAS PAIN, WRACKSAW, AND NOW I RETURN IT!
LOP!

When she finally reaches Wracksaw, he's ready—his many armacles thrashing and flashing in a blinding blur. He is a terror to behold.

Suddenly, Rover *woof*s.

I glance down and realize—*oh no*—we're floating upward. I grip Rover tighter. His claws pierce the ground, trying to hold us firm, but it's not enough.

We're lifting off when I hear Quint's voice boom—

"STATIC CLING!"

I feel a sudden buzz of energy around me—unlike anything I've ever felt before. I glance down, and—

"*Whoa!*" I exclaim.

If you think this is cool, you should see what he did to the Drakkor.

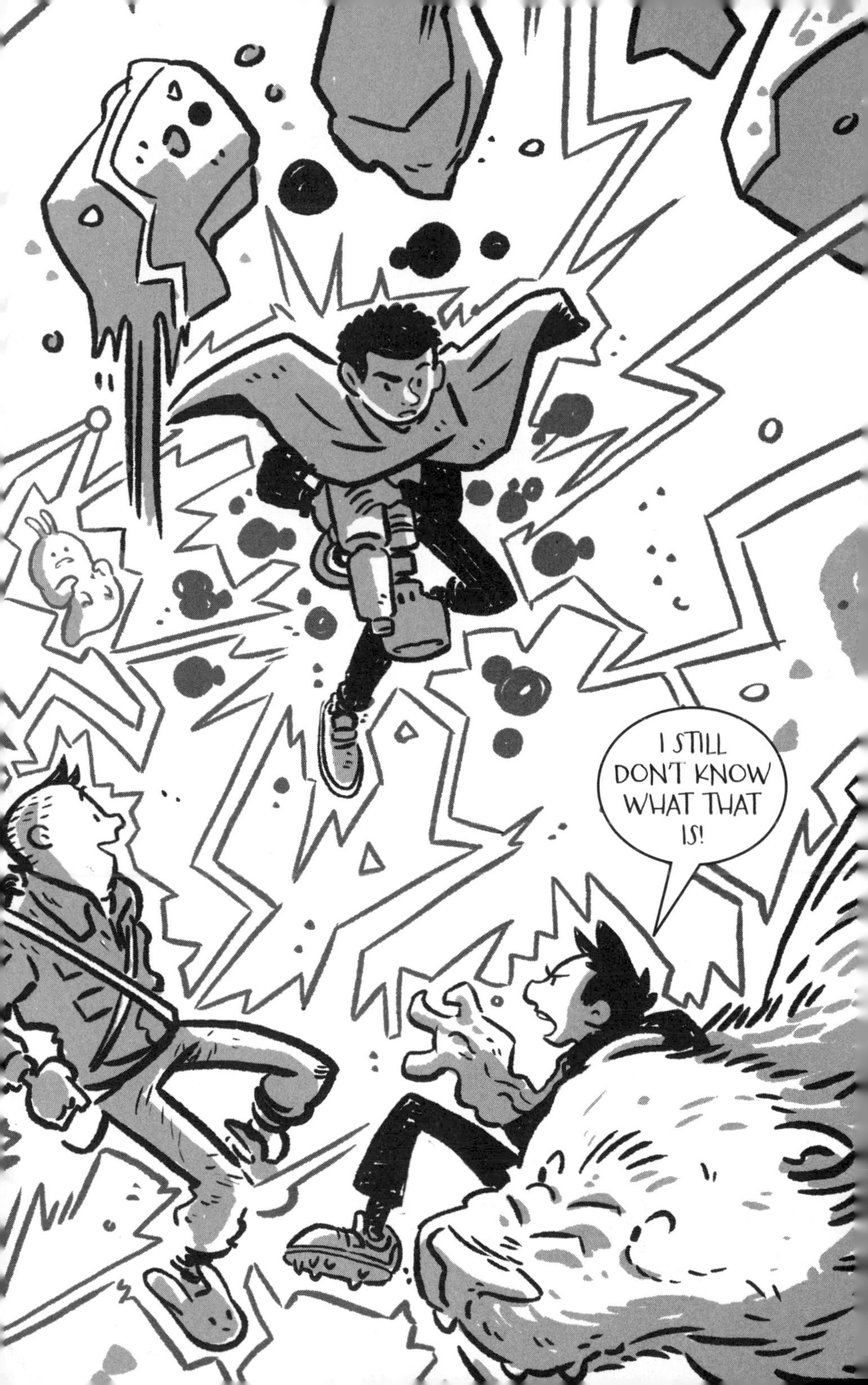
I STILL DON'T KNOW WHAT THAT IS!

The sound of steel crashing against steel sings out as Skaelka's ax clangs off Wracksaw's razor-lined armacles.

"Forget him, Skaelka!" June shouts. "If we don't leave now—we won't be able to leave at all!"

Skaelka glances down for a split second—her feet are starting to lift off the ground. She brings her ax crashing down, splitting open the ground beneath Wracksaw. It drifts apart—his tentacle-legs stretching like rubber bands until they reach their limit.

Skaelka raises her ax, ready to bring it crashing down once more, when—

WHOOP!

The weapon is yanked out of her hand—carried up, toward the portal.

"Darn," she mutters. "I liked that one."

"NOW, SKAELKA!" Quint calls. "The conjuration won't hold much longer!"

Wracksaw roars, "Yes, Skaelka! Run again! It is all you can do! I could have made you so much more! I could have removed the cowardly parts of your—"

And then Wracksaw is silenced.

"Time to go home," Peaches says as—

SNIKT!

Her six sword-appendages flash at once, severing the tips of Wracksaw's tentacles. That's all it takes. His grip is broken.

Cannonhead Johnson grabs three of the severed tentacles before Wracksaw can regrow them and pulls them tight around Wracksaw, like a balloon-animal straitjacket. Peaches leaps onto Wracksaw's back, her swords jamming into his fleshy, gelatinous body. Dave swoops up, grabbing hold of Wracksaw's head.

But Debra is long gone, along with Eye-Bulb, and about 98 percent of the fortress, soon to be 99 percent because Wracksaw is now drifting upward, the Goon Platoon draped all over him.

"Uh-oh," Dirk says. "Skaelka's going up with 'em!"

"Hey, lady, I dig your fightin' moves," Cannonhead Johnson says to Skaelka, then—

THUNK!

Cannonhead's fist slams into Skaelka's armored chest, sending her pinwheeling wildly through the air, and then—

"Gotcha!" Quint exclaims as Skaelka is caught in the pull of his conjuration.

We watch in stunned awe as Wracksaw and the Goon Platoon pick up speed, sucked skyward by the vortex, falling *up*.

Dave looks down at me. His beard flaps in the wind and his eyes flicker mysteriously. "I got a hunch we'll be seeing you soon, Jack," he calls.

What the huh? What's *that* supposed to mean?

I cup my hands over my mouth, shouting at Dave, but the roar of the dying fortress drowns out my words—

Wracksaw is gone, carried up into the portal, ushered home by the Goon Platoon.

"Whoa," June says.

Dirk holds Drooler tight. "Yeah."

Just like that, they're gone. Soon, they'll be landing in another dimension. If the Goon Platoon doesn't finish Wracksaw once they land on the other side, who knows what he'll tell Ṛeżżőch . . .

But there's no time to think about that. Not yet. The portal has been greedily devouring the fortress—and it's close to finishing its meal.

Suddenly, we're drifting again. Quint's conjurer's cannon shudders. A battery light flashes red. "No more I can do," he says.

Rover barks twice—like he's telling us, "I'll handle it from here."

In a flash, we're on top of him—gripping his fur tight as the portal's pull tries to rip us off. Rover kicks out, his paw finding an uprooted hunk of train track, and he launches toward the exit.

He hits the ground once more, bounding off it like he's leaping across the surface of the moon, sending us through the exit with enough speed that we escape the pull of the portal, and—

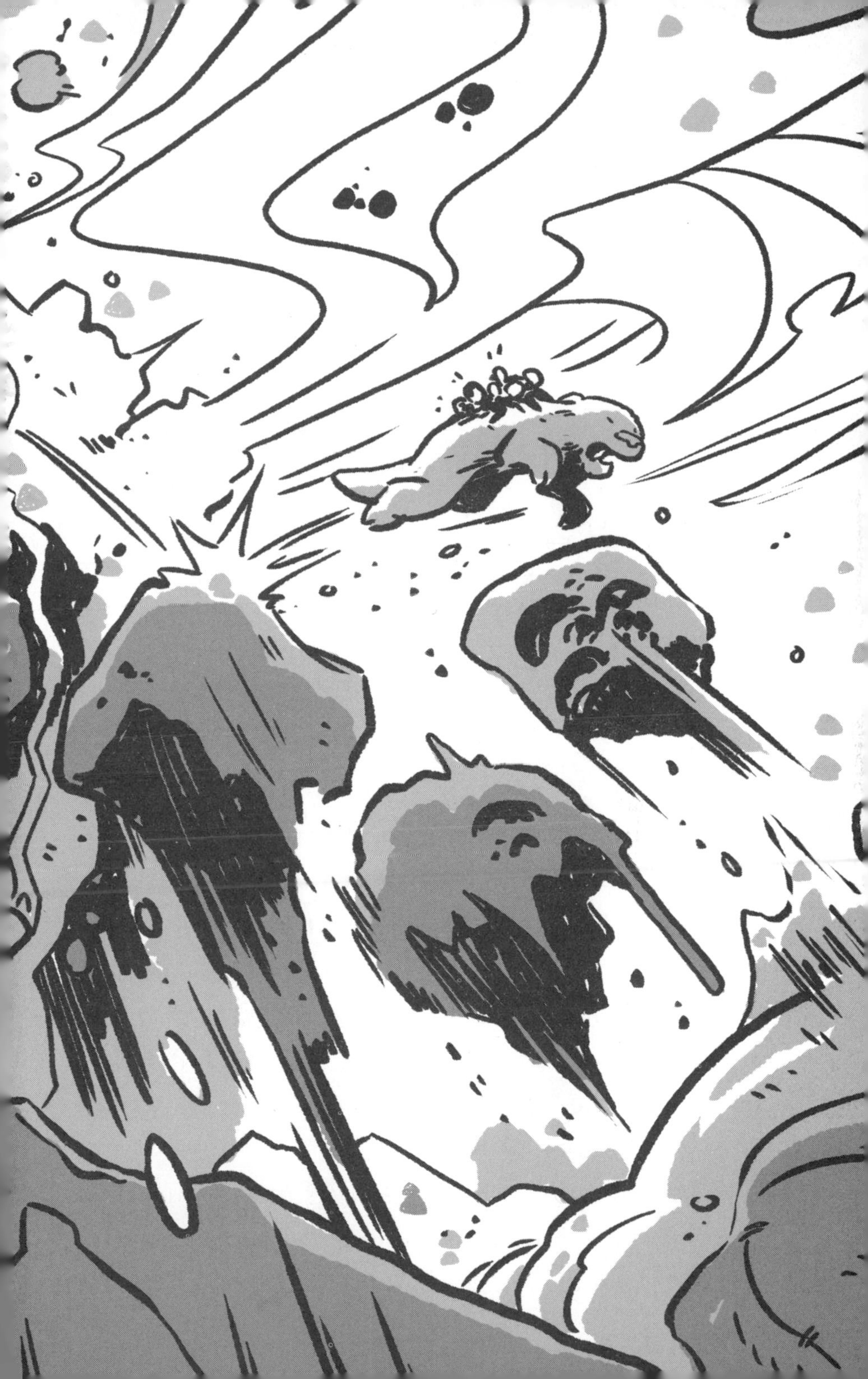

chapter twenty-nine

We hit the roof of the Mallusk hard.

The instant we land, the Mallusk's pincers crash into the ground, and its mighty hull raises, everything tilting as it turns, beginning a speeding getaway from the portal's grasp.

Cruise-ship-sized slugs aren't known for their speed, but the Mallusk's pincers pound away like they're tattooing the ground.

With one collective moan, we slowly sit up. Johnny Steve, Smud, and other monsters hurry over to greet us. Yursl winks at Quint.

"Skaelka . . ." June says. "Why didn't you tell us the fortress was *ALIVE*?"

Skaelka scratches her head. "I really don't think I could have been any clearer."

Dirk groans. "I landed on my helmet. Ow." He pulls it from under him and sets it on his head. "Gonna need to keep this on all the time now, huh, Jack?"

I swallow. He's right. There are zombies marching toward the Tower. Alfred, Lefty, and Glurm are about to make a lot of new friends.

The portal has nearly finished its devastating, destructive devouring of the fortress. The remaining ruins are torn from the earth.

"Fortress . . ." June says. "Broken."

In that final cluster of wreckage—I can just barely make out Ghazt, still strapped to the slab. Despite the furious vortex, the slab spins slowly; it's carrying the weight of a god.

For a second, it's like all the air is sucked out of the world. White and purple lightning splits the sky. Everything crackles, and the hair on the back of my neck stands on end.

The portal contracts, closing, the final remains of the fortress sucked in. And finally, when it's no bigger than a pebble in the sky—

An eruption!

A supernova of cosmic terror, exploding outward in a great ring of energy, turning night to day—blindingly bright.

I see Ghazt one last time. But he looks the same way we saw him back at the ABC theater, when Evie summoned him into this world. Before the summoning went sideways and he found himself in the body of an oversized rat.

He looks nothing like that now, here, in his true form . . .

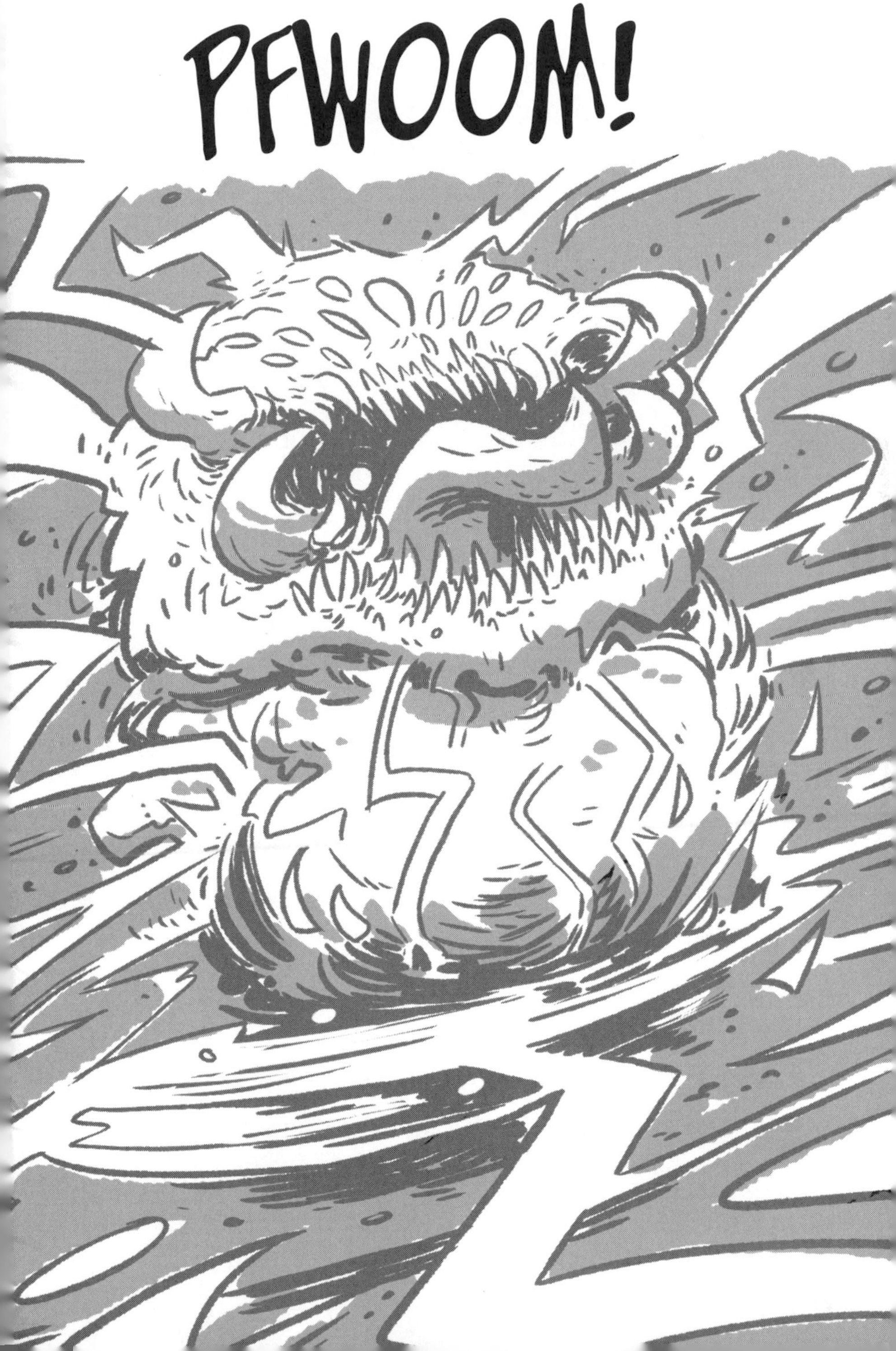
PFWOOM!

And then it's gone.

All of it. Ghazt. The fortress. The portal. Like it was just a tear in the sky that someone stitched up.

Everything is suddenly very quiet.

Ghazt the General, Cosmic Terror—our mortal enemy turned unexpected ally—is dead. For *real* this time.

Wracksaw? I'm not sure. The Goon Platoon? I sure hope not.

We had a chance to stop Ṛeżżŏċh from coming—and we failed.

In the immortal words of that random dude who gave Indiana Jones his hat—on the same day Indy coincidentally developed a fear of snakes, got his rad chin scar, and first snapped a bullwhip—"You lost today, kid. But that doesn't mean you have to like it."

I don't like it.

But now . . . I'm a general? A leader? Or I'm supposed to be?

And a leader wouldn't sit idle.

So I put on my best camp counselor voice. "Full speed ahead," I bark, starting to stand. "We're gonna need some Carapaces. We gotta

head for the Tower. Thrull has the schematics—
and a head start. There's no time to rest, no
time to delay, no time to—"

But June wraps her hand around mine. Her
human hand on top of the monstrosity that
my Cosmic Hand has become. A monstrosity
that's . . . also me.

"We did enough today," she says, staring out
at the star-speckled sky. "Take a breath."

"Take five breaths," Dirk says

Drooler *meeps* sharply.

"Or six, sure," Dirk adds.

"I concur. We must . . ." Quint starts to say,
but before he can finish—his body is slumping
against mine, his head flopping on my
shoulder, and he's breathing softly.

Rover wriggles behind me, a great big pillow.
I forgot how warm he is. And how soft his fur is
against my skin. And how curling up with him
always felt like home.

Skaelka collapses against him. He licks her
face. She licks him back.

The creature-brigade forms a giant snuggle
pile around Rover. And soon, they're all
snoring.

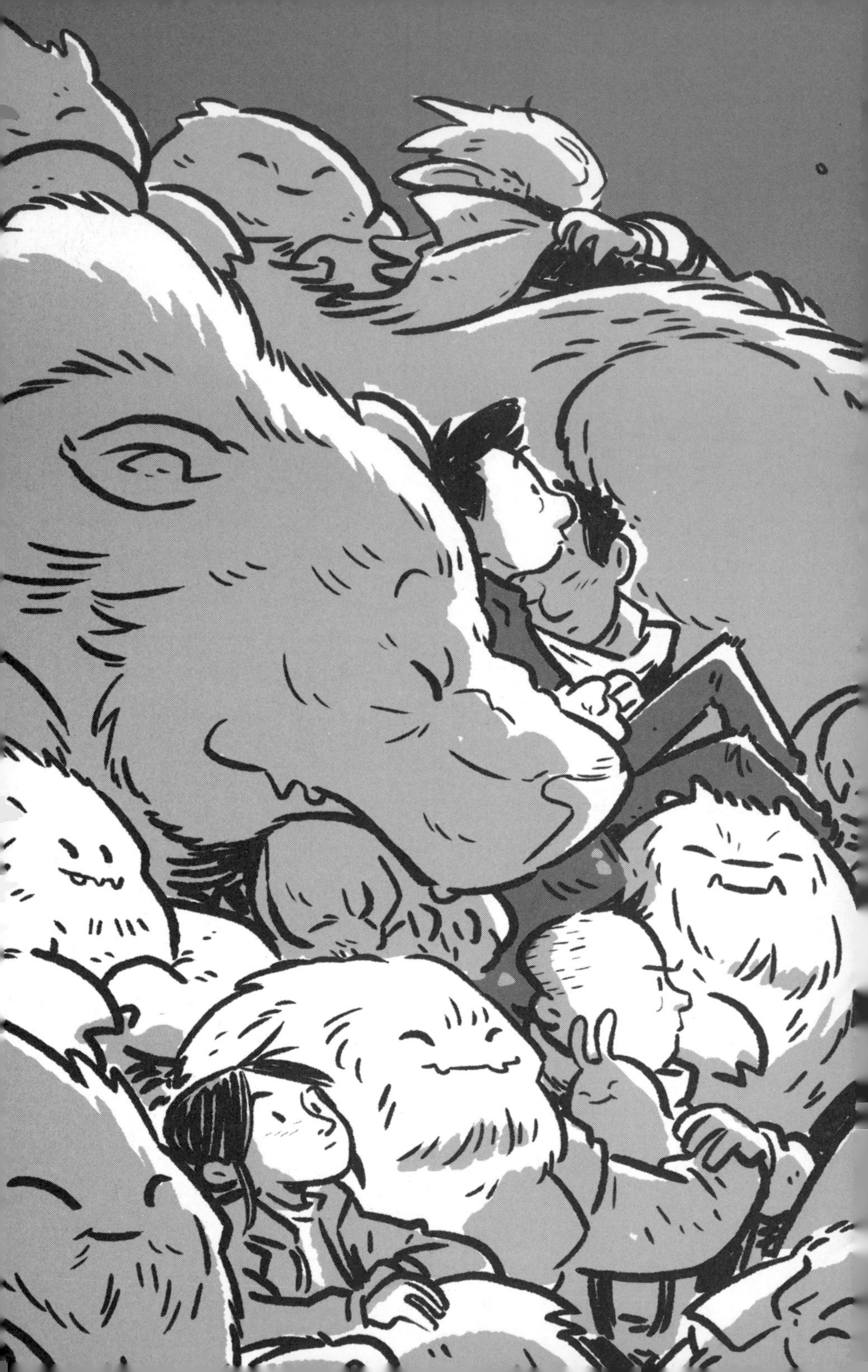

The Mallusk rocks us gently as it rumbles through the night. The air is fresh, the wind is cool.

My Cosmic Hand beats in time to my heart.

I hear it clearly. I feel incredibly . . . alive.

A single bubble of slime dribbles out of Drooler's nose as he breathes: big bubble, little bubble. I laugh. I should poke Quint and June so they don't miss it.

But it's so peaceful now.

I think I'm just gonna shut my eyes for a little bit . . .

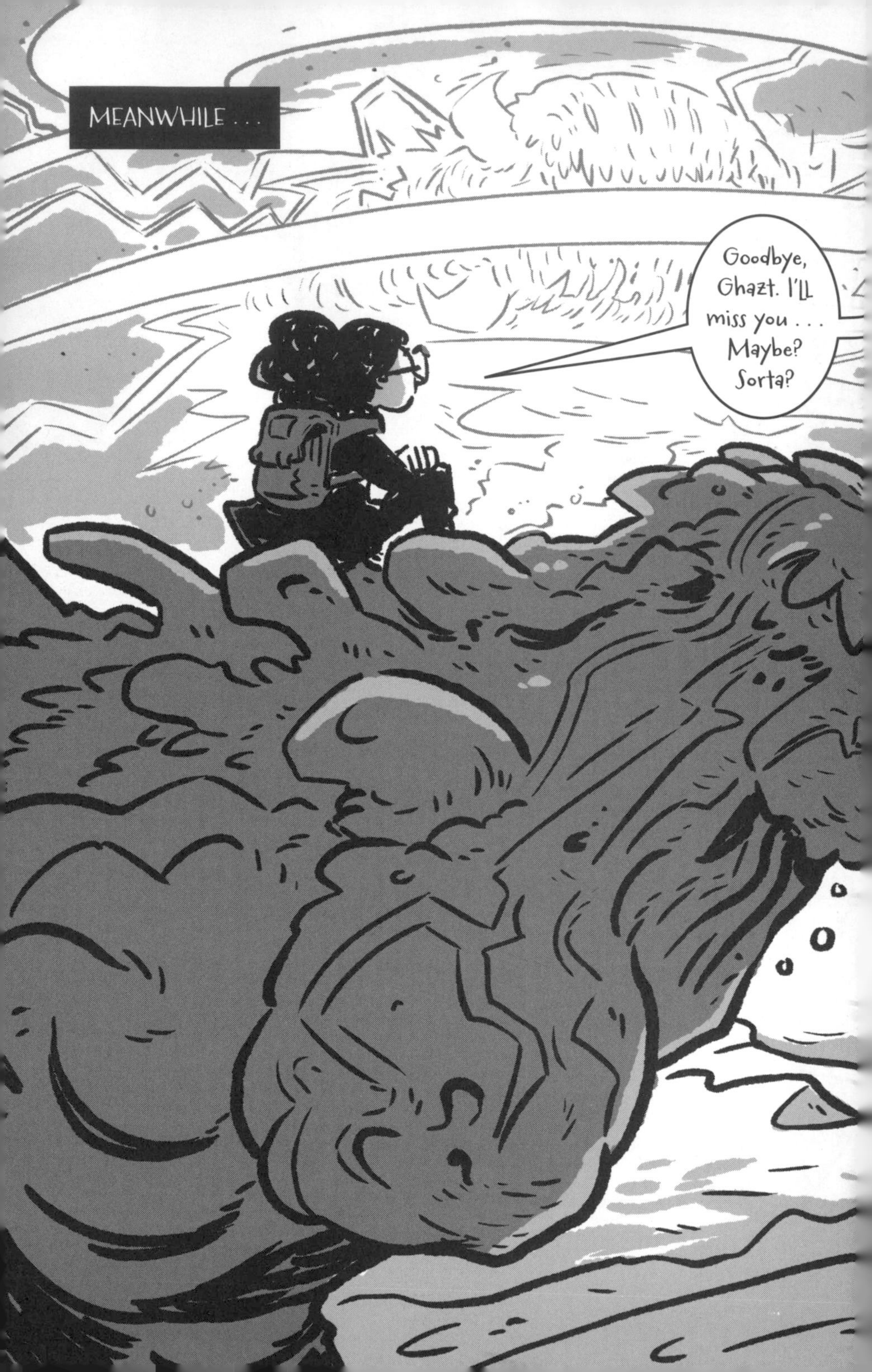
MEANWHILE . . .
Goodbye, Ghazt. I'LL miss you . . . Maybe? Sorta?

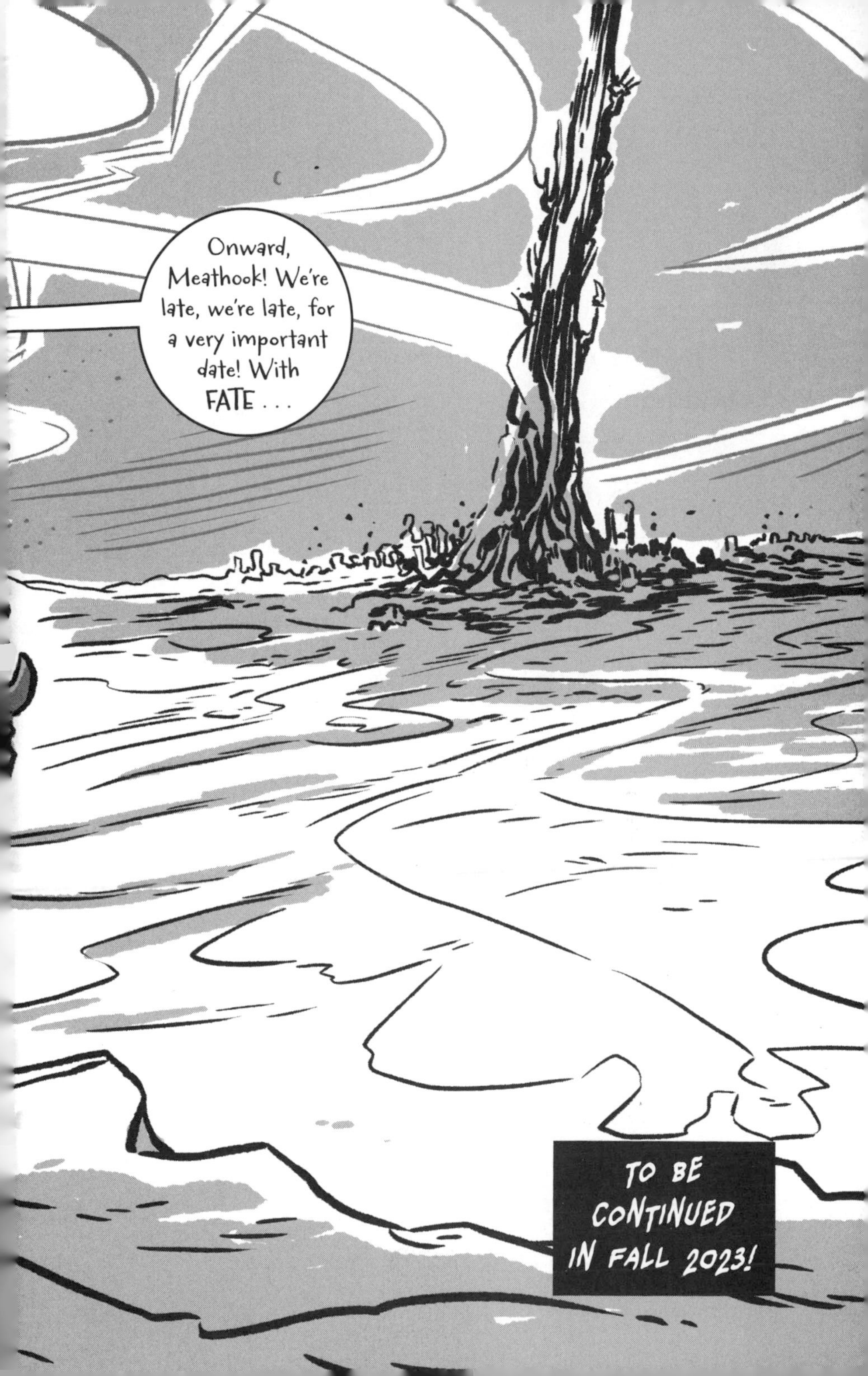
Onward, Meathook! We're late, we're late, for a very important date! With FATE . . .
TO BE CONTINUED IN FALL 2023!

Acknowledgments

Thanks to so many people for doing so much: Douglas Holgate, Dana Leydig, Jim Hoover, Ken Wright, Jennifer Dee, Josh Pruett, Haley Mancini, Felicia Frazier, Debra Polansky, Joe English, Todd Jones, Mary McGrath, Abigail Powers, Krista Ahlberg, Marinda Valenti, Sola Akinlana, Gaby Corzo, Ginny Dominguez, Emily Romero, Elyse Marshall, Carmela Iaria, Christina Colangelo, Felicity Vallence, Sarah Moses, Kara Brammer, Anna Elling, Alex Garber, Lauren Festa, Michael Hetrick, Trevor Ingerson, Rachel Wease, Lyana Salcedo, Kim Ryan, Helen Boomer, and everyone in PYR Sales and PYR Audio. Hugely appreciative, as always, of Dan Lazar, Cecilia de la Campa, Alessandra Birch, Torie Doherty-Munro, and everyone at Writers House. A huge thanks to Stuart Gibbs, Karina Yan Glaser, Sarah Mlynowski, and Christina Soontornvat for letting me bounce ideas and other boring stuff off them. And above all: thank you to my incredible family.

© Ruby Brallier

MAX BRALLIER!

is a #1 *New York Times, USA Today,* and *Wall Street Journal* bestselling author. His books and series include The Last Kids on Earth, Eerie Elementary, Mister Shivers, Galactic Hot Dogs, and Can YOU Survive the Zombie Apocalypse? He is a writer and executive producer for Netflix's Emmy Award–winning adaptation of The Last Kids on Earth.

DOUGLAS HOLGATE!

is the illustrator of the #1 *New York Times* bestselling series The Last Kids on Earth from Viking (now also an Emmy-winning Netflix animated series) and the cocreator and illustrator of the graphic novel *Clem Hetherington and the Ironwood Race* for Scholastic Graphix.

He has worked for the last twenty years making books and comics for publishers around the world from his garage in Victoria, Australia. He lives with his family and a large, fat dog that could possibly be part polar bear in the Australian bush on five acres surrounded by eighty-million-year-old volcanic boulders.

You can find his work at DouglasBotHolgate.com and on Twitter @DouglasHolgate.

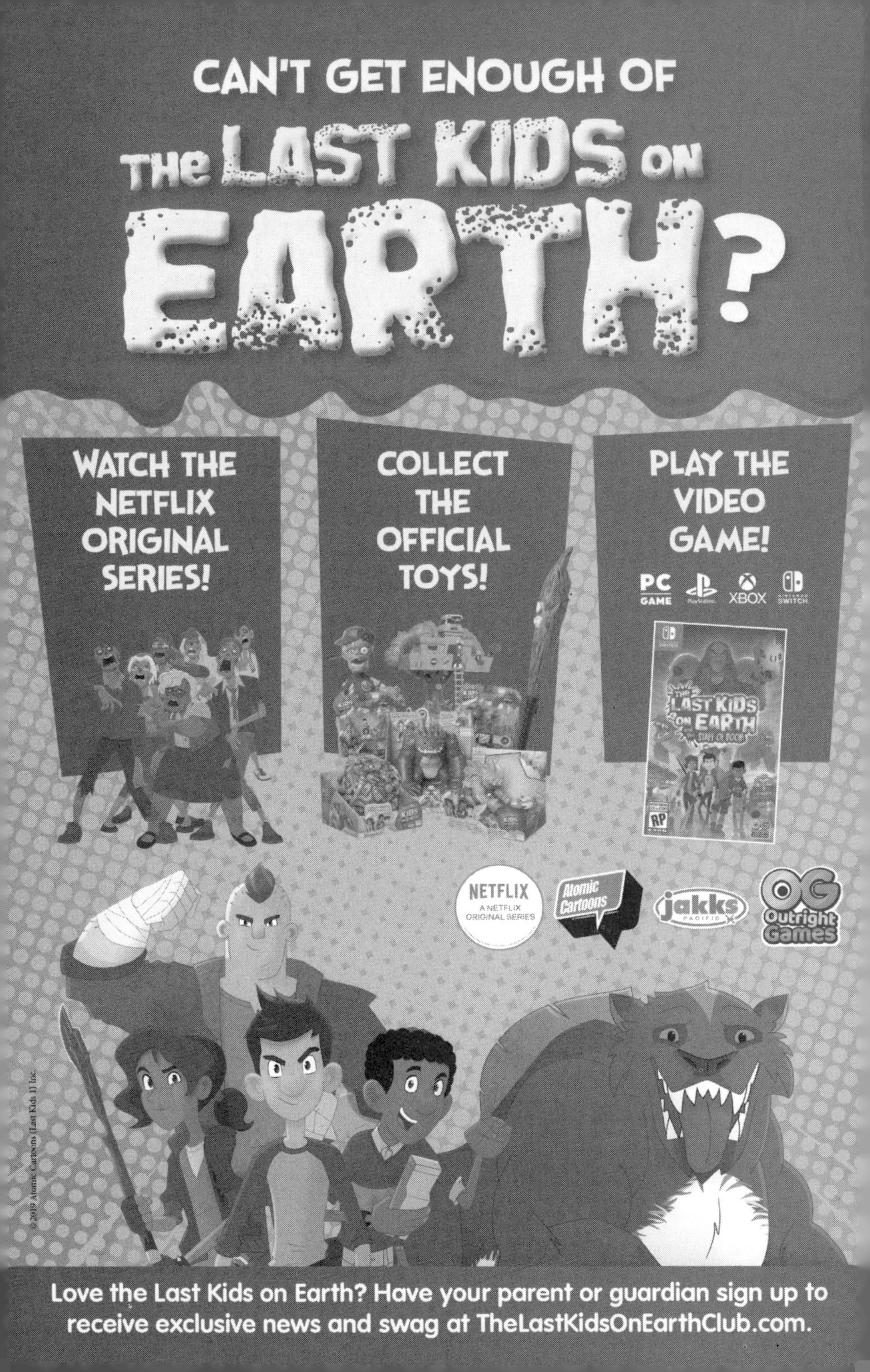
CAN'T GET ENOUGH OF
The LAST KIDS on
EARTH?
WATCH THE NETFLIX ORIGINAL SERIES!
COLLECT THE OFFICIAL TOYS!
PLAY THE VIDEO GAME!
PC GAME
XBOX
NINTENDO SWITCH
LAST KIDS ON EARTH
STAFF OF DOOM
NETFLIX
A NETFLIX ORIGINAL SERIES
Atomic Cartoons
jakks PACIFIC
OG Outright Games
© 2019 Atomic Cartoons (Last Kids 1) Inc.
Love the Last Kids on Earth? Have your parent or guardian sign up to receive exclusive news and swag at TheLastKidsOnEarthClub.com.

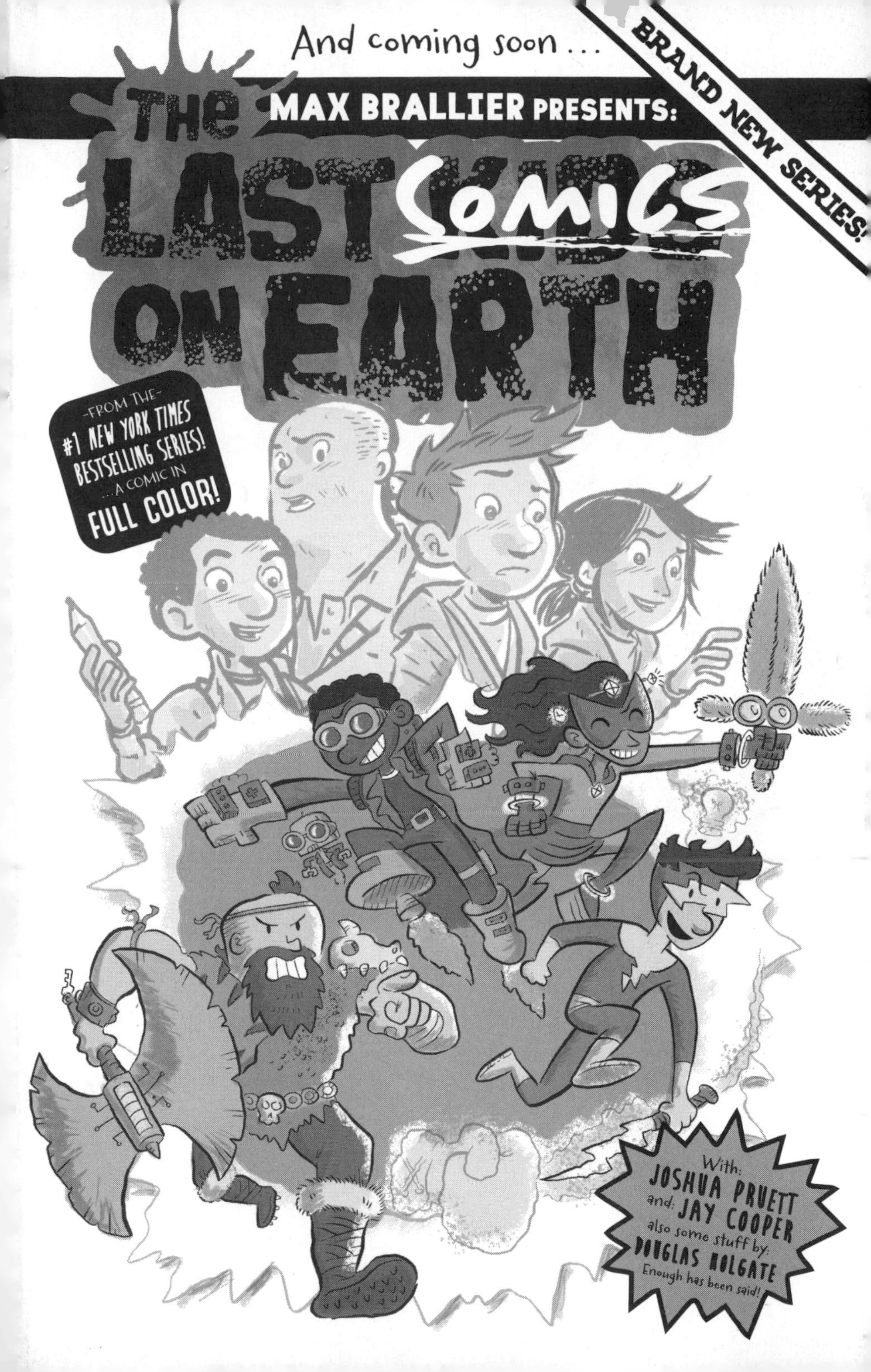

And coming soon . . .
BRAND NEW SERIES!
MAX BRALLIER PRESENTS:
THE LAST COMICS KIDS ON EARTH
-FROM THE-
#1 NEW YORK TIMES BESTSELLING SERIES!
...A COMIC IN
FULL COLOR!
With:
JOSHUA PRUETT
and: JAY COOPER
also some stuff by:
DOUGLAS HOLGATE
Enough has been said!

JOIN TODAY!

MAX BRALLIER'S
THE LAST KIDS
FAN CLUB
ON EARTH

Have your parent or guardian sign up now
to receive a Fan Club Welcome Kit and swag
mailings with each new book release!
Plus, exclusive Last Kids news, sneak previews,
and behind-the-scenes info!

VISIT TheLastKidsonEarthClub.com
TO LEARN MORE.

SCAN QR CODE

TO VISIT TODAY